SEA TRIAL

Fourteen days and nights adrift in the seductive seclusion of the sea – just the four of them:

the lovers

Tracey – young, beautiful, willing to leave her guilt about her husband behind this one last time
Phil – smooth, successful, risking ruin if this affair is ever discovered by his wife

the hosts

Captain McCracken – tough, gruff, amiable, almost a caricature of what he is meant to be – but what is he really?
Penny McCracken – so pleasant, so tactful – a nice, normal, middle-aged lady? or is there something more?

Aboard the *Penny Dreadful* the romantic dreams of Tracey and Phil slowly give way to the nightmare realities of the McCrackens . . . out there on the calm and quiet sea, with no one near, nowhere to turn for help, no one back home who even knows where they are . . .

D0717070

SEA TRIAL

FRANK DE FELITTA

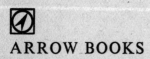

ARROW BOOKS

Arrow Books Limited
3 Fitzroy Square, London W1P 6JD

An imprint of the Hutchinson Publishing Group

London Melbourne Sydney Auckland
Wellington Johannesburg and agencies
throughout the world

First published by Gollancz 1980
Arrow edition 1981

© Frank De Felitta 1980

This book is sold subject to the condition
that it shall not, by way of trade or
otherwise, be lent, resold, hired out, or
otherwise circulated without the
publisher's prior consent in any form of
binding or cover other than that in which
it is published and without a similar
condition including this condition being
imposed on the subsequent purchaser

Made and printed in Great Britain
by The Anchor Press Ltd
Tiptree, Essex

ISBN 0 09 924910 3

For Grace

I wish to express my
thanks to Joyce Lukon
and Joe Wizan, who went,
and to Robert Wise, for
his chance remark.

SEA TRIAL

Advertisement

Sun 'n' Fun magazine, December 14, 1979

Board a beautifully appointed private yacht for a relaxed two-week voyage through the sparkling Caribbean. Travel in ease and perfect anonymity. Your hosts, two friendly, expert seafarers, enable insights unattainable aboard large cruise ships. The weather will be brilliant, the sun's disk uniquely visible this perfect of all seasons. And when the sun goes down, life aboard our yacht rises to the occasion. Our nights are filled with epicurean delights, clinking glasses, and scintillating conversation, or—if you prefer—restful silence. Send resume of interests. Couples only.

Inquire Box 212 Coral Gables, Florida

ONE

It's not going to happen, Phil thought. He checked his watch. Nearly five. Sweltering in the lowering Florida sun, in clothes designed for a northern climate, Phil stood motionless on the patio of the Hotel Flamingo. Through the file of tiny palms, he stared bleakly out at the bleached white dust that rose with the passing cars and settled on the baking asphalt. He put his sunglasses on, feeling conspicuous, his ears catching the frivolous voices drifting from the lush dining rooms.

"Darling . . ."

Phil turned. A young woman stepped onto the far end of the patio. She wore a lacy white blouse, a blue skirt, and a broad-brimmed sun hat. She looked diminutive, and for the briefest moment, afraid.

"Tracey . . ." Phil whispered.

They ran into each other's arms, and he squeezed her until her shyness was gone. Pressed against his body, he felt her warmth through the fragile lacy blouse.

"I didn't think you'd come," Phil said.

"I didn't think I would, either. But here I am."

Phil covered her neck with kisses, then held the sides of her face.

"Would you like a drink?" he asked. "Are you hungry?"

"No. Let's just go."

"All right. We'll have to get a taxi."

"My suitcase. I left it at the desk."

"We'll take care of it later."

Phil found a taxi, and soon the bright heat of the marina and the bay fell away behind them.

"Have you seen the boat?" Tracey asked.

"Yes. It's all decorated inside. Far out."

"What about the captain?"

"An older guy. Easygoing."

Tracey leaned voluptuously against Phil's chest. She knew what Phil was thinking. His fingers trembled slightly as they stroked the back of her neck. She saw the taxi driver glance at them in the rearview mirror. Outside, the bustling avenues gave way to fruit markets and then to massive, cool gardens.

The taxi stopped. Tracey got out and saw a dark lagoon in front of them. Her eyes flitted about, nervously probing the dense walls of hibiscus, willow, and broad-leaved tropical plants that lined the lagoon and hid white cabin cruisers at the docks.

Phil smiled. "Don't worry," he said reassuringly. "Nobody knows us here."

"Did you give the captain our names?"

"We're Mr. and Mrs. Williams."

At the foot of steps leading down to the water was an outboard moored to the pilings. A tall, square-built man in a white shirt extended his hand to Phil.

"Captain Jack," Phil said. "This is my wife, Tracey."

The Captain smiled broadly. His forehead was blotched by the sun. Deep creases lined the handsome face. He was well over fifty, but the barrel chest and strong forearms revealed a man at home in the elemental seas.

"I'm so pleased to meet you, Mrs. Williams," he said. "My name is John McCracken. 'Captain Jack' to my friends."

"Hello, Captain Jack," Tracey said, a trifle uncomfortably.

Tracey modestly held her skirt down and stepped into the small boat. She sat, facing forward, beside Phil. Mc-

Cracken pushed off from the steps. Suddenly, the engine roared and the boat glided forward through the tranquillity of the lagoon. Fans of bulged green reflections spread out beside the boat.

The curves of the lagoon unbent majestically. Birds called raucously overhead as they dipped low over the water and disappeared beyond the willows. Now the boat glided into a smaller side canal. Impenetrable walls of trunks, roots, flowers, and glossy leaves nearly hid the white cabin cruisers moored, utterly still, to the white docks.

"It's like a dream," Tracey whispered.

It had taken her less than three hours to arrive in Florida, meet Phil, and now find herself skimming through this picturesque waterway. Events had happened so fast, the great divide was crossed, and Tracey was both exhilarated and bewildered at the sudden fast pace of life. Already her husband was in the vast ice wastes near the Soviet Union, incommunicado in the radar installations for the Air Force. Nor would he return, even to where a telephone was located, until mid-January. By then, Tracey could live three lives at this accelerated pace.

McCracken curved the outboard in a wide arc into the dense regions of the oldest part of the lagoon. The houses and docks were elaborately walled from one another by banks of flowers and palms. A few of the owners reclined on lounge chairs. Everywhere was a hidden order, tranquillity, and privacy. McCracken cut the engine, and there was no sound but the outboard gliding slowly forward on its momentum.

"There she is, Mrs. Williams!" McCracken said. "Now isn't she a sight to make the heart soar like a hawk?"

The *Penny Dreadful* floated at peace, white and sensuous, aloof from all things, in the cool shade, nestled in a stand of tangled cypress at the farthest end of the lagoon, and well away from the eyes of neighbors. The decks were immaculate, the hull dappled with hazy circles of sunlight shafting through the palms over her. Deep-red strips of woodwork lined the cabin, adding a touch of luxury to the sharp, powerful lines.

It was larger than Tracey had imagined. "It's lovely," she said. "Can we go on board?"

"You must, Mrs. Williams. She will be your home for two weeks. You must get to know her."

McCracken deftly secured the mooring rope, climbed onto the dock, and helped Tracey and Phil from the outboard. A pleasure from being near the long, white cruiser illumined McCracken's tough face.

"You must be completely pleased with her," McCracken said with an air of certainty.

"I'm sure we will be."

"Because it is important to match the people to the boat."

Tracey stepped clumsily onto the white decks of the *Penny Dreadful.* It was a long cruiser, nearly eighty feet, and solid. Shadows from the palms hovered over the railings and the doors. She stepped past a luxuriously appointed wheelhouse and went down the steps into the main salon. The interior had a faint resinous smell, like a varnish, sumptuous, that grew pungent as they descended.

Down below it was cool. Everything was finished in deep-red wood that enlivened the senses. The salon contained a bar, a glass-enclosed case featuring a display of antique weapons, a wall of books, a long side table on which were models of clipper ships, and two long, comfortable couches. In the center of the room a large table was encompassed by four sturdy captain's chairs. Maps, a pipe rack, and nautical charts decorated the walls, the sides of which were occasionally interrupted by curtained portholes presenting a knee-level view of the deck.

Phil provided a running commentary on the layout and various points of interest. Tracey learned that the McCrackens' stateroom was tucked into the forward end, and theirs was at the far rear of the boat—a generous separation insuring privacy. Between the two staterooms, a narrow corridor connected into the main salon. On one side of the corridor, aft of the salon, was the entrance to the galley, a compact room with cabinets and gleaming stainless steel fixtures.

Their state room was finished in a darker wood, and the green light from the lagoon outside shimmered on the ceiling. Resting under a porthole was a large double bed with two ruffled pillows and two plaid blankets. A trunk at the foot of the bed was very old, scarred by the sea, banded in thick black iron straps. On the walls hung a lantern, its glass smoky, twirled inside from black stains. Next to it hung twin swords, the long blades eaten ragged with time, the hilts chipped and twisted.

"These things are real," Phil said. "The captain collects them."

On a heavy, massive dresser, iron handles hanging from carved shelves, were old nautical instruments, pieces of compasses, lens caps, and ancient maps of the West Indies, all discreetly fastened to the surface in case of storm.

"It's beautiful," she whispered.

"Look at this."

Under the smaller porthole by the washbasin stood a barrel, inscribed in Old English script, that once had carried rum. On the barrel was another lantern, this one functional, also well over a hundred years old.

Phil stepped onto the red and black braided rug over the hardwood floor. He gestured toward the room.

"I was afraid we would get something that looked like, you know, a motel."

"It's so quiet. So clean."

Several bolts from a capstan two hundred years old, and Dutch belaying pins lay along the far corner, as though waiting to be used again. The door handles were carved from wooden pegs. Now, in the growing gloom of the Florida twilight, Tracey saw that the bed, tucked under the large porthole, was scratched and carved along the top with old Spanish script.

The silence was palpable. Not even the breeze was heard as it shook through the willow fronds overhead. Tracey stood apart, like a Madonna or a doll. She looked fragile, unsure of herself, as though waiting for Phil.

He stepped to her, so that his chest was against her back. His hand moved smoothly down her neck into her blouse. She closed her eyes, and a tremor went through her. She turned. His hand slid further under her blouse, and they kissed long and passionately.

"I don't know what to think any more," she whispered helplessly.

"Let's not think. We've done too much thinking."

"Let's stay here. Forever."

But slowly the spell was broken. Tracey smoothed her skirt and buttoned the top button of her blouse. Phil smoothed her hair and they kissed again.

"I think the Captain's waiting," he said.

Tracey and Phil went up to the deck. The twilight had already come, cool and alive with chirping, buzzing sounds.

"Are you in love with her?" McCracken asked.

"Excuse me?" Phil said.

"Isn't she a lovely ship? Seventy-seven feet of pure seamanship. Cut sharp and clean as an ocean breeze."

"It's a fine boat," Phil agreed. "Just what we were looking for."

"The decor was my wife's idea. Isn't it charming?"

"Dreamy," Tracey said, finding the Captain somewhat amusing.

McCracken studied Tracey for a second. He seemed pleased by the trim lines of the pretty woman in front of him.

"Yes," McCracken said. "Charming and dreamy. Come. Let's go to my house. We'll drink to a fine voyage."

McCracken led them up a stone path, across the cool moist lawn. Lights were on in the garden. Nothing was visible beyond the palms and hedges. Phil and Tracey held hands and breathed in the delightful perfume from the willows on the banks.

McCracken paused at the door.

"My wife's name is Penny," McCracken said. "On board she's first mate."

Phil smiled and McCracken opened the door. Inside it was warm, though an air conditioner hummed at the far end of the living room. Trophies lined the mantel. Photographs of sailing vessels were hung in the corridor leading into the back rooms of the house. It was a modest home, decorated with potted plants and macrame holders, but there were unmistakable signs of wealth in the exquisite tables and antique furniture by the fireplace.

"Penny," McCracken called. "Mr. and Mrs. Williams are here."

From the back of the house came a woman, youthful in appearance, with a calm, symmetrical face. She had the bright, piercing eyes, the tanned features, and the certain aura of the self-reliant. She took in Phil and Tracey with a single glance, smiled, and extended her hand. Her voice was deeper and softer than Phil had expected.

"I'm Penny McCracken," she said. "I'm so pleased to meet you."

"How do you do," Phil mumbled, shaking hands.

McCracken cleared his throat. "They like the boat, Penny. I like them. I propose we drink to that."

"Yes, yes. Of course," Penny said with delight. "To our new guests."

McCracken rummaged among opaque bottles in a crystal glass cabinet. After rejecting several, he settled for a squat black decanter and brought it forward with four short glasses.

"Please be seated, Mr. Williams," McCracken said.

They sat on a plush, dark, almost black sofa. On the walnut table in front of them, McCracken poured with delicate relish the deep golden liquor. McCracken held up a glass. They all clinked together and sipped. It was extremely strong, and Tracey held back a cough.

"Jamaican rum," McCracken grinned. "Duty free."

Phil laughed. This was going to be a good trip, he thought. He sipped more of the rum and so did Tracey.

"Is the boat named after you?" Tracey asked Penny.

Penny leaned back and laughed. "In a way."

"I was originally going to call her *Pretty Penny*," McCracken said, leaning forward, "in honor of my wife."

"And my expensive tastes," Penny added.

"But when I saw the final bill," McCracken chuckled, "the shock of it changed my mind."

Phil could not quite place the careful enunciation. It was nearly clipped in the British manner, but definitely American.

"Is this a honeymoon?" Penny asked, smiling.

"Not exactly," Phil said. "It's a sort of second honeymoon."

"Well, the *Penny Dreadful* is made for comfort."

McCracken leaned forward to refill the rum glasses.

"Are you a sailor, Mr. Williams?"

"I wouldn't know a jib from a mainsail."

"Since neither is on board," McCracken drawled, "you're safe in that respect."

"And you, Mrs. Williams?" Penny asked. "Have you sailed?"

"Not really. I mean, when I was a child. Freshwater sailing."

"But not on the high seas?"

"No. This is the first time."

Penny looked at the Captain to engage his attention.

"Pehaps we should stock up on Dramamine," Penny said. "What do you think?"

"I suppose. Although I'd hate for our guests to sleep through their first day in the islands."

Phil had now relaxed completely. He had expected the McCrackens to be more formal. Instead, there seemed nothing about them that was not in the open. It was evident that he and his wife liked and understood each other very much. They seemed part of the same harmonious attitude toward life.

"Are the terms satisfactory, Mr. Williams?" McCracken asked pleasantly.

"Fine. Two weeks, two thousand dollars. I think that's very fair."

There was a comfortable, even an intimate silence, save for the hum of the air conditioner. The rum was beginning to mellow the room even more. Phil held hands with Tracey.

After a long silence, McCracken stirred like an old dog and picked up the black decanter. Tracey declined, but Phil accepted.

"You see," McCracken said gently, "we began this charter business, Penny and I, quite accidentally. Originally, we had just gone out ourselves. Then we started taking friends. And then we became a charter. But we never thought of it as a business, only as a way to meet people and make friends."

"It is one of life's great pleasures," Penny said, "to find people with whom you can share life, even though it's only for a week or two."

"I'll drink to that," Phil said amiably, raising his glass.

"Well," McCracken said conclusively, raising his own, "to a good ship and fair weather."

"And to our noble captains," Tracey added, holding her glass high.

McCracken grinned, pleased with her rejoinder. They finished their rum. Phil stood and shook McCracken's hand.

"Captain Jack. My wife and I were wondering whether we could stay on board tonight."

McCracken paused, a smile creeping into his hardened face. "You liked her, didn't you?" he said, pleased. "Of course you can stay."

"We'll pay you, of course."

"Forget it. Which hotel were you staying at?"

Phil dug into his pocket and pulled out the key.

"Flamingo," Phil said. "Room Twelve D. My wife's suit-case is being held at the desk."

"Your luggage will be outside your door in the morn-ing," McCracken said.

"And if you should want to nibble on something," Penny added, "feel free to help yourself to anything you find in the galley."

"We'll be hoisting anchor rather early," McCracken said, accompanying them to the door. "But you can sleep as late as you wish."

Phil and Tracey stepped down the stone walk lined with floodlamps embedded in the cool, perfect lawn. He put his arm around her shoulder. For a while, neither spoke. Then they stepped onto the *Penny Dreadful*.

"What do you think?" Tracey whispered.

"I suppose they know."

"Do you think it matters?"

"No."

He was right, Tracey thought. Nothing mattered. Not now. It was her new strategy in life. Ever since Phil had worked his way, first to a close friendship with her, then to an intimate relationship, she had drifted into a new destiny. She saw everything coming and did nothing to stop it. Why should she? When it was over, she would return to her former life. She would pick up a life in the large formal apartment, the regularity of an immaculate, well-ordered life. It was reality, perhaps, but for now Tracey had opted for her new and unquestionable destiny. With Phil there were no questions, no answers. It was just a two-week cruise. That was how they both wanted it.

They stepped down into the darkness. They did not know where the lights were so they moved gingerly, close together, down the long corridor toward their stateroom. Phil pushed open the door and a bit of blue-black reflec-

"We're probably moving down the coast," Phil mumbled huskily.

She pressed closer and became warmer, softer, enveloping him until it seemed the sunlight turned to honey and was dissolving him in its luxurious sweetness. Tracey wrapped her arms around him and enclosed him with surprising strength. All the way through until they were spent, breathing slowly in one another's arms, she said his name softly over and over again.

Phil sat up on the edge of the bed, smiled, and ran his hand down her calf. Tracey smiled as well, the hair around her temples dampened from perspiration.

A beam of sunlight, finding its way through the curtain, performed a sultry dance upon the carpet. Mesmerized, Tracey was reminded of another square of sunlight moving across the deep pile carpet of her and Larry's duplex apartment high above Central Park West. Especially after making love, it took only small suggestions to trigger the playback of that lovely winter afternoon.

She had been staring at the yellow light streaming across the carpet and over the ebony sculpture near the stairs. In a sudden pause in the conversation, she realized that Phil Sobel was staring at her, appraising her. Then he and Larry continued discussing the breakup of the Vietnamese army. Phil was vehement, curious, and sarcastic; Larry cool and analytical. Politics had been a division between them since college. The discussion mattered little. They argued for the friendship of it. In the soft sunlight, Tracey felt Phil's thoughts reaching out, enveloping her, as he talked. Larry saw nothing. He could not feel and think at the same time. Phil amused Tracey in the way his emotions led him on, exuberantly, a little boy's smile curling his lip. Underneath it he frankly studied her, and she knew it.

Several times he came for dinner. Every time they pleasantly argued the latest news out of Washington. Phil was a cynic, believed nothing he was told. Larry was a professional intellectual. He believed in expertise and he defended the Senate. As the months drifted by, Tracey began to realize how much she looked forward to Phil's visits, and the moment she did, she became nervous and tried to find excuses for not being present when he came to the apartment.

During a rainstorm, Phil and Tracey waited for Larry. A nervous, awkward silence maintained itself as they watched the empty street. It was as though he were torturing her, waiting for her to speak first. Then he told her, directly and simply, his feelings for her. He told her all that he guessed about her as well. Tracey denied everything, and he fell into silence. But she became openly nervous, and even when Larry arrived she did not calm herself. She kept stealing looks at Phil throughout supper. In her mind she was already compromised. Desire, she thought, was like hypnotism. She was not responsible for her destiny any longer.

It was a cold, bitter evening in New York. The tiny snowflakes were sweeping up against the bleak skyline when she made her choice. She had only a blurred memory of the luxuriant hotel lobby, the night lights of the city outside the window, what Phil said or did. But she did remember the dark red wine, and the scent of her own perfume. To her surprise, she felt no guilt, only comfort in Phil's presence. He was less a clown than he liked to appear. Making love to her, he softened his ambition with genuine tenderness.

Tracey hoped that, by flying to Florida to be with Phil, she would be able to love him to her heart's content. In that way, she might be able to exorcize him and to return to her former life.

"Let's go up on deck," Tracey said softly.

Dressed in new white trunks and marine-blue T-shirt, Phil felt oddly like a boy in this room full of lanterns, doubloons, and sea instruments. Tracey dressed similarly

in a newly purchased outfit, closed her suitcase at the foot
of the bed, and followed Phil into the companionway.

The immaculate galley and dining area were deserted.

Phil went up the steps to the deck. He saw a hot, ashen
sea laden with heavy white light. Off the right side the
Florida coast rolled by, ragged bunches of foliage dropping
nearly to the surf line. Hard beaches untwined for miles in
both directions, with twisted driftwood bleached bright
from the sun.

"Good-morning, Mr. Williams!"

McCracken waved from the wheelhouse. The visor of
his cap threw a heavy shadow across his eyes.

"Sleep well?"

"Like a babe," Phil answered. "What time is it?"

"Seven-thirty."

"Is that all?"

"Morning comes early to the sea, Mr. Williams. Come
and join me."

Phil helped Tracey onto the wheelhouse platform. Mc-
Cracken's extended hand gently but firmly assisted her the
rest of the way. The interior of the wheelhouse was larger
than it seemed from the outside, and easily accommodated
the three of them. McCracken's brawny arms were draped
familiarly over the old-fashioned mariner's wheel with antique writing along the base. The instruments were a mix
of modern and antique, featuring an old-time binnacle with
compass, a scratched ebony chart table with slots for rolled
maps and ledgers, and a number of gleaming brass instruments of more recent vintage. A large brass bell of uncertain ancestry was ceremonially placed and shone brightly
no matter what kind of light floated into the wheelhouse.

"An old ship's bell," McCracken said. "Early eighteenth
century, I'm sure. British. Not a very large ship. That's all
I can tell you. I picked it up at an auction in Miami, of all
places."

Phil pointed to a dark screen on which a green line
traced, from right to left, a rounded line.

"That, Mr. Williams, is a picture of the ocean floor under us. This indicates the depth. I can switch to numbers if you like."

With a flick of his thumb, McCracken snapped a black switch and a digital readout appeared in green-lighted numerals over the moving line. The ocean bottom was approximately thirty-five feet below them.

"What's this?"

"It's a radio. It picks up sending stations at various points. I use those to arrive at a location fix."

Phil folded his arms and admired the gleaming instruments.

"This is the radar," McCracken went on. "This, the ship's log. I keep a continual report on the ship's progress."

"Marvellous," Tracey confessed. "It all gives me confidence."

"What does 'auto' refer to?" Phil asked.

McCracken smiled. "You just set the course, switch this part of the console to 'auto' and it will keep the engines running at the desired speed, in the desired direction. And, I might add, correcting all the while for currents and winds. It does that through a constant compass check."

Phil whistled softly.

"You see," McCracken confided, "boats today practically run themselves—once you understand the principles of the instruments. With two weeks' training, you could run the *Penny Dreadful.*"

"Me? Never," Phil protested. "I don't know anything about tides, or winds, or—"

"Marinas are well protected. You just follow the information they give you and avoid bad weather," McCracken said. "In the old days, one risked one's health, even one's life. Today, well, it's very much safer. And duller, I may add."

McCracken looked sadly down at the instruments. He suddenly looked out of place, a gruff, bulky figure with bushy white eyebrows, in the midst of gleaming, transistorized instruments.

"Good-morning!"

Penny McCracken, wearing sunglasses and a red bandana around her hair, looked up at them from the foredeck.

"Good-morning," Tracey answered. "Have we missed breakfast?"

"Coffee in half an hour."

Down below, it was cooler. Shimmering light cascaded over the white stove. The blue sky poured in through the portholes and the open hatch, a striking well of bright light. Phil and Tracey sat on the brown-cushioned benches. Penny McCracken carefully lit a burner and placed a yellow pot over it.

"Where are we going first?" Tracey asked eagerly.

"The Captain has to pick up supplies," Penny said. "Fuel, fresh fruit, canned goods. Things like that."

She set down two heavy mugs of steaming dark liquid in front of them. The handles of the mugs were carved, like entwined vines, and there was a suggestion of the moon rising in the tropics on the mug faces.

"Caffeine at last," Phil said, breathing in the rich aroma.

"That's not really coffee," Penny said. "It's a kind of bran that the Captain brews. It improves the circulation."

Phil looked down at the dense, swirling brew. Bits of bran floated in the bubbles. Beneath the table, Tracey squeezed his leg.

"Drink up, darling," she said. "It'll help your circulation."

"I circulate just fine," Phil said, sipping dutifully.

To his surprise, the hot liquid was slightly sweet, thick, almost a dull honey. It was quite pleasant and he drank it down.

The morning passed in drowsy relaxation. Luncheon was at twelve precisely in the aft salon. A refreshing fruit compote and thin slices of ham on buttered brown bread were served. A cold Norwegian beer accompanied the meal.

Now he realized how much he preferred not to see shopping centers, gasoline pumps, and slick yachts. The coolness of the delicate breeze through the porthole and Tracey beside him were all he wanted for a long, long time. Around two o'clock, there was the sound of another engine on the water. The *Penny Dreadful* slowed. Phil could hear the low talk of men above.

"We're landing!" Tracey said as she peered out the port-hole.

"If you'll excuse me," Penny said, removing her apron.

The boat turned around. All Phil saw was a tangled mass of decaying seaweed that rose and fell in a glassy swell.

There was no metropolis. There were no yachts. There were no landing slips. There was only a shack against a tangled cove, and a rickety dock that sloped into the water. Men labored along the shore, carrying crates into the *Penny Dreadful*. The curve of the shoreline cut the boat off from sight of the rest of the coastline. Garbage moved with the waves.

"What an ungodly looking place," Tracey whispered.

"Not exactly your upper-crust marina, is it?"

Against the corrugated tin shack stood McCracken. He fanned himself, watching over the laborers on the shore. Tin cans, wire, and pieces of bottles lay on the hard sand. It was blistering hot. Tracey's blouse became soaked with perspiration, plastered to her skin, revealing the forms underneath. Self-consciously, she buttoned the top button.

"What the hell is this place?" Phil mumbled.

Feeling foolishly pampered in their Fifth Avenue cruise wear, Phil and Tracey walked onto the dock, past the sweating men, and stepped down onto the beach. It was rough beneath their feet. Tiny black mites hopped from the bulbous seaweed where they stepped. An unpleasant odor rose from the depot as they approached.

"Mr. Williams," McCracken said. "Had there been anything on shore for you, I would have told you."

"Just exploring, Captain."

"Very well, but this is just a loading depot. Just a lot of hot and sticky work, that's all."

Through the screen door of the depot Phil saw an accumulation of barrels, boxes, lanterns, engine parts, spools of wire and rope, and canned goods on precariously leaning shelves. A black man sat in the corner. His yellow eyes blinked thoughtfully.

"Mr. Williams!" Penny called.

Behind the depot shack, Penny McCracken took inventory, clipboard in hand, over crates stacked up against the wall. At her direction, bare-chested men heaved the crates to their shoulders and took them to the *Penny Dreadful.*

"Since you came on shore, you must work," Penny said conclusively. "That's the rule."

Phil felt suddenly awkward. Tracey looked at him worriedly.

But Penny smiled and handed Phil a small bunch of bamboolike sticks. She brushed the dirt from the tips. "Lick the ends," she said.

Through the bitter roughness came a full, sweet honey taste. It reminded him of the Captain's bran coffee. It revived ancient boyhood memories that elusively wavered away in the bitter heat.

"And for you, Mrs. Williams."

She gave Tracey a small bunch of pink bananas. From them a thick, almost overripe aroma flowed, sensual and enticing, yet with a hint of decay.

"West Indies bananas," Penny explained.

Tracey sampled a banana and found it meatier than any she had tasted before. It was cool, refreshing. Her eyes widened with delight. "It's certainly a delicate taste!"

Penny walked among the crates, turned, and seemed surprised to see Phil and Tracey still there.

"That will be all, Mr. Williams. You are discharged until dinner."

"What? Oh, thank you. I mean, aye, aye."

Phil saluted her with his bundle of sugarcane and followed Tracey into the shade of the depot's overhanging roof at the front. For fifteen minutes they remained, swishing flies from their faces. The ennui of the heat, the brilliance of the day, and the darkness of the shade made them uncomfortable. The ground below them was hard. Soon crawling ants filed busily in streams around their feet.

"Not much of a start," Phil observed.

Tracey's hand lightly touched Phil's. He squeezed her hand softly.

"Do you want to go back on board?" she whispered.

"Yes."

Once on board, Phil closed the door to the stateroom. He watched Tracey undress. Her small breasts hung down and quivered as she bent over to slip off her sandals. Her belly rounded ever so slightly. It was quiet in the stateroom. Only the humming of the blood in their ears seemed to make any sound. Their skins were vibrant, pulsating from their encounter with the tropical heat.

Phil walked to the porthole, closed the curtain, and snapped the hooks. He stripped and stood naked in the soft diffuse light. Tracy blushed to see him in the mirror, strutting shamelessly the way men do, the semidarkness closing him in at the window. He came forward.

"Phil," she whispered, laughing, "I'm all sweaty . . ."

Phil was behind her. The last piece of sugarcane was in his mouth. He took the cane and put it into her mouth. It was a bittersweet, sticky flavor over the rough bamboo. She laughed as his hands took her by the breasts and pressed her backward. She closed her eyes, his cheek nestled against her, and moaned softly at his vigor.

Then they breathed more slowly. Opening their eyes, they saw themselves in the mirror, in the dim light, shamelessly and luxuriously intermixed together. Tracey stretched herself languorously backward, yawning with pleasure, watching her own lithe, petite body, taking delight in its supple lines and soft curves. She pressed lightly backward, kissing Phil's cheek, holding his arm over her chest. She would not let him go, but leaned drowsily against him until she felt his desire grow. Then she laughed softly and felt herself picked up in his arms.

Phil took her to the gleaming shower stall where they soundlessly bathed each other in mild soaps and lotions, lost in the timeless universe of the senses. The water cascaded in cool sheets over their bodies as they rhythmically pressed against the pebbled glass walls. The shower spray sounded like thunder in their ears. Exhausted, Tracey felt herself softly being wrapped in a thick white towel and carried like a babe toward the bed.

When they awoke it was a different twilight. The sun had gone over the *Penny Dreadful*. Insects buzzed at the screened windows behind the curtains. It was a different kind of sound. The air compressor was turned off outside, and only the mild wash of water sounded against the hull of the boat and the mooring piles. Outside there was a babble of men's voices. Phil rose through the levels of consciousness until he focused on the sounds. It was a hard, abrupt language, neither Spanish nor English. He thought he heard McCracken's voice angrily snapping in that foreign tongue. Then Tracey gradually awoke at his side.

"Are we still here?" she asked, surprised.

"I'm afraid so."

Tracey sat up and peered out through the curtains. The evening was dark blue, and the rolling thunderclouds almost black. A sultry, sulphurous weight was palpable in the air. From time to time, a sheet of white flared over the horizon, lightning from far away.

"What are they arguing about?" she asked.

"Probably money. That's all people ever argue about, honey."

Tracey looked at Phil strangely, but Phil was already dressing at the side of the bed. She looked out the window again. McCracken was gesticulating in sharp jerks, his powerful shoulders expressive, and his brows knitted together over his eyes. The water lapped steadily now against the shore and threw refuse in sharp waves onto the dark sand.

"Maybe we should stay on board," Tracey said.

"Why? What's to be afraid of?"

They went up the stairs to watch the scene on the dock. McCracken stood towering over what seemed to be engine parts, spread out on blankets on the dock, the nuts and bolts in compact bunches. Lanterns illuminated his sweat-drenched shirt, made his skin glisten. Their faces unreadable, the laborers stood or sat, unmoving. Behind them all the depot was swallowed in darkness and the palm trees merged into a black silhouette against the deepening twilight.

McCracken now stepped against the railing of the *Penny Dreadful*. There was a manic glint in his eyes.

"Anything the matter, Captain?" Phil asked.

McCracken looked up sharply, striving for control. "What do you know about labor disputes?" he asked dryly.

"I've been involved in a few in my time."

"These apes have ruined my engine."

Phil weighed the consequences. The dark mass of the cove's foliage seemed to have blocked into a sturdier mass in the last few moments. On the dock, the men remained motionless, sullen, defiant. Tracey now came on deck.

"They damned well ruined the distributor," McCracken spat out. "They dropped a bolt through it. Can you believe that?"

"Well, accidents happen . . ."

"No accident, Mr. Williams. Damned carelessness."

Phil looked at McCracken. A kind of uneasiness squeezed around Phil's chest. He looked down at the dark water, massing and relaxing below the boat.

"Exactly how far *are* we from another distributor?" Phil asked softly.

"I'm having one shipped in. By outboard," McCracken said irritably. "By *outboard!*"

The night seemed to surround them all with an impalpable darkness. McCracken turned around, staring balefully at the men.

"In the old days, the culprit would have been seized and made to walk the plank."

Phil grinned. "That doesn't repair your distributor."

"No," McCracken snorted. "But the damned fool would never make such a mistake again!"

Phil and McCracken laughed awkwardly. The men watched them. Tracey leaned against the railing, watching the reflections of the lanterns on the black sea.

"Is it going to be long?" she asked.

"A few hours, I'm afraid," McCracken said. "I am heartily sorry . . ."

"Forget it, Captain," Phil said. "It wasn't your fault."

"Thank you," McCracken mumbled. "These men. They only learn mechanics by trial and error."

For a long moment the eerie silence of waiting grew. Time grew as dense as the night settling on the cove. Still, the men on the dock did not move, as impassive as water birds facing the northern sea. The moon now rose above the horizon, and the *Penny Dreadful* threw its dark shadow against the water massing below them.

McCracken studied Phil and raised a single bushy eyebrow quizzically. His arms were folded, giving him an appearance of brute strength.

"You're in the leather business?" he suddenly inquired.

"Design, really. Suede, different kinds of leather. Ladies' fashions."

"I would imagine that winter would be your busiest season."

"The holidays, to be sure. Of course, most of the work is done months in advance."

McCracken had trouble lighting his pipe. He puffed vigorously, frowned, and turned back to Phil.

"Would you like to place a call to New York?" he asked. "There's a phone in the shack."

"Hell, no," Phil laughed. "Nothing doing. I'm on vacation!"

"Suppose there were an emergency?"

"There's always an emergency, Captain. But they'll work it out. To tell the truth, no one knows where I am."

McCracken sighed, said nothing for a while. He seemed to be thinking.

"Well, Mr. Williams. You certainly have cut yourself off. I do hope you'll enjoy the cruise."

"I hope we will."

Phil experienced a vague feeling of having just been grilled. Probably his imagination, but he found it unsettling nonetheless. Tracey gave no indication of being troubled. The men on the dock sat on empty crates. One of them sipped from a dark bottle. Penny McCracken came back to the stern railing of the *Penny Dreadful*.

"The Captain and I should like to add a day to the excursion," she said. "To make up for today."

Phil was visibly touched. "Not necessary," he mumbled. "We enjoyed—"

"We insist," McCracken added. "The matter is closed."

For several moments they stood, a bit awkward, at the stern railing. Then Penny went below and returned in a few minutes with a tray and four squat glasses filled with a smoky brown liquid.

"Drink slowly," she warned.

It was thick, sweet, a heavy blend of liqueurs that burned the throat. Tracey coughed. In a matter of moments Phil's head swam. He was not at all hungry and, in fact, looked forward to being drunk.

"To our new distributor," Tracey toasted.

The McCrackens raised their glasses.

For an hour there was no sign, not a sound of an approaching motor from the north. Many of the men slept against the empty crates. Penny rose.

"I'd better see to dinner."

"None for me," Phil said. "I'll wait for breakfast."

"Me, too," Tracey agreed. "It's too hot to eat."

"Get some sleep. We'll be out before the morning tide," McCracken promised. "Guaranteed."

In the quiet of the stateroom, Tracey paused. Her thinking went back to the final arrangements. Should Larry call and no one be home, he would call the neighbor. Therefore, Tracey had told them that she would be visiting her sister. As she had two sisters and did not say which one, Larry would probably not call them at all. But if he did, if there were an emergency, ought she to have dropped a line to one of her sisters to cover herself? She would make up a story about getting lost in Boston, becoming depressed, and turning back again. How terribly complicated it all was. What if Larry were to return early? And what about her tan? How would she explain it? A health club, perhaps.

"What are you thinking?" Phil asked.

"Nothing," Tracey said, removing her stocking.

"Are you sorry we came?"

"Not at all."

"I mean, it's not their fault."

"I didn't say it was."

Phil lay down beside her. Desire returned as the golden, smoky liqueurs chased away his depression. He felt comfortable with Tracey beside him. Through the curtain a cool breeze drifted down over their feet, their hands, and their faces. It smelled of distant oceans, of zephyrs dancing far away under the moon, slim bands of dark-colored currents twisting among the coral reefs.

"It would be so nice to have breakfast on the open sea," Tracey said.

"You heard the Captain. It's guaranteed."

She nestled against his shoulder, her cheek against his chest. Soon she was asleep. Her breathing softly warmed his skin, her breasts gently rising and falling under her white nightgown. Then the moon rose high enough to send its silver light through the porthole. Silver light bathed her legs and face. Phil stroked her face. Then he fell asleep, too.

In a dream, Phil saw his two sons crawling across the lawn of his Long Island summer home. The sun was cruel, the shadows long, and the two moved like cripples, haltingly, toward the front steps. They were looking for him. Phil awoke, sweating. It was cold in the stateroom. The doubloons glinted in the pale reflections of lanterns outside. Through the porthole Phil saw only two sleeping laborers on the dock. The McCrackens slept on lounge chairs.

Phil lay back down. Then he had a second dream. His two sons were swimming in Long Island Sound. A shark gained rapidly upon them. Phil awoke with a start. The *Penny Dreadful* was moving. The soft, rhythmic beat of the engine penetrated from below.

So the distributor had arrived, Phil thought vaguely. He was about to sink back into the lulling sound of the engines when another sound began to insinuate itself into his brain. It was the sound of a voice—deep, masculine, unintelligible, with only the cadences, lilting and melodious, rising above the steady thump-thump.

Tracey slept soundly. Phil quietly got out of bed and put on his robe. He went to the door and pulled it open a crack. The voice belonged to McCracken and seemed to originate from somewhere above the stateroom. Phil walked silently up the corridor and into the main salon. The first pale shafts of dawn softly illuminated the quaint furnishings. Phil made his way to the farthest porthole and peered out.

On deck, partially obscured by the bait box, Captain McCracken stood in sharp silhouette against the blue and pink line of horizion. He was reading from a small, well-worn book. His ramrod body listed slightly into the still ocean breeze as he thrust his words forth at the boundless waters ahead.

"... *Those who go down to the sea in ships, who do business in the great waters; they see the works of the Lord, and His wonders in the deep ...*"

Phil crept back down the companionway and crawled into bed. Tracey snuggled close to his body and murmured sleepily, "We're moving."

"Yes," Phil replied. He tried to will himself back to sleep, but sleep wouldn't come.

THREE

Spray shot over the bow as the *Penny Dreadful* crossed into the Gulf Stream. Tracey squealed and laughed as she stood at the wheel. The boat bounced forward under her hand and plowed into the blue-green sea ahead. Each wave smashed into white spray flying over their heads.

"Hang in there, Mrs. Williams," McCracken said, smiling, "she handles slower than a car."

Tracey turned the wheel. It took a few seconds for the boat to turn its tonnage of wood and steel.

"Which way?" Tracey called.

"Five points east," McCracken said, eyeing the compass.

"It's so powerful!" Tracey shouted into the spray.

Phil, standing behind them, looked over the edge of his beer can. The sea was unending. At the far horizon nothing seemed to move. A few whitecaps danced and dissolved into the dark blue mass, but the bow of the *Penny Dreadful* thundered through wave after wave without a shudder being felt on board.

"Nice boat," Phil said amiably.

"Ah, yes. She's a classic," McCracken said. "Built in the twenties by a master. There are those who prefer glossy acrylics and fiberglass jobs, but I'm satisfied with good old impractical wood. Of course, I've had to modify to conform to safety standards, but I tried to do it without compromising her charm and beautiful sense of the past."

Phil nodded. He lay his head back so it fell into a square of sunlight, warming his face. At the same time, he felt the cool sea wind invigorating his cheeks. He could do this forever, he thought.

"You try it, darling!" Tracey said.

Phil opened his eyes. "Time for a new skipper?" he said.

Phil put down his can of beer and ambled to the wheel. He was just drunk enough to find the dials embedded in the wood panel slightly amusing. He found the compass, a circular wheel with two needles in it, one trembling slightly.

"Due east, Mr. Williams," McCracken said.

"Let's see," Phil mumbled. "That must be this way."

It took a little time to get used to the boat's handling. In a few minutes Phil felt at home. He relinquished the wheel to McCracken when he went below for more sunburn lotion.

When he came up, Tracey had unbuttoned her shorts and blouse and was sunning herself in her bathing suit on the top deck. Penny sat in a lounge chair. Her eyes were closed, her skin well-tanned, and her sun-bleached hair gently streamed over the side of her face.

"You'd better put more of this on," Phil suggested.

Tracey smeared the golden cream over her arms and neck. Phil crouched down and kissed her under the ear. She smiled.

"Want to swim?" he asked.

"Now?"

"Sure. I'll speak to the Captain."

Phil walked to McCracken who eyed him from under a white visor.

"What's the chance of taking a swim before lunch?" Phil asked.

"Pretty good."

McCracken cut the throttle. Abruptly the engines were silenced. The boat plowed into the waves, slower and slower, and finally stood, rocking ever so slightly, in the immensity of the blue ocean.

"Are you good swimmers?" McCracken asked, removing his white shorts, revealing a pair of red and yellow bathing shorts beneath.

"Fair."

"The water is a bit rough here. We'll lower the dinghy. You can rest on that."

McCracken and Penny untied the dinghy from its boom and lowered it into the water. Tracey and Phil climbed slowly down the accommodation ladder which Penny had let into the water. The Gulf Stream was surprisingly warm as Tracey slowly descended into the seawater.

"Hey, are there sharks in this ocean?"

Phil grinned. "Now, the Captain wouldn't let us swim in shark-infested waters, would he?"

Tracey hesitated, almost embarrassed.

"What's the problem?" McCracken said, rowing the dinghy along the side of the boat with one hand.

"My wife wants to know if there are sharks in these waters," Phil said.

"There are sharks all over the ocean."

"I mean, is it safe?" Tracey asked, smiling hesitantly.

"I believe so," McCracken said, edging the dinghy away from the boat. "But if you've cut yourself, or have come to your time of the month," he added, "it would be better to go back on board."

McCracken rowed the dinghy to a spot about seventy feet away from the *Penny Dreadful*. Tracey treaded water for a few seconds, then back-stroked away from the boat. Phil stood on the last step of the ladder and jumped in.

"It's amazing," he said softly. "There must be a mile of water under our feet."

"Yes, and there's all those living things in it."

Phil laughed and kept to Tracey's pace as she stroked leisurely toward the dinghy. The water rippled sinuously

over her shoulders and down her chest. She moved effortlessly and gracefully, though she did not have the stamina
for more than a hundred yards. The two paused and
treaded water. Their legs wavered weirdly into the greenish
depths under their bodies.

"Can you kiss me while treading water?"

"Not with the whole world watching."

Phil turned to see McCracken, his burly body hairy over
the chest and upper arms, sitting in the dinghy. He seemed
almost unaware of them as he floated on his second home,
the sea.

"Where's the first mate?" Phil asked.

"There she is. She's going to dive in!"

From a spot adjacent to the top of the accommodation
ladder Penny McCracken stood briefly to adjust her swim
cap and the top of her light orange suit. Almost without
bending her knees, she abruptly kicked herself off the boat
and dove cleanly and perfectly, knifelike into the water.

"Did you see that?" Tracey murmured. "I'll bet she's a
champion swimmer."

"She certainly has form," Phil admitted.

With long, sure strokes, Penny gracefully approached
them.

"Why don't you swim out to the dinghy?" Penny said.
"It's a good place to rest."

"Good idea," Phil said and kicked forward through the
water.

When he looked up, Penny was already at the dinghy,
leaning on its edge, speaking to the Captain. Tracey side-
stroked alongside Phil. The waves lifted and lowered her as
she swam. It occurred to him that her skin would tan and
her hair would probably bleach after a few days. What
kind of complications might that cause when they returned? Phil submerged into the Gulf Stream, feeling his
own arms push behind the water, the infinity of ocean, the
depth of translucent water all around him. He felt wonder-

fully lost and insignificant. There were no more complications in his mind. Breaking the water, he threw his head from side to side and laughed.

"Need a hand, Mr. Williams?" McCracken asked.

"No thanks," Phil said as he pulled himself into the dinghy.

Though less tanned, Phil's body was trimmer, the pectorals tighter than the older man's. He was conscious of his youth and his health. He sensed Penny's watching him, almost unconsciously taking note of his shape—the way an athlete makes evaluations by habit. Phil reached down and pulled Tracey aboard. Tracey shook her hair, throwing seawater off.

"That's farther than it looks," she laughed.

"You'll be able to swim twice as far with a few days' practice," Penny said kindly.

Though it was crowded with four in the dinghy, by alternating the direction in which they sat, they were able to recline comfortably, their legs on the opposite gunwhales. The brief swim had made Tracey sleepy and she leaned her face drowsily against Phil's leg.

"Were you an athlete?" Phil asked Penny. "I mean, in competition, or something?"

Penny blushed slightly and smiled. "Many years ago, Mr. Williams. For the state of New York."

McCracken suddenly lowered himself like a seal over the side into the water without rocking the dinghy.

"Have the mate show you how to row one of these things," McCracken said. "It's a special trick."

"You're leaving us?"

"Duties call."

McCracken abruptly dived under the dinghy and swam with an awkward but powerful kick toward the *Penny Dreadful*. Phil surmised that either the Captain had taught himself to swim or had long ago sustained an injury, because the right leg kicked powerfully downward while the left came in sideways in a kind of side kick. The old boy,

nevertheless, was already halfway across the expanse between the boat and the dinghy and moving effortlessly.

"Was your husband also in competition?" Phil asked
delicately.

"No, he has incredible endurance," Penny said, in a
strange flat tone. "But I'm still faster."

Phil felt the dinghy bob pleasantly under him. The motion made him drowsy. He felt the warmth of Tracey's face
against his legs as he closed his eyes in the heat of the
day.

Shielding her eyes from the sun, Penny observed, "I believe the Captain is signaling us. Would you like to row us
back?"

Phil opened his eyes. His arms and shoulders felt hot,
burning. The sea danced lazily around until it looked like a
flat edge at the horizon. Phil felt his leaden body drained of
energy as he sat up.

"The Captain said there was a trick involved," he murmured sleepily.

"It's very easy," Penny said, placing the oars in their
locks. "Just remember when to turn your wrist."

Penny easily pulled the oars back and forth several
times, twisting them at the end of the stroke so they sliced
back through the water for propulsion. Phil took the oars
and struggled with them manfully. The dinghy swung side
to side at the same spot on the ocean.

"Don't these things have outboards?"

"Many do. But Cap'n Jack doesn't believe in being
overly mechanized. See, you're getting the hang of it,"
Penny said, changing the subject. "It's a rhythm. It becomes very natural."

Phil stopped, then started again, consciously trying to
find the rhythm. The blades, though, pushed the dinghy
sideways. Frustrated, he grabbed the oars tightly and studiously synchronized their motions. Gradually the dinghy
progressed toward the boat.

"I think I'll leave," Tracey teased.

"You'll stay right here, young lady, if it takes the whole goddam afternoon."

"When the oars clear, twist them. That's right," Penny instructed. "Now twist. Wait. Twist. Hold it. Twist and pull. You've got it!"

After several moments Phil was close enough to let Penny pull the dinghy to the accommodation ladder.

"Hard work, Mr. Williams," Penny said pleasantly. "You're earned your lunch."

Inside the dining salon the sunlight bathed the teak walls, making the glassware sparkle on the table. Light glittered from the silverware and stainless steel fixtures. A bowl of fruit was set in the center of the table. A stew steamed at four place settings.

"Mmmmmmm," Phil sniffed appreciatively. "Crab?"

"And a few other things," Penny said. "Try the salad."

Tracey dipped her fork into a huge bowl of greens at the side of her plate. "My goodness," she said with a full mouth. "This is superb. It's so tangy. There's different kinds of fish in there. I can taste three kinds."

"Well, it's most appropriate," Penny said, drinking a deep red fruit punch. "You were swimming among their friends a little while ago."

Tracey laughed. The tangy fruit punch was full-bodied, with pieces of watermelon fiber throughout it. Phil helped himself to another portion of the stew. Penny placed a small basket of woven bread rolls on the table.

When they had eaten their fill, McCracken went to a cabinet and pulled out a small bottle of an almost clear brandy. He raised the bottle and looked questioningly at Phil.

"By all means, Captain," Phil said.

McCracken reached for four small glasses from a high shelf and brought them to the table. The brandy gurgled as it flowed into the glasses. Phil raised his glass to Tracey as the sunlight caught in her hair, making it flame a dazzling white.

"To you, darling," he said.

"To you," Tracey answered, blushing slightly.

After a moment McCracken cleared his throat. Phil declined a second drink. Penny took the dishes and bowls away, leaving the bowl of fruit. Phil helped himself to an orange, slicing broad peels with a knife.

"It is right that we eat these fish and pluck these fruit," McCracken observed, lighting his thick black pipe which, Phil noticed, was well worn and scratched with the years.

"Excuse me?" Phil said.

"Species develop over the ages. Someday there will be no men."

"I don't quite follow you, Captain."

"Quite simply, Mr. Williams. Once there was a time when there were no men. Now there are. But in a few million years, why, it will be all different again."

"I suppose you have a point."

Phil and Tracey subtly exchanged glances, secretly amused at the Captain's philosophy. Phil handed her a large, cool piece of peeled orange.

"How does that make it right for us to eat fish and fruit?" Tracey asked. "It must be criminal from their point of view."

McCracken puffed dourly at his pipe. Seeing it was out, he relit it with a large match lying atop the stove. He puffed with satisfaction a few times. Evidently, he was not accustomed to philosophical debate, and the sudden realization that Tracey might be more nimble than he somewhat dampened his willingness to venture an opinion.

"They have no point of view," McCracken said. "Only the ruling species has a point of view."

"Surely the sharks and octopuses would disagree," she said amiably.

"Then let them, Mrs. Williams. I tell you, intelligence is what rules the world. That is how they end up in our salad dressing and not we in theirs. It's intelligence that built the *Penny Dreadful.* Intelligence lets us sport where once there was only the struggle for sheer survival."

Penny smiled indulgently as she swept crumbs from the table into a silent butler, as though she had heard this all many times before. Phil shared a smile with her. Mc-Cracken reddened slightly.

"Maybe someday it won't be intelligence that rules the world," Tracey suggested. "Maybe something else."

"Like what?" McCracken asked.

Tracey shrugged. "How could I suggest something I can't even imagine? But there was a time when it was the ability to reproduce that ruled the species. Then it was the ability to change. Now it's intelligence. Maybe in a few million years some new trait will be the dominant one."

"But in the meantime," McCracken concluded dryly, "intelligence makes the rules. The rules of the games we play."

Tracey took another segment of Phil's orange.

"And enjoy playing," she added.

"Quite right," McCracken said amiably.

Phil thought he heard the conversation through some vague, attenuated barrier of absurdity. He wondered if Tracey found the old man as amusing. It was like being drunk. You could carry on a conversation for quite a while before you crashed in the realization that everything was totally disconnected.

"Might I ask you what you are smoking?" Phil asked.

Startled, McCracken looked up. His thoughts broke from the train of recent conversation.

"Does it perturb you?"

"No, no. On the contrary. Only it's not something I've smelled before."

"It's a Jamaican blend. Several tobaccos from South America and a few local species. Not very rich, but striking in its taste."

"I'd like to try some if possible."

"That may be possible, Mr. Williams," McCracken said. Obviously pleased, he made no move to accommodate him.

Tracey yawned. "All the swimming and the sun," she murmured drowsily. "If you don't mind, I'm going to take a nap."

"Enjoy your rest, Mrs. Williams," McCracken said, half-rising from the chair.

Penny went into the stateroom at the end of the hall and soon Phil heard the shower beat against the glass walls of the bathroom. McCracken turned to find Phil gazing out the porthole.

"Mr. Williams," McCracken said.

"Yes?"

"I'll let you try some of my tobacco if you'll step up to the deck with me."

"All right."

McCracken went into the stateroom and returned with an ivory-handled pipe which he handed to Phil Then they went up on deck.

The afternoon was still hot, but there was a breeze again. Reveling in the feel of the sun on his body, Phil took off his shirt. He felt the warmth fill out over his shoulders and arms. McCracken went up to the wheelhouse and turned the ignition key. Suddenly the *Penny Dreadful* kicked to life. The boat slowly moved into the small waves, until McCracken further pulled out the throttle and the hull smashed through the water. Spray flew from both sides.

Ducking into the protected wheelhouse, Phil allowed McCracken to light his pipe. There was something invigorating about the dry, scratchy tobacco. It seemed to have an aroma of something else, like black, twisted trees in it, Phil thought. It raced his blood and was stimulating.

"Do you find me a bit odd?" McCracken asked.

"What? Of course not. Why do you say that?"

"I believe you and your wife exchanged glances during our conversation."

The man may be odd, Phil thought, but he's sharp as an eagle.

"Oh, that. You should know that my wife studied moral philosophy. In fact, taught it."

"A philosopher?"

"No, just a researcher into ethical studies. When I met her she was working on a book," Phil lied.

"On moral philosophy?"

"Yes."

"Ever published?"

"I don't believe so. I mean, chapters have appeared, you know, in journals and such. But not as a book. No, it hasn't been published."

Phil took another drag on the pipe and pretended to admire it. He knew he was a terrible liar and he did not know why he even bothered to lie. McCracken observed him pleasantly. His small, sharp eyes observed Phil's face.

For a while the two men sat in silent communion, bonded together by the pounding weight of the boat under them, the mutual appreciation of the sea stretching around them to infinity, the heat of the sun, and the taste of salt in the air. Then too, it was the first time they had been on board together without the presence of women. This added a gruff, relaxed kind of intimacy to their company.

"Great weather," Phil observed.

"Mark my words, Mr. Williams, the day will come when you will want to be closer to it."

"It wouldn't be impossible."

"There is really nothing in the north worth having except the money," McCracken said. There was a peculiar note of bitterness or unusual hardness in his voice. "And the day will come when that isn't enough."

Phil was not certain what McCracken meant. He feared another labyrinthine philosophical discourse.

"There are compensations," Phil said.

"What?"

"The theater. The art. The society—you know, the people who work there."

As if in answer, McCracken took the wheel off automatic and steered by hand.

"Be assured, Mr. Williams," McCracken said starkly, "you'll view life differently . . . one day."

Phil shrugged.

Far away on the horizon, over the port side, small dark clouds chased through the deep blue sky as though trying to keep up with the *Penny Dreadful*. Dark patches of shadow followed them on the water's surface, contrasting oddly with the shimmer of the waves around them.

"Rain, Mr. Williams. Far away. We probably won't see any of it."

Toward late afternoon, Phil observed that the clouds became darker, but smaller, and the sky a deeper blue. McCracken had given him a light jacket to ward off sunburn on his arms and upper shoulders. Phil briefly considered some exercise. He was utterly content to do nothing for the rest of the afternoon.

"You'd best attend to your wife," McCracken suggested. "The ladies like a little time to prepare themselves before dinner."

Phil glanced at his watch. "You're right, Captain. The afternoon just disappeared. I'll go and wake her up."

Phil left McCracken at the stern railing, gazing at the departing sea.

Down in the stateroom, Tracey slept under a single sheet, her sheer nightgown barely covering her shoulders and hips. Phil placed a hand on her thigh, and she woke up immediately with focused eyes.

"You won't believe this," Phil said softly, "but it's almost time for dinner."

They dressed. Phil showered last and combed his hair before the mirror.

"By the way, honey, if McCracken asks, you're in the process of writing a book on ethical philosophy, parts of which have already appeared in journals."

"Why on earth did you tell him that?"

"I got trapped when he started prying. Before I knew what I was doing, I'd made that up."

"Hell, I haven't thought of any of that since I graduated."

"Fake it," Phil chuckled. "That's what you did then."

A pillow flew through the air against his head. Phil laughed and combed his hair again. They went out to dinner.

There was no dinner on the table in the aft salon, however, when they arrived. Nor were here any pots or pans on the stove in the galley. Only a cutting board with a knife and a few red stains.

Penny emerged from her stateroom wearing a beige dress. Her hair was neatly combed and gathered in a bun.

"Won't you join us on deck, Mr. and Mrs. Williams?" she said.

"Dinner on deck!" Tracey said. "What a marvellous idea!"

"It may get cool," Penny said. "Perhaps you would want a wrap."

"Right. Thanks."

Penny went up to the deck while Phil went back to the stateroom for Tracey's white knitted shawl. Tracey stood for a moment where the metal steps joined the open area that led to the galley. On her side were the cabinets that housed the fire extinguishers, rain gear, spare fishing tackle and poles. There were shelves of aluminum wire, fittings, and an array of wrenches and pliers in carefully placed wooden holders. From where she stood she saw the door ajar to the McCrackens' stateroom at the distant end of the companionway, at the bow of the *Penny Dreadful*.

The twilight was descending and no lights were on, so it was dark as she felt her way toward the door. Suddenly she worried that the Captain might still be in his room. She peered cautiously around the door and saw it was empty. Ancient rifles lay bolted to the walls, knives in series alongside a deep mahogany desk, and a deep glass-enclosed bookcase along the far wall stocked with thick, red books whose bindings were obscured with age, the titles long ago faded into the cloth. Several quills protruded from an inkwell on the desk. The ink on the quill appeared to be wet. Curious, Tracey noticed that there was an old sea map affixed to the wall, showing an area of the Great Bahama Bank. Perhaps a dozen dark lines had been etched over it in meandering curves. She surmised various voyages had been made into the region.

"Tracey," Phil whispered from the corridor, "where are you?"

She appeared in the doorway, put a finger to her lips, and gestured Phil to come closer.

"Look!" she said. "It's just like an old-time movie set. You know, an Errol Flynn flick."

"Come on. I don't want to be seen poking around like this. Besides, they're waiting for us."

Tracey reluctantly followed Phil into the corridor. As they climbed the stairs, she turned to him and whispered, "You didn't see his logbook."

"What logbook?"

"The one on the desk next to the quill pen. And the quill was still wet. He must have just finished writing with it."

"So?"

"Don't you think that's quaint?"

"Utterly."

"You have no curiosity, that's your problem."

They were advancing around the wheelhouse when they saw the McCrackens seated at a small table on the foredeck. Dishes and glassware sparkled upon a table laid with

a white tablecloth. A steaming casserole dish and several
side dishes were visible. A maroon and magenta series of
clouds provided a perfect make-believe backdrop.

"Oh, isn't this lovely?" Tracey whispered.

The Captain, as was his habit, half rose from his chair
when Tracey approached the table.

"Good evening and *bon appétit*," Penny said. Gesturing
to an empty chair she said, "Won't you be seated, Mrs.
Williams?"

"Thank you."

The white wine was poured gently into their glasses.
Semi-dry, it was suited to the relaxed atmosphere of the
evening. Phil noticed that the table was laid to favor the
Captain so that, instead of four people being seated
equally, McCracken undeniably sat at the head of them all.
McCracken's back was to the sunset. Gazing at him, they
saw the ragged wisps of orange cloud emanate from behind like an ancient aureole, but McCracken's face had
taken on a stern visage, as though cut from granite. He was
moody, silent.

"Anything wrong, Captain?" Phil ventured.

"Oh, there is a bit of a storm possible."

"Is that a problem?"

"Not if it's a squall."

"You're expecting something really big?" Tracey asked.
A curious excitement was audible in her voice.

McCracken shrugged. "That's what I'm thinking about."

"You mean a hurricane, Captain," Phil said.

"Possible, Mr. Williams. Possible."

"You see," Penny said matter-of-factly, dishing out a
swordfish steak with a thick sauce from the casserole dish,
"we're near the area where most of the big storms are
born."

"It's not the season for them," McCracken added hastily.

"But sometimes *they* don't know that, is that it?" Phil
said.

"That's about it, Mr. Williams," McCracken chuckled.

"Still, it presents no problem. There is no definite storm yet—only the possibility of one being born."

"And if it happens," Penny said, "we would have to go to port. Probably Nassau, I should think."

Phil and Tracey exchanged quick glances.

"You might enjoy that, Mrs. Williams," Penny said. "Give you a chance to do some shopping. Nassau is duty-free, you know."

"Oh no," Tracey said quickly. "I prefer to keep away from all those big places. I'm really enjoying the solitude."

McCracken winked at Phil. "Now there is a wife worth her weight in gold. Take a lesson, Penny."

Penny smiled and sat down. The swordfish steak was served with potatoes sautéed with a creamy dressing, thin, twisted bread rolls with whipped sweet butter, and a mixed vegetable dish from which the aroma of spices rose like a heady perfume.

Phil, unable to resist the steaming dinner before him, hastily dug his fork into the swordfish steak. He was munching it with gusto when he felt Tracey's restraining hand on his arm. The McCrackens were observing a silent grace.

Phil choked gently, swallowed, replaced his fork, and dutifully lowered his head for what seemed like an eternity. Tracey had to look away to keep from bursting out laughing. Then McCracken raised his head and began eating. He noticed Phil's head was flushed.

"Are you well, Mr. Williams? Your face is just a touch red, I think."

"I . . . I'm allergic to discussions about storms."

They ate for a few seconds in silence. McCracken exchanged glances with his wife.

"A rather peculiar allergy, Penny. I don't believe I've ever encountered it before."

Tracey finally burst out laughing, covering her mouth with a white napkin.

"It's been in the family for generations," Phil muttered.

"I believe Mr. Williams is joking," Penny said, smiling at McCracken's expense.

"I see," McCracken said uncertainly.

After a few moments the sunset turned to a dark purple. The evening stars were visible in the east. The *Penny Dreadful* bobbed gently on the smooth and darkening sea. The clouds had nearly dissipated, save for some tortured trails at the western horizon. It was hard to believe, Phil thought, that there could be a storm for miles around.

"I should think it would be exciting," Tracey said, "to be at sea in a storm. I mean, not a hurricane, but a small storm."

"A nice, pretty little storm," Phil chided.

"You know perfectly well what I mean."

"I believe the moon is rising," McCracken said.

Tracey turned. Over her shoulder, along the knife edge of the eastern sea, a crescent bulged up out of the water. It was silvery white and clear in its visible purity.

"One thing about the ocean," she said, "is it makes you appreciate infinity. That's not a thing you normally think about."

"But the ocean is finite," McCracken said.

"Ah, but the vastness of it, Captain. It changes your perspective."

"It does, Mrs. Williams."

"How long have you been on the sea, Captain?" Phil asked.

McCracken paused. "I would say my whole life, Mr. Williams. Because my life began the day I went to sea."

"And before that?"

McCracken gestured vaguely and sipped wine.

"Lived and worked in a variety of places, but that was another age ago."

"It's not only the vastness, Mrs. Williams," Penny broke in, "but the aloneness, the isolation. It is like a force all around you. That, too, changes your perspective on human life."

"We are all playthings," McCracken said, with a sudden and surprising undertone of strange bitterness. "We play, and are played with according to the rules we discussed at lunch, Mrs. Williams."

"Possibly, Captain," Tracey said, wary that she was supposed to be a published author on the subject of moral philosophy. To her relief, McCracken only frowned.

The moon had risen far over the horizon. Its color had noticeably brightened, an almost blue-white, with subtle pockets of deeper blue barely visible on its surface. A pale glow shimmered over the *Penny Dreadful* and entangled it in its slow wake. Tracey's arms were illumined by the pale moonlight.

"Wouldn't it be nice to drift along in the dark?" she said. "I mean, just for a moment or two? Just the boat under the stars?"

"Unfortunately," McCracken said sympathetically, "certain lights are required by law to be shown."

"But Captain," Penny said, "just for a minute. Go turn them off."

McCracken looked at Penny. With a trace of fondness at the younger woman at the foot of the table, he smiled. "Well, just for a moment."

McCracken went to the wheelhouse, fumbled in the dark for a moment, and then suddenly the deck lights on the *Penny Dreadful* went out. Tracey saw only vague suggestions of shadows in a deeper darkness. Then the ocean appeared deep blue, not black and she saw the white outlines of the deck and the cabin. McCracken sauntered heavily toward the table.

"You see?" McCracken said softly. "The ocean is never completely dark."

Tracey saw that the moon dappled far-off waves with a silver crest. In large areas of silvery blue, it rode on the sea's dark immensity. There was an overwhelming sensation of subtle light, blue and vast, that seemed to permeate the ocean and rise through the night skies.

"What are those silvery patches? Far away, against the horizon?"

"Those are actually reefs, Mrs. Williams," McCracken answered. "The water is breaking just a bit as it hits the shallower area."

"It seems to glow in the night."

"The moon is exceedingly bright out here. It has no competition."

Tracey sighed. Her hand reached over the table and fell lightly into Phil's. For a moment no one spoke. Each was wrapped in silent communion, an unselfconscious observation of the dappled surface mass of the Atlantic Ocean. Phil felt himself relieved of small burdens. A kind of nervousness evaporated from him and he felt purified, alone, and strangely exalted. Embarrassed, he reached for another glass of wine. The sound of his pouring was amplified, and rose over the gentle wash of the ocean all around.

"Since the mood is upon us," McCracken whispered mysteriously.

He walked back to the wheelhouse and cut the engines. Sound slowly died away, leaving only the watery movement below them. The *Penny Dreadful* lifted once or twice, slowed, then seemed to hang suspended under the stars.

"Do you feel it?" Penny whispered. "The isolation? Magnificent, isn't it? Now you begin to see why we could not go back."

"One could not feel grand there," McCracken said, sitting once again at the head of the table. "Here, one is larger than life."

The wine was consumed. It had grown late. Phil pressed Tracey's hand. She exchanged looks with him and returned his signal. For a few moments they sat under the stars, which seemed to sway overhead when they raised their glances to look.

Phil affected sleepiness.

"I believe the rowing knocked me out," Phil said amiably. "With your permission—and thanks for the most enjoyable supper of my life, Captain—I will retire."

"Do sleep well, Mr. Williams."

Trying not to show haste, yet slightly embarrassed at having ended the evening, Phil and Tracey made a show of walking slowly around the deck, looking out over the railing. They talked there for a moment before going below. After they closed the door to the stateroom, they embraced.

The stillness was extraordinary. Silence seemed to emanate from the ancient dresser, the bed, and from the curtains at the porthole. From time to time there was a crinkle of sound as a tiny wave rippled against the sides of the *Penny Dreadful*. Above, the McCrackens must be sitting in the darkness like captains of old, Phil thought.

His warm lips met and pressed together with Tracey's. Kissing, they undressed one another.

Half the night they made love, unable to account for their extraordinary desire, their suddenly unlimited physical strength. There was no fatigue, no sleepiness, no bone-wrenching weariness. And when the engines finally started deep in the boat, chugging lowly through the sea again, it was well past three in the morning. Tracey's hand slowly brushed her hair from her eyes. Phil returned from the bathroom, smiled at her, and sat down at the edge of the bed. Laughing quietly and almost embarrassed, her desire grew yet once again. She rose to where he sat and, half-climbing from the bed, enclosed him once again. They rocked with the motion of the boat.

Never had Phil known such utter well-being, an exhaustion that knew no bounds. Lying drowsily beside Tracey, the night still seemed to give forth an invigorating and tantalizing perfume, an intoxicating silver quietude. He lay with his head on her breast. Neither fully asleep, fingers interlocked, they drifted with the darkness.

When the cold red sunrise slanted through the porthole,

Tracey's hands were pressing Phil closer and closer against her. Her breath came in shorter and shorter gasps.

Phil cradled her head in his hands. Surprised even more at their capacity, together they made love again and once again on the bed and by the bureau, before they showered and dressed for breakfast and the new day.

FOUR

The *Penny Dreadful* cruised along the cold, blue Atlantic fringe of the Gulf Stream. Though the sun beat down directly, a cool breeze whisked over the white-dotted ocean and onto the warm decks of the boat. Phil lay with his bare back against the boards, sunglasses over his closed eyes, his chest and legs feeling the heat of the sun.

Tracey's eyes were closed as she lay beside him on the warm deck. A low-brimmed straw hat reached down almost to her sunglasses. Her two-piece bathing suit was trimmed in red slanted stripes along the top, over navy blue. She lay with her arms spread out for an even tan, feeling the utter peace of drifting with the motion of the boat.

"Mr. Williams!"

Phil looked up toward the wheelhouse.

McCracken had cut the engines of the *Penny Dreadful* and was climbing onto the deck. A long, green shaft was cradled in his arms. Phil saw a trigger mechanism at the front end and a double groove down the shaft. McCracken indicated for Phil to join him at the stern, away from Tracey, who slept soundly.

"Are you a good shot, Mr. Williams?" he asked genially.

"Can't say I've ever tried."

McCracken rapidly loaded the harpoon gun. He fit a two-foot lance down the slot and pulled back a squat, black lever, bending a metal strip to a sharp tension. Then he snapped a small rope onto an eye hook at the base of the spear.

"Did you get that? Load it pointing down, but never at your foot."

McCracken made Phil practice loading the gun. It was lighter than a rifle, naked-looking somehow. The prongs of the lance glittered at the end of the shaft. Against Phil's armpit rested a bare metal handle.

"Is there much recoil?" Phil asked.

McCracken shook his head. "Keep your nose out from behind. That's all."

"What are we shooting at?"

McCracken winked. "Depends on what we find below, doesn't it?"

"Below? You mean, under water?"

"Of course."

"But I've never—"

"Then it's about time you did."

McCracken provided scuba suits from the gear box. The mask felt uncomfortable over Phil's face. A thin line of pain circled around his forehead and cheeks. With the tank on his back and flippers on his feet, he could hardly walk. McCracken had to assist him down the accommodation ladder.

Phil suddenly entered the world of water, and that world had no horizon, no sun, no air, only a perpetual green twilight.

McCracken swam powerfully. Carrying the spear gun, he beckoned Phil on. The bed of the ocean was far below them, a dim brown with vague waves of light over the sand.

McCracken paused abruptly. Treading vertically in the water he pointed to a school of striped fish. The fish were tinged with black along their backs and lower fins, energetically darting then stopping in the water and gazing stupidly around them. Flashes of green separated them into disparate, flying blurs of color. A single fish remained, as motionless and dead as a theatrical prop. A long spear stuck out of its side. Slowly the spear's weight turned the fish side downward. McCracken pulled on the rope, and the fish fluttered toward his hands.

Phil had not seen the spear leave the gun. McCracken worked the fish free of the prongs and rubbed his stomach with his hand, signifying a good meal. McCracken set the spear again, cocked the gun, and dumped the fish into a canvas bag at his side.

"It's your turn," McCracken indicated as they treaded water.

Phil demurred, but McCracken pressed the spear gun into his hands.

Phil felt the weight of the gun disappear in his arms. Under water everything was lighter, dreamlike. It was hard to believe that in this green, shimmering ballet, he held in his hands an instrument that could kill even a man. It made his arms go cold. Then, strangely, it gave him a manly confidence. It was as though he had entered another world, a world of danger and risk, of killers and victims. Now, with McCracken's guidance, he was no longer a victim.

McCracken pointed ahead of him.

Silver fish, only inches long darted by in a blazing display of sunlight along their backs. Behind them a dour-looking fish, like an old man without teeth or memory, wallowed, drifting down toward the ocean floor. McCracken gestured again. More striped fish now emerged from the eternal twilight and gazed at Phil. Their mouths worked up and down as though talking to one another. Phil pulled the trigger. The spear shot forward. It reached the end of its tether, and the jerk pulled the gun out of his arms.

McCracken retrieved both spear and gun and followed Phil to the surface. Embarrassed, Phil explained that he had misjudged the distance.

"I could remove the rope," McCracken laughed, "but I'd lose a lot of spears that way."

The minutes passed quickly. Phil wounded one fish at the base of the spine, but found that he could not get close enough to improve his aim before the fish flicked their tails and shot away. McCracken bagged another and they climbed back onto the *Penny Dreadful*.

"Don't feel bad," McCracken said, clapping Phil on the shoulder. "It takes practice. We'll do this again. I promise you."

On the foredeck Penny gently touched Tracey's arm.

"Mrs. Williams?"

"Yes?" Tracey murmured, opening her eyes.

"Would you like to give me a hand with the fish?"

"The fish?"

"Yes. Your husband and the Captain caught a charming pair of sea bass."

Tracey sat up and sleepily rubbed her eyes. Awakening fully, she sighed, leaned against her arms folded on her knees, and squinted out at the sparkling sea.

"I'll be waiting in the galley."

"All right. I'll be down presently."

Penny was grating cheese at the galley counter. Tracey saw an oblong knife and a blocklike scraper on a chair nearby. In a pail of water were the two large, striped fish, one of which slapped its tails against the metal.

"It's alive," Tracey said in disgust.

"Meat keeps better that way—until the last moment. That's the secret."

"Poor thing."

Penny had prepared a large broiler with cheese, various spices, sliced shallots, and a bit of wine. She worked quickly and efficiently. Occasionally Tracey looked down at the thrashing fish in the bucket.

"It's the last moment for it, isn't it?" Tracey said. "How sad."

Penny smiled. "Do you want to say last rites?" She held

out a large, broad-bladed knife with a heavy black handle.

Tracey waved it away with her hand. "No, please. I couldn't."

"I'll teach you how. They feel no pain."

"I'd rather not."

Penny reached down and with both hands lifted the squirming, kicking sea bass onto the counter. She picked up the knife and with a single whack slammed through the skin, meat, and neck bones down to the wood of the counter. With the knife she separated the head from the body. With her left hand she held down the quivering body, which shook and then lay still.

Blood flowed onto the counter into a fluted edge, and down into the sink. Flowing for several seconds, it thinned, dripped, and then spread out on the counter and onto Penny's hands and apron.

"The trouble has become that we hide death," Penny said, "as though it were some mystery. That's falsified our lives." She glanced at Tracey. "What's the matter, Mrs. Williams? You look pale."

"I forgot that fish have blood."

"The sight of blood makes you queasy?"

"Yes," Tracey said, turning away to the wall.

Penny picked up the second fish. To Tracey's horror, she felt the wet tail brush against her hair.

"A real beaut," Penny said.

Tracey heard the hard tail slap ferociously against the wooden counter. Then there was a long silence. It seemed as though Penny were taking a long time. It became unbearable. Then there was a tiny swish, a solid thud, and the motions of the tail subsided. There was a drip, drip, drip into the sink. When Tracey heard Penny washing the counter, she turned back.

"You do that very well," Tracey said, limply.

"Lots of practice. The thing is not to hit your finger when the seas are riding hard."

Penny held up the neatly decapitated sea bass. "Can you gut the fish?"

"I suppose."

"Most of the blood is gone."

Penny set the two fish on a tray and placed it on the chair next to Tracey. She demonstrated how to remove the fins and how to scrape the scales. With the knife she began to scrape the interior.

"Be sure to remove all the innards but leave the bone."

The sensation of Penny's voice was that of a disembodied, authoritative voice, floating around her. Tracey began to scrape.

"Scrape *away* from yourself."

The innards clung to the point of the knife. Tracey banged the blade against the rim of the bucket, and the guts dropped cleanly into the water, and they slowly sank, turning over and over.

Penny quickly shook ground seasonings into the saucepan. She seemed to be deliberating on something because she stood with a finger to her lip, as if debating with herself. Finally she reached into the shelf and produced a small packet of nutmeg. She considered a moment, then decided to try it, and lightly sprinkled a bit into the pan on the counter.

"Be sure to remove any dark tissue," Penny said as she stirred the ingredients in the saucepan. They amalgamated into a light, yellow creamy sauce. Then she put the pan on the stove and let it simmer. She began to prepare a large, oversized pan for the two fish.

"Do you have children?" Penny asked.

"No."

"Your decision, or God's?"

Tracey couldn't help smiling at the childlike nature of the question.

"Ours," she said finally.

Penny brought down a large bag of flour. She washed her hands before continuing. She stopped, as though to remember something. Then she quickly added salt to the simmering sauce in the pan.

"I always forget the salt," Penny said.

Tracey smiled. "I guess it's just not exotic enough to remember."

Outside the sea had grown colder, flatter, and an even more leaden gray. Penny looked through the porthole for a moment. Her eyes were fixed on the horizon and concentrated on a distant thought.

"The Captain and I had a son. He was killed in the war. Vietnam. But we're grateful for the years he was with us."

Tracey said nothing.

"The joy of seeing him in the morning, bathing him, watching him grow and change, seeing him learn, become an individual—it was the great joy of our lives. I don't think we could have lived without that."

Tracey wiped an imaginary piece of fish flesh from her cheek. She jabbed at the interior of the gutted fish.

"Especially during the winter," Penny said, casting a glance at Tracey, who leaned over the chair. "I used to see his face by the window, just looking out while the snow fell, and we were so happy just to be there in peace—all of us together—while the snow fell. No, I couldn't have lived without that kind of joy."

Penny stepped back, wiped her hands, and smiled.

"That should do it for now. Would you like a cup of fruit punch? With a dash of red wine in it?"

"I—well, I'd better not. I think I need some air."

"A delicate constitution, I see. Well, in that case, you may rejoin your husband. I'm sure he's wondering what's happened to you."

Tracey left. The sea breeze on deck was surprisingly cool and brisk. Phil had put on a light white jacket, and he lounged in a long chair against the cabin.

"We're going to have an *exquisite* lunch," Tracey said with an edge of sarcasm, "thanks to you and the Captain."

"Thanks to the Captain. The bass were his victims."

She sat down in a lounge chair next to Phil and put on her sunglasses.

"And I gave them their funeral. I never gutted a fish in my life! Did you know they have *blood*?"

Phil's head leaned away. He was drifting into a light sleep. She looked for half an hour over the dark blue waves around her. They seemed bluer than those of the previous day. She thought she saw tiny breaks in the vast expanse of rolling water, something dark and hard, but she did not know what they were. Then she must have drifted as well into a light sleep because McCracken's voice, though gentle, seemed to come breaking down on her like a shot of ice water.

"Mrs. Williams? I'm truly sorry, but the sea bass won't keep."

She shook her hair free of her eyes, removed her sunglasses, and prodded Phil into opening his eyes.

"Captain Jack," Phil said, slurring his first words, "your ship induces sleep."

"It's the fresh air," McCracken said. "That and the sun and the rolling motion."

"And not getting much sleep at night," Tracey added.

Phil gave her a look that she missed. McCracken caught the glance and smiled.

"Perhaps more exercise," he offered. "In any case, won't you join me below?"

McCracken spoke more like a captain now, with a kind of politeness, a sense of formality kindly reduced for their sake. His smile seemed to resemble the smiles of captains the world over—boyish, engaging, but somehow vague and well practiced.

They went down to the aft salon where the table was laid with a gay blue-checked tablecloth. The matching blue-checked dishes and pans gave the kitchen area a festive aura. A few flowers, perhaps dried seaweed, curved gracefully from tiny ceramic bowls. A fresh breeze rustled through the currents.

"We are officially out of the Stream," McCracken said, pulling back a chair for Tracey. "I suppose you didn't even notice?"

"No," Phil said.

"I think the water changed color," Tracey said.

"You see that, Penny? The makings of a true sailor. Yes, the water does change color. Now, can you tell me, what color does it change to?"

McCracken sat at the head of the table. His massive head nearly blocked out the deep blue of the sky visible through the right porthole.

"I believe it changed from blue-green to dark blue," Tracey said.

"*Bravo.*"

Penny set down the pan of fish, still bubbling under the lid, on a decorated hot plate.

"Mrs. Williams is a quick learner," Penny said. "She was my assistant with this meal and was an excellent observer."

"Was she now?" McCracken said jovially. "Splendid!"

Phil dropped his napkin, bent down to pick it up, and saw McCracken's foot gently touch Penny's. Then her foot gently responded and touched his.

"That's very important," McCracken was saying as Phil returned to the table, "to be able to observe and respond to command. Why, I could tell you stories where the failure of a single crewman to properly execute an order resulted in the loss of over a dozen lives. Not to mention the company's entire cargo."

"Well," Tracey said, smiling, "I hope I never become responsible for anything like that."

"Let's hope not," McCracken said, picking up the carving knife.

Penny poured the wine. "How did Mr. Williams perform?" she asked cheerfully.

"Well. Very well," McCracken said. "I'd rate him at about a six."

A burst of laughter exploded from Phil.

"So you've joined the rating game, too. Six, huh?" Phil winked at Tracey. "Not bad considering I'm not a buxom blonde."

Ignoring Phil's comment, McCracken fell to cutting the sea bass and handing a large portion to Tracey, then to Phil.

"You did very well," McCracken said, pouring himself wine. "Very few score above a six. Now then, I'd advise you to try this with a little bread first. If it doesn't seem too hot, go ahead. Jump into it."

Warned, Phil nibbled cautiously. His cheeks filled with the Captain's dark, heavy bread. The sea tang of the fish assailed his nostrils and tongue at the moment the burning sensation of the spices flowed into his mouth. His eyes began to water and he reached for the fruit punch.

"You were warned," Tracey laughed.

"You'll get the hang of it," McCracken said, smiling. His mouth worked with gusto around the seafood. "You'll find that many of the islands in the tropics have learned to spice up the sea's bounty."

"It certainly does spice it up," Phil agreed.

The Captain automatically shot his hand out to stop a wet-bottomed glass suddenly sliding in a small wave.

For the next quarter hour they ate steadily in silence. Then Phil leaned back in his chair. His mouth agreeably tingling, he pulled two large, crooked cigars from his jacket pocket.

"Captain?" he offered. "A little something from New York."

"For me?"

"They look like they've been sat on, I know. But they're made that way."

McCracken laughed as Phil lit the cigar for him.

"I believe the first mate would approve this better up on deck."

"Good idea. I could use a stretch."

Phil and the Captain rose from the table.

"You coming, honey?" Phil said pointedly.

Tracey was picking up dishes from the table and handing them to Penny at the sink.

"I'll be there in a sec," she said.

Hiding a flicker of displeasure that passed like a wave over his face, Phil puffed on the cigar, turned, and followed the Captain up the steps.

Below, Tracey put the dishes away quickly and wiped along the edges of the counters and the table, under Penny's direction. Penny scoured the pots, closed the cabinet doors, and rinsed the sink. Tracey checked over the counter, took off the apron she had tied around her waist, and then went to join the men.

Phil helped Tracey up to the top deck where McCracken had set two pairs of lounge chairs.

"K.P. duty wasn't included in their ad," Phil softly grumbled.

"Oh darling, don't be angry. It feels good to help out."

"Well, don't make a habit of it. They'll begin to take it for granted."

Tracey picked up a cushion from the lounge chair, plumped it up, and sat down, stretching her legs out toward the open sea. A few darker clouds were ranged over the horizon, as though tracking the *Penny Dreadful* which drifted at slow speed on automatic pilot.

"You see, Mr. Williams," McCracken said, emerging from the wheelhouse. "Intelligence. It boils down to survival, sooner or later. Men of the sea knew about these things in the old days."

Phil sighed. Being stuck in the center of the sea with a garrulous host was more serious than, say, at a cocktail gathering in the city, Phil thought to himself. Here, there was no escape.

"Yes, Captain, I know," Phil said.

Penny now sat by the Captain's side as the perfect help-mate. She did not disturb his train of thought, nor was he oblivious to her presence. Phil could only remark on the perfect teamwork the two embodied. Penny stared pleasantly over the ocean at the invisible spot that had engaged the Captain's attention. Though they appeared relaxed, each kept a sharp eye out for any incongruities in the waters ahead.

"Those were good days in a way," McCracken finally said, quietly.

"Sure. Scurvy. Mutiny. Pirates."

McCracken raised a hand, as though to obliterate Phil's objections.

"There was no . . . no . . . how shall I say this, Mr. Williams? There was no *falseness*."

"I don't follow you, Captain."

"There was no *protection*. No civilization. Not on the sea."

"There were laws. Codes of conduct."

McCracken scratched the back of his head in mild frustration. "I seem to have difficulty expressing myself, Mr. Williams. I mean that all the boundaries were removed when a man was on the sea. It was a struggle of the intelligence and will over the elements."

"And over other men," Penny added.

"Yes," McCracken went on. "Over other men as well. No radios. No communication with land-bound authority. Not on the high seas of those days. Just brute power and intelligence."

Phil coughed and slowly let his cigar die out. He tossed it out into the water and lost sight of it.

"Well," Phil said, "I, for one, vote for modern methods. I'm not sure I'd care to be on a ship that ran on 'brute power and intelligence,' as you put it."

McCracken turned suddenly to Phil. His eyes brightened, enticing and friendly. His stubby fingers jutted toward Phil with the cigar. "That's because you've never *tried*, Mr. Williams. You don't know the thrill of isolation, or risk, or mastery!"

"I suppose that makes my life incomplete," he said with an edge of sarcasm.

"It does, Mr. Williams," McCracken said, relaxing once again, and returning to his former demeanor. "It does."

For several minutes they only sat. Tracey seemed oblivious to Phil's discomfort. Perhaps, Phil wondered, she was asleep under the sunglasses. The sun had cooled. Looking up, Phil saw a few tiny puffs of cloud cover the sun, until a white-hot disk showed plainly through them.

"I'll give you an example," McCracken said.

McCracken hunted for his lighter, having difficulty with the remainder of the black, crooked cigar. As he lit it, Phil cupped his hand around the flame, protecting it from the wind. McCracken puffed and nodded his thanks.

"Blackbeard," he mumbled over the cigar butt.

"The pirate?"

McCracken nodded. "Now this was in the days when the navy was afraid of the pirates. And for good reason. Blackbeard was smarter than they were. He was cruel. A lot of good sailors fed the sharks trying to bring in Blackbeard."

"How awful," Tracey

Phil turned and smiled. "Thought you were asleep, honey."

"I was. I heard something about sharks."

"Your husband and I were discussing a famous pirate, Mrs. Williams." McCracken paused. "Blackbeard," he said softly. "Wore firecrackers in his beard. You could smell him twenty feet away. Clothes matted with filth and blood. Over six feet tall. Castrated the sailors he caught. Most of the ladies committed suicide before he got to them.'"

Tracey shivered. She laid her blouse over the swimsuit top, covering her shoulders.

McCracken leaned back, folded his hands, and gazed

down at the dark water rolling swiftly by. His concentration seemed complete, as though Phil were hardly at his side.

"A man without so much as an *idea* of morality," McCracken said. "Not even to his own crew. Keelhauled his men for the tiniest infraction. And when Blackbeard got drunk, he saw infractions everywhere."

"What's keelhauling?" Tracey asked.

"What? Oh, you tie a man's hands to one rope, his feet to another. You pass him back and forth under the keel of the ship, from side to side, under the water. Scrape the barnacles off."

Phil winced. "Barnacles? Those are spiny."

McCracken shrugged. "I never figured out if that worked. You've got to remove the growth somehow. Of course, you'd need a different man the next time."

Tracey winced and looked away, trying to avoid picturing a man scraped into ribbons under the immense keel of a sailing vessel.

"Why didn't they mutiny?" Phil asked. "Seems to me—"

"Because sailors had no rights. And pirates were even lower than sailors. Some mutinied, of course. But what happened to them I can't relate in front of Mrs. Williams."

Phil was oddly fascinated in spite of himself by McCracken's tales of the old, lawless sea. He knew without looking that Tracey, discomfited by such things, was probably avoiding them both.

"Tell me, Captain," Phil asked, "what happened to this demon? I can't believe that such an evil monster found a peaceful end."

McCracken chuckled. "It has nothing to do with being evil, Mr. Williams. Quite simply, Blackbeard was caught by a more intelligent man.'"

There was a long silence. McCracken puffed deeply, trying to extract the last draws of the diminished cigar butt. At length, he flipped it over the railing and watched it tumble in the air. Penny sat as a silent accomplice, listening, encouraging, and saying nothing at all.

"You ever lift that old cutlass in your stateroom, Mr. Williams?"

"No."

"For a normal man, it's a heavy weapon. Meant to be used once in a battle. Maybe twice. No more." He made a sweeping gesture across his neck and down his chest. "A strong man, a really strong man, will cut through the shoulder, neck, and chest with a single blow.

Phil nodded.

"Now, the thing is this. Blackbeard and his crew used cutlasses nearly twice as heavy and a foot longer. So you see, when you got hit by a sword like that . . ."

"It would discourage you from continuing."

McCracken eyed Phil, decided Phil was trying to be humorous, and then cleared his throat.

"These were very powerful men, Mr. Williams. And very cruel."

McCracken turned away, not to look at Penny, but in her direction. A wall of clouds seemed to have arisen in the west, despite the *Penny Dreadful*'s steady clip eastward.

"What would you have done, Mr. Williams?" McCracken asked.

"I?"

"If you had been given the assignment of bringing Blackbeard in?"

Phil felt the darkened eyes searching his own, as though examining him there for something, for that something McCracken called intelligence but in reality was something closer to cruelty.

"Well, I suppose the secret *is* intelligence," Phil said. "Isn't that the gist of what you're trying to say?"

McCracken smiled broadly, showing a row of gold-capped teeth on the side of his mouth. "Excellent, Mr. Williams, you do learn. I may be an imperfect instructor, but you do learn."

"Thank you."

McCracken leaned back in the lounge chair, closer to Phil, assuming a confidential, relaxed attitude.

"You're right, of course," McCracken said. "What happened is that Maynard, the man who caught Blackbeard, trained his crew with rapiers."

Phil looked at McCracken. "Those thin, little fencing swords?"

"Precisely."

Phil thought it over, blinked, and then shook his head.

"A rapier is very light," McCracken gently explained. "You can fence for a long time with a rapier."

"So?"

"A cutlass is extremely heavy. Even if you're built like Blackbeard. Fifteen, twenty pounds. You swing that around for more than a minute and your arm grows weary. You tremble with fatigue. You pause. You switch the weapon to your other arm."

Phil waited.

"And in that split second of vulnerability," McCracken said insistently, "in that one instant of unguarded stance, you slip in the rapier. Like that. Puncture a lung. Poke a vein. Blind your opponent."

Phil nodded, trying to imagine the scene.

"Is that what happened?"

"Yes," McCracken said. "Not far from where we've been. Maynard caught him in a low tide, boarded the ship, and fenced him. It took courage to persevere with such a plan. When your men are rolling in bloody stumps around your legs. But in the end, Maynard prevailed. Intelligence, Mr. Williams. A simple idea like that."

"Amazing, Captain."

"Isn't it?"

Phil felt an odd kind of mesmerization, a flavor of the Captain's tale, the rushing of the wind, the surging of the boat, and a kind of diminished dreaming. He was barely conscious of anything but the Captain's powerful personality next to him.

"Mr. Williams," McCracken said cautiously.

"What?"

"A bit of exercise, eh? What do you say?"

"I don't think we're up to that."

"Nonsense," McCracken laughed. "Up now!"

There was a subtle note of command in the Captain's voice that caused Phil to pick himself up and follow McCracken toward the wheelhouse. McCracken paused at a white-painted cabinet to the left of the wheelhouse door. Inside the cabinet was a jumble of beach balls, red and yellow umbrellas, Hawaiian sport shirts, Bermuda shorts, water polo balls, a volleyball net, and a medicine ball.

"Here's the net," McCracken said. "You take it while I look for the ball."

"I'm not sure I can run around much. That lunch was really—"

"Here's the ball," McCracken said, pulling out a white ball and pounding it energetically with his fist. "In excellent condition, too. Follow me."

At the stern deck there were two pairs of eye hooks set into the flagpole and into the rear of the cabin. McCracken merely hooked the net, top and bottom, to each.

"Rather neat, isn't it? Don't worry. The ball floats."

Cutting off the engine, McCracken called Tracey forward. He and Tracey played against Phil and Penny. They slipped off their sandals and put on Hawaiian sport shirts and broad-brimmed hats made of woven straw.

The rear deck was soon a blaze of riotous color, and the white ball arched back and forth over the net. Once McCracken dived overboard to retrieve the ball. The game ended when McCracken lifted Tracey bodily up, enabling her to spike a return at Phil's head.

"Score!" she laughed when the ball bounced off Phil's forehead.

"Invigorating, isn't it?" McCracken said. His face

flushed with merriment as he came under the net to shake hands.

"Great," Phil agreed. "I've never felt so—well, so great in all my life!"

In truth, when Phil looked out at the turquoise horizon, the endless soft blue that surrounded the white deck, he felt himself expanded, as though his chest were cleared of the burdens and worries he had assumed to be a permanent part of him. It was like being young again, filled with a potential for living which had barely been tapped.

By late afternoon the air had noticeably cooled. Dark washes of seawater were observable far away, sucking the coral reefs jutting only a few feet into the air. For broad stretches, brown masses extended under water, never breaking surface, but lying below it like endless, motionless sharks.

"I believe you'll have your wish," McCracken said. A rope was in his hand.

Phil put his finger on the line of the novel he was reading. He wore a light blue sweater over his bathing suit.

"What do you mean, Captain?"

"A tiny squall," McCracken said with a twinkle in his eye. "Just what your wife ordered."

Phil looked up. The sun still shone but a host of tiny, rapidly moving clouds were fleeced around it like vicious little fish.

"Where *is* my wife?" Phil asked.

"Down below. She's been made second mate."

"Second mate?"

"Under the first mate, of course. They're scrubbing out the heads, going through the staterooms."

Phil put down his novel and scratched the beard forming on his chin.

"Scrubbing out the heads?" he said.

"You'd be surprised how much you learn about a ship when you get down on your hands and knees."

"Listen, Captain—"

"Did you know that the engine heats the water through pipes that you use for a hot shower?"

"No, I didn't. Captain McCracken—"

"Well, your wife knows. Because she's learned. The hard way."

McCracken was giving Phil an unpleasant sensation. Phil was so geared into relaxation and even drowsiness that he found it hard to assume the sharp demeanor that was his habit in the north. He sat forward and put the novel down.

"It was her idea, Mr. Williams. She meant for me to tell you."

McCracken's gaze seemed to challenge him.

"Well, she certainly has a peculiar way of enjoying her cruise," he murmured.

McCracken laughed. It was a strong, hearty, and friendly laugh.

"What is work to some is enjoyment to others. What is relaxation to some is boredom to others," McCracken said.

Phil glanced at his book, now pelted with two individual, bulging drops of clear rainwater on the slick cover.

"I personally like to read," he said defensively.

"So do we all," McCracken said enjoyably, "when the time is right. Now we have work to do."

"We?"

McCracken held up a heavy three-inch braided rope with a hard plastic cord around it.

"I've noticed the dinghy rope has worn a bit," the Captain said. "Would you care to help me replace it? If you're through reading, of course."

By now several more convex bulges dotted the slick cover of the novel. The eyes of the heroine illustrated on it smeared into a weird configuration as the rain began. Phil took off his sweater to protect it and looked for a place to stash it.

"In the wheelhouse, Mr. Williams," McCracken advised. Phil followed McCracken to the wheelhouse where he tossed his expensive sweater down among the maps on a protected bench. A few drops fell on his sunburned shoulders. Cool, hard, bracing drops pelted his arms. Each gave off a tiny shiver due to the unaccountable coolness of their impact.

"To the stern deck, Mr. Williams," McCracken said in a clipped voice.

"That's the left side?"

"That's the rear side."

"Excuse me. Stern deck on the way."

The rope that wound through the metal eye and into the dinghy was in fact badly worn, frayed where the metal had rubbed after countless risings and fallings. It looked as if a knife had hacked laboriously through the strands of the fibers. Phil marveled at the strength of the sea, that placid arena in which dangers and hidden strengths, not to say peculiar wonders, lay masked to his own land-habituated eyes.

"Pass it through and throw it here," McCracken ordered.

With difficulty Phil squeezed the fat rope through the eye, pulled out about a foot and a half of it, and held the weight of the dinghy. McCracken twined the new rope around a small, sturdy metal cleat.

"Fine work, Mr. Williams."

"Thank you, sir," Phil said, panting. His blood raced, and his arms ached from the weight of the heavy dinghy. He was pitifully out of shape through he strove to hide it from McCracken, as if a test of his manhood were at stake.

The brute elements grew darker minute by minute around them.

"Where is my wife?" Phil asked.

"I think she's on her way."

Phil turned. Tracey was wearing an absurdly large yellow oilskin slicker. Phil was pained in a subtle, disturbing way. They had dolled her up. She looked silly. Her big boots flopped on her feet and she could barely make her way forward in the mass of heavy yellow rubber. A large yellow slick hat flopped over her eyes. She looked as helpless and uncertain as a child.

"This one's for you!" Tracey said, holding out a big bundle of oilskin garb.

Phil saw that Tracey's hands were red and roughened by the brutal effort below. Her eyes, behind the merriment, had a different quality. Something less assured, something frightened. She *wanted* him to take the oilskin and put it on, as though it would prove she had done the right thing by doing it herself. She was suddenly afraid of looking ridiculous.

"Yellow," Phil said, pretending to examine the rain gear like a possible purchase in a department store. "My favorite color!"

"Put it on. Penny says the rain blows hard."

"It can't blow *that* hard."

"Oh, put it on, silly. Don't be embarrassed."

"Nothing can embarrass me," Phil said, putting on the floppy hat and the long black boots.

Tracey held a delicate hand to her mouth as she laughed.

"No laughter from the second mate," Phil growled.

Phil glanced carefully at Tracey. The sparkle in her eyes hardened for a second. He guessed now it was simply fatigue from physical labor that had drawn her face and made the complexion wan under the floppy hat.

"They made *you* the *third* mate," she chuckled, "so you have to take orders from me."

"They did? I wasn't present at the ceremony."

"That's what you get for absenteeism."

Tracey snapped on the front of the huge raincoat over Phil's chest, and realized that his hands had slipped in between an opening in her own oilskin. His hands gently moved over her breasts.

"Third mate forbidden to do that," Tracey said.

"You going to court-martial me?"

"Yes."

"Would you like to go below and begin the hearing?"

Tracey giggled lightly, broke free, and ran down the length of the starboard deck. Her hair was wet, flouncing under the broad-brimmed hat. Her oilskin already was pebbled with many drops of rain. Phil heard, rather than felt, the increasingly steady rattle of rain against his coat. He turned and saw the McCrackens with wide-brimmed hats, bathing suits, and tennis shoes, discussing something at the wheelhouse door. They looked as ridiculous as he did, Phil thought. Somehow all pretension was gone. All elegance was washed away in this cool, refreshing rain. They were only civilized beasts, intelligent beasts, bouncing forward into the darkening sea.

Tracey ripped off her wide-brimmed hat and laughingly faced into the rain, which now blew in at an angle.

"A squall!" she shouted joyously. "A real squall!"

Suddenly Tracey was happily tired. Exhilaration turned to a deep, wonderful fatigue. At this moment Phil was her world, he made it for her, drew its limits, explored it for her. It was a limitless world. The boundaries had dropped. It shocked Tracey how seldom she thought of her home. Partially from guilt she made herself conjure an image of Larry, sitting studiously over his drafting table. She wanted to conjure a cozy scene but all that came to her was a vague sense of darkness, perhaps a winter's night and an endless waiting. For what had she been waiting: to break out of something nameless like a glass shield between herself and the outer world?

A violent blow of spray suddenly shot past the bow and whipped past Tracey's face. She squealed with delight. Larry disappeared even as an image. Running to Phil, she hugged him.

FIVE

The full force of the storm awakened them at three o'clock in the morning. Phil knew it was severe when he felt tremors shooting down through the shell of the boat. The sea smashed at the portholes, and the wind screamed ahead.

"I'm frightened," Tracey whispered.

Phil sat up on his elbow and peered through the curtains. The black sea rolled as high as the deck. He put his hand on her shoulder. "It's not a hurricane."

Suddenly there was a violent smash at the front of the boat and Tracey threw herself into his arms.

"What was that?" she gasped.

"A deck chair coming loose, I guess."

"It sounded like the whole front half broke apart."

Phil kissed her lightly on the nose. "Why don't we go and make ourselves a cup of tea? You'll see it's a lot better there than it sounds in here."

Tracey nodded. They dressed with difficulty, clinging to furniture for support, then went out into the corridor. A dim light had been left on over the galley counter. It seemed strange how steady everything looked when they could feel the pitching underfoot and hear the whining of the sea wind overhead. Then Phil realized it was because the light was fixed to the cabinet and was rolling with them, and that was why the shadows were immobile. They carefully made their way to the dining table.

"You just sit here," Phil whispered.

Tracey sat with her slippers planted firmly on the floor. The pitching was reduced at the center of the boat. It was restful, like a rocking cradle. On the table were lemons in a deep bowl for breakfast, and Tracey squeezed juice into her cup. A vicious gust of wind reverberated overhead.

"Romantic, isn't it?" Tracey whispered.

"I wonder where old Captain Jack is."

"Probably up in the mainmast, checking the rigging."

They giggled irresistibly. The *Penny Dreadful*, in only a few short days, had become their boat as well. The walls, galley, and stateroom had become extensions of themselves, a floating home. It seemed as though it had been years since they had had any different home.

"Want to go up on deck?"

"Are you crazy? In that storm?"

"Sure," Phil grinned. "When is the next time you're going to sea a storm on the ocean?"

"I'd get blown over the rail."

Tracey watched Phil dress in the thick oilskins that hung in the cabinet. He soon peered out from under a broad yellow brim.

"I'll be right back."

"Be careful. Hang on to things."

Phil went up the stairs. The noise of the storm increased as he approached the hatch door. He hesitated, then pushed the door open. With unexpected violence, the door was ripped from his hands and crashed against the bulkhead. Phil struggled into the murky light.

The noise was deafening. Water was everywhere, churning around the boat, flying at a steep angle across the deck, dripping from the cabin and rails. Phil stood against the hatch door and observed the violence. He had never seen the entire earth in such an uproar. It was frightening and yet the most stimulating thing he had ever seen. The blood raced in his veins. It was difficult to breathe, unprotected from the wind, and yet it did not occur to him to move.

Mountains of deep water rose to the height of his head and rolled down under the boat. It seemed that any one of the waves was big enough to pull the entire bow under the sea. Spray lashed at his face. He turned away, shielding himself with his arm. In the far distance, by the bow, he thought he saw two vague forms in the vaporous gray.

A wall of spray caught a glimmer of light from the boat lights overhead and threw itself along the length of the deck. When Phil opened his eyes, he saw once again what appeared to be two bundles of canvas nearly obscured by the shrieking ocean froth.

All around the storm crashed out of clouds that rolled into an impenetrable mass. Yet somewhere there was the beginning of daylight, for the sea was not black but deep gray, glittering along its crests like something cruel and evil. Now Phil saw that a rope had been stretched from the hatch door to the wheelhouse, alongside the cabin wall. Pulling himself hand over hand, he took several careful steps toward the bow.

In the storm, only five yards ahead of him, unprotected by any tarpaulin or roof, were the McCrackens, kneeling on the foredeck. They were well bundled against the cold ocean, but their hats were off and their faces turned away from him. They knelt, unmoving. Phil wiped the salt spray from his eyes and was unmindful of the water filling his boots. A sudden wave smashed across his vision. When the water receded, he saw that the McCrackens had not moved. Gradually he noticed that they held hands. He took a step forward, then froze when McCracken stirred slightly and turned his head. Phil ducked behind the cabin wall. After a long time, Phil peered fearfully once again into the howling maelstrom.

Apparently they were through for they turned to one another, kissed lightly on the lips, and began to rise.

Phil quickly made for the hatch door, wrestled it open and took a last look into the dark turmoil. The McCrackens strolled, heads down, into the wind. They had not seen

him. They still held hands. Phil ducked into the hatch and
slowly caught his breath.

In the silence his ears rang. Gradually he became aware
of the sound of water dripping from his rain gear. Tracey
looked at him from the bottom of the stairs.

"Are you all right?"

"What? Oh, yes. Fine."

"I've made some toast."

"Just the thing," Phil said, rubbing his hands.

When he hung up his raincoat, he became worried that
McCracken would notice the puddle. And why then should
he be worried, Phil thought. He had just blundered into
them. They certainly weren't doing anything to be ashamed
of. And yet Phil felt uneasy and checked the amount of
water collecting at his feet.

"Wasn't it dangerous up there?" Tracey asked.

"No. They've strung a rope across the deck. You can
just hang on to it."

Phil sat down and began devouring the small, crisp
pieces of toast, spreading copious amounts of red jam on
them.

"The McCrackens are up there," he said.

"Thank goodness. That's where I'd want them to be in a
storm."

Phil swallowed his toast and reached for the butter dish.

"They were praying."

"Praying?"

"On their knees."

Tracey laughed.

"What's so funny?"

"We're in pretty bad shape when the Captain has to pray
during a storm."

"Storm or not, they do a hell of a lot of praying, those
two."

Tracey smiled. "I think it's nice to be religious. I used to
be once. A long time ago."

Phil shrugged. "It's not against the law, I suppose."

Just then there was a roar of wet wind and a blast of air hurled itself, cold and bracing, down into the galley. Mc-Cracken stopped halfway down the stairs, surprised to see them there. He wore heavy yellow rain gear, now dripping wet. He took off his rain hat. His white hair stuck together, matted with rain and salt spray.

"Up a little early, aren't you?" he asked.

"It's pretty hard to sleep in the middle of an eggbeater," Phil said.

"Made yourselves some tea, I see."

"Yes," Tracey said. "Care for some?"

"Does the first mate know?"

"No. Why?"

McCracken frowned. He came heavily down the stairs and removed his boots. He hung his coat on a hook, and the water flowed onto the floor into a small drain at the foot of the stairs. The shadows made his bulk huge, like an impenetrable block.

"She really should be informed," McCracken said.

Phil and Tracey exchanged a quick glance. Tracey shrugged, drank her tea, and leaned back, raising her legs onto the far end of the bench. But McCracken did not let the matter drop.

"She likes to know what goes on in the galley. It's her province, you know."

"Well, we'll clean up—"

"Could be a breach," McCracken said, pouring some of the tea for himself. "Might well be a small breach."

McCracken sat down at the table. He rubbed his eyes wearily. He looked very tired and his face was reddened from the storm. He warmed his hands against the cup of tea.

"A breach?" Phil asked.

McCracken turned to Phil and smiled softly.

"Isn't this excellent tea? It's from Venezuela."

"A breach of what?"

"To get good tea you have to know the right people. I

buy the leaves directly from the plantation. They save a bit of the best for me."

"Captain."

"Yes?"

"What about not telling the first mate we used the kitchen?"

McCracken looked at Phil, puzzled for a second. "Oh, that. Well, listen. Just be sure to clean up after yourselves and I'll cover for you."

"Thanks," Phil said with undisguised petulance.

Tracey handed him a cigarette. He leaned forward as she lit it for him, then he exhaled a clean puff of white smoke. Phil eyed the Captain curiously.

"I thought you said we'd miss the storm," Phil said.

"The *hurricane*," McCracken said. "We missed the *hurricane*. This is just a winter blow. Nothing much."

"Don't these things show up on the radar?" Phil pursued.

McCracken cleared his throat. "They do," he admitted. "But they get born so quickly. Cover a huge area. No place to run to."

"Any chance of this developing into a hurricane?" Tracey asked.

"Always a chance, Mrs. Williams."

Tracey shivered. "I don't think I want to go through a hurricane."

"Nobody does," McCracken said, rising from the table and putting on his boots and his raincoat. He appeared to be concentrating on several things at the same time. Several thoughts he seemed to dismiss. He turned to Tracey.

"We have contact by radio," McCracken said in a kindly tone. "If there *is* a development, we'll dash to the leeward side of an island about fifteen miles south. We'll just wait it out there."

"Then I'm not worried," Tracey said.

"Good. No reason to be. And Mrs. Williams. If you please. The counter top is wet."

"I'll take care of it."

"Right you are," McCracken said jovially, swung around, and clambered up the stairs. There was a howl as he opened the door, then it was muffled again.

Tracey reached for the sponge. Phil shook his head.

"Leave it," he said. "Remember, we're paying guests."

"Don't be silly, darling." Tracey quickly wiped the counter. She made certain everything was clean and dry. Then she sat down again and in the silence they rode, rising and falling, through the storm.

The light of day crept into the galley, a gray, bleached light from the clouds. Overhead the storm continued to blow, neither growing nor abating.

"Try for some sleep?" Phil murmured.

Tracey shook her head. "I wish I could. Do you realize we've hardly slept for two days?"

"And my head feels it."

Tracey threw her hair back and lit a cigarette from Phil's.

"You know what I'd like? I'd like to be floating in two feet of water over an ocean floor of warm white sand. Just like in the travel folders. Baking in the hot sun—"

There was another crash on deck. Something metal rolled ferociously over the wood until it banged against the hatch.

"Go on," Phil encouraged.

"And we'd make love under the water, in some coral bed. And all the little black and yellow fish would go swimming around us, and the sea flowers—"

"Sea flowers?"

"Yes. Glorious underwater orchids and begonias. And a big sea turtle to keep us company. And us . . . in the white sands . . ."

"Sounds good to me."

Tracey sighed. The wind now howled across the deck as McCracken turned the boat. The waves struck more to the broadside, and the *Penny Dreadful* rolled more violently until the bow turned back into the waves.

"What was that?" she whispered.

"I think he's changing direction."

Tracey put a hand on his arm. "Do you think he's running to the island? That there's a hurricane coming?"

"I don't know. I really don't."

Tracey now showed signs of nervousness. She listened carefully to the wind, trying to determine if it had grown in pitch or volume. Her eyes darted toward the portholes, glazed with smashing rain and a bleak light.

"Come on, honey," Phil reassured her. "Everything'll be all right."

"Then why is he changing direction?"

"Well, if he is, it's to find protection behind the island. One thing about him—he's very capable. He seems to know what to do."

Tracey smiled gratefully at his effort to cheer her. "I won't worry," she said. "I promise."

"Good. Now I'm going to go and shave. You put on a brave front if the first mate should arrive. I don't want you to lose your rating for drooping confidence."

He kissed her and went to their stateroom.

The hatch overhead opened and in the shriek of the wind Tracey heard Penny say, "It's time, Captain. Time to begin." McCracken followed her down the stairs. They hung their rain gear over the drain. Penny surveyed the galley to make certain nothing had fallen or spilled from the shelves. She smiled at Tracey.

"Time for what?" Tracey asked.

"Time to begin going for the island," Penny said.

McCracken shook his head. "I'm not certain, mate. Temperature's rising to the south and west. I'd say this storm is dying. In any case, let's give it an hour and see how it develops."

Penny went to the galley and began bringing out eggs

and cheese for an omelette. McCracken looked tired now. He leaned against the cabinet in the corridor, his gaze fixed steadily upon Tracey, and attempted to penetrate the too-cheerful facade.

"You must trust me, Mrs. Williams," he said in a kindly tone. "There really is a sun over these waters."

Tracey laughed. "There'd better be. I've got two more bikinis to try out."

"You will get your suntan, Mrs. Williams. That's a pledge from Captain Jack."

Eating was made difficult by the battering waves. Phil and Tracey clung to their cups which Penny had half-filled to minimize sloshing. Throughout the meal McCracken left the table at fifteen-minute intervals to study the instruments and check his radio contact. Clearly, he only returned from the wheelhouse to be sociable. Evidently he felt bad about the poor weather on the cruise and wished to make it up to Phil and Tracey.

"Don't you tink it's time?" Penny insisted, looking significantly at McCracken.

McCracken coughed almost silently. "Perhaps," he said slowly. "I'll take one more look. Excuse me."

McCracken walked slowly to his rain gear and dressed. His movements were deliberate, weary, and strangely definite as though he had made up his mind even before checking his instruments. Phil wondered at the intricacy of decisions made during a storm at sea. Currents, winds, changing tides, sudden changes in the weather—he wondered now what McCracken had decided. Phil guessed they were not going to run for the island, partly because he could not believe that McCracken could be wrong.

But when McCracken returned, very quickly, he took off his coat and sat down at the table with his rain hat still on.

"We're drifting to the left," he said to no one in particular.

Phil paused in mid-bite. No one said anything. Penny

continued to shake pepper over her omelette. Phil put down his fork.

"Drifting?"

"To the left."

Tracey looked at Phil. McCracken simply sat there. It was impossible to read the expression on his face.

"Is that serious?" Phil asked.

McCracken said nothing for a while. Penny watched them all. Finally McCracken sighed.

"The boat shouldn't drift to the left," he said.

"Well, I mean, is it a current? The wind? Or what?"

"It's not the wind or the current."

"Then what?"

McCracken rubbed his hands into his face. His eyes looked bloodshot. He sat calmly and looked blankly at Phil for a moment.

"It's the propeller," he said simply.

Phil waited, his expression betraying nothing. Tracey continued to eat, but listened carefully.

"The propeller," McCracken repeated. "It's pushing to the left."

"Maybe it's the shaft," Penny said softly.

"Let's hope not."

Above them a moaning wind assailed the bow, throwing a wave of seawater furiously at the boat. McCracken winced.

"Well, if it *were* the shaft," Phil said, "what then?"

"We'd have to have it repaired."

"Out here? In the middle of the ocean?"

"No. We'd have to nurse her back to Nassau. That's the nearest large port."

"Would we have to register with the authorities?" Tracey asked.

McCracken and Penny exchanged glances.

"No," McCracken said. "You could stay on board."

"For how long?"

McCracken shrugged. "A day. Two days. More. Depends on whether any welding needs to be done. Or if the whole shaft needs replacing. It's a big job."

Phil reached for his coffee. A knot was forming in his stomach. He tried to ignore the implications of what had happened.

"Well," Phil said with a matter-of-fact air, "let's assume the best. Suppose it's the propeller?"

"I would beach the boat. Fix it myself. I can do small-scale welding."

"When would you find out?" Tracey asked.

"As soon as the storm falls."

There was a moment of silence. Penny scooped the remainder of the omelette into Tracey's dish. It seemed absurd to be eating calmly when disaster appeared to be hovering so close.

"There's nothing to do now but enjoy your breakfast," the Captain said. "I'm going back. I'll be there the rest of the day."

McCracken went up the stairs. The breakfast was finished in silence. Penny's brow was furrowed. Instead of cleaning up briskly, she leaned back in her chair and studied the clouds outside the porthole.

"The Captain was right," she said calmly. "The storm is dying."

The the *Penny Dreadful* took several hours more of battering weather before the wind lessened and the rain slackened.

When the storm had calmed and the seas rolled without wind, like billows of sail, McCracken lowered himself in the dinghy into the water. Penny sculled him to the underside of the stern where he leaned out dangerously over the side. Fascinated, Tracey and Phil watched from the stern railing.

McCracken climbed back up the ladder, ripping off his drenched sweater and wool cap. He did not seem worried, which reassured Phil and Tracey.

"Can't see a thing," he said to them. "Water's too

rough." McCracken paused as though thinking of a solution. "With your approval, I'm going to beach the boat. Take a look at the propeller."

"Well, we don't have an alternative, do we?" Phil said.

"We could steer, try to compensate by taking the drift into account. But there's no telling. Perhaps something more serious will develop. I would rather play safe."

"Of course," Phil agreed quickly.

"Is that all right with you, Mrs. Williams?"

"Certainly, Captain."

"All right, then. With luck you can find a pretty beach all to yourselves."

"We'd love that," Tracey said.

Nevertheless, they were apprehensive as they heard McCracken start the engines. Soon the horizon was dotted with tiny islands, some as large as atolls, bits of a reef breaking through the surface.

Phil went to the wheelhouse to watch McCracken. Maps and tide charts were spread over the benches. Obviously the Captain had been calculating, because several sheets of his elaborate handwriting filled the panel over the instruments.

"Have you decided where to beach her?" Phil asked.

McCracken looked around, startled. "Oh, hello, Mr. Williams. Yes, I have. A little place I noticed several years ago."

"Several years ago?"

"Yes. A good seaman always keeps an eye out for likely shelters."

Phil watched McCracken steer. According to the sonar, they were in water only ten fathoms deep. The water was now relatively calm, rising and falling like a spasmodic breathing, and getting calmer as they went south. The radar was picking up several of the islands.

"What do you do, cruise slowly until you hit sand?" Phil asked.

McCracken smiled. "You beach a boat, Mr. Williams. Not crash it."

Phil smiled at his own naiveté. "Fill me in on the details. This is my first beaching operation."

"What we're going to do, Mr. Williams, is anchor her at the high tide on a smooth bed. Let the sea fall away. Should give me time enough to evaluate the damage."

"Very clever."

"Quite rational, Mr. Williams. Everything in navigation is. Now you enjoy the cruise. I expect we can look forward to some good swimming by this afternoon."

Phil watched with Tracey as the horizon line became more and more frequently dotted with sandy projections. It was warm now, the cloud cover dispelling slowly to areas of light blue. A gradual laziness descended on them. While they changed into swimsuits down below, they felt the engines cut off.

"We must be at the beach," Phil said.

"How long are we going to be here?" Tracey asked.

"As long as it takes for the tide to ebb and return, I guess."

When they ascended the stairs, the sky overhead was a uniform light blue. Trails of faraway clouds lined the horizon but the sun bore directly down on them, warming the decks. In the dinghy McCracken and Penny were returning to the boat. Phil saw the anchor high up on the beach rather than in deeper water. Below the dinghy was the green, clear water, pure and crystalline, and then the white sands. Starfish and a few small seaweed were visible. Behind the dinghy was a small beach, white and short, and several clumps of grass beyond the sand.

McCracken looked at his huge wristwatch.

"About two hours, Mr. Williams! We should be grounded by then. I'd advise you to take advantage of the water. It's seventy-four degrees!"

Throwing a towel over his shoulders, Phil climbed down the accommodation ladder. He hooked the towel over the last rung, letting the ends get wet. With his foot he felt the water, which bobbed pleasantly over his ankles. With a shout, he threw himself backward into the water and swam away from the boat.

"Stay close to me," Tracey called.

Tracey stroked neatly into the water, her arms knifing superbly into the clear surface. She had little stamina, however, and was relieved to find Phil standing in two feet of water.

As the tide lowered, the *Penny Dreadful* settled lightly, then heavily, into the sand. The boat tilted slightly, but as the water lowered the final foot, the boat righted itself, resting on the keel. The propeller, protected by the out-reach of the stern, stuck out into the air. McCracken walked in the sandy water and carried a tool box. Phil and Tracey eavesdropped with concern.

"Let's hope we don't have to go to port," Phil said, floating on his back. "I don't feel like spending two days inside the stateroom going crazy with the heat."

"We'll soon know," Tracey said, trudging toward the sands.

Phil swam a few feet, then walked onto the beach with her. It was an eerie feeling to see the clumps of wild grass growing so naturally from the soil, and then to see the blue horizon all around it.

They kissed in the shade of tall, broad-stemmed leaves on the far side of the tiny island.

McCracken walked toward them. They saw him as he rounded the edge, the water lapping at his ankles, and Tracey waved to him.

"Ah, there you are," McCracken called and walked through the surf, which was broken into many tiny wavelets by the long, shallow plateau under the ocean surface. He walked to Phil and kept his voice low.

"I'm afraid the shaft is bent," McCracken said. His steely eyes bored into Phil's.

"Are you certain?"

"Yes. What's worse is that we're going to have to pull the boat through the channel."

Phil stood up. He was not sure that he understood the Captain.

"Pull the boat?"

"A standard method, Mr. Williams. As you can see, there is coral all around us."

"Why can't you just steer out? The way we steered in?"

"Not with a bent shaft," McCracken said, illustrating an angle with his hands. "On the open sea, I can adjust. Here, among these obstructions, I need pinpoint accuracy."

"I don't understand. You got in here just fine."

"The truth is, Mr. Williams, that the shaft was so bent that a retaining plate sheared off as I was working on it."

Phil whistled softly. For a second the balmy breeze seemed cool. Now he felt genuine alarm.

"So we're crippled," he said softly.

Tracey approached, sensing Phil's changed expression.

"What is it, darling?"

"The Captain says that—"

"That we must hand maneuver into deep water, Mrs. Williams. Nothing more. Once we're clear we have to head for Nassau."

"Oh dear," Tracey said.

Phil dug his toe into the sand. It turned up a darker, cooler brown. He watched his own motionless shadow over tiny white seashells at his feet. Something felt ominous the way the silence hung over them all.

"And in the deep water?" Phil asked. "What then?"

"The shaft is not broken, Mr. Williams. We have full power. It's just that the angle is uncertain at best."

"But in deep water you could correct?"

"You have the essence of the situation. It's just here, among the thousand projections, sandbars, and the shallow water . . ."

"What are we going to do, darling?" Tracey asked.

"We have to pull the boat," Phil said morosely.

"You're in good shape, Mr. Williams. We'll split the labor. I estimate four hours—"

"Four hours?"

"At least."

Finally Phil felt the words burst forth, as though a log-jam had broken. Petulant, frustrated, helpless, he confronted McCracken.

"I don't understand," Phil sputtered. "How could the shaft bend? I mean, that's the backbone of the boat, isn't it?"

"How? *How?* What do you mean, *how?* A flaw in the linkage. Accumulated strain. Faulty machining. I don't understand you, Mr. Williams."

"A shaft . . . a shaft can't break down. It just can't!"

"Everything that's mechanical will break down sooner or later. Worn, or sheared, or snapped, rusted, buckled, or ground up!"

Phil gestured helplessly. "But there must be a reason," he continued lamely.

"Do you want an analysis? Do you want to know which rivet? Do you want me to draw you a picture of the ruptured seam? What difference does it make? The point is that the shaft is now damaged."

Phil slumped helplessly onto the sand. "It doesn't make sense," he mumbled in despair.

McCracken sat down next to him.

"Come, come, Mr. Williams," he said kindly. "Mechanical things have no intelligence. They go round and round, up and down, slaves to electromagnetic forces. Blind, stupid hunks of metal. And they break down. That's all there is to it. Perfectly natural. Don't despair."

Tracey took Phil's arm. "Perhaps we should have lunch first."

"Yes. I would suggest that," McCracken agreed.

Silently they walked back to the near side of the island, into the water, and climbed the ladder. They ate a brief lunch on a table set on the foredeck, which faced the island. Hot steaming vegetables, tea, cheese, and thin slices of a carrot cake were attractively offered on a white table-cloth. Before touching his food, McCracken advised his guests, "You will have noticed that we observe grace before a meal. You may join us if you wish." All four lowered their heads.

After lunch, Penny brought out a bottle of suntan lotion and gestured to Tracey to put it copiously on Phil. Phil waved the bottle away with a surly motion of his hand, and Penny took the suntan lotion away. Then she cleared the table. Soon, McCracken stood, put on a small visor over his eyes, and took off his baggy trousers, revealing a well-worn pair of checkered swim trunks over his muscular thighs.

When he was out of earshot, Phil turned to Tracey in a burst of anger.

"Goddammit!" he snapped. "Do you see what's happening? They've got you washing dishes and scrubbing the heads and cleaning fish, and now they expect me to pull this goddam boat! Well, I don't think it's the duty of us as guests to do that! After all, when you travel on an airplane, you don't have to clean out the jet tanks or push the plane down the runway. That's included in the price of the ticket!"

Tracey flushed in embarrassment.

"You mean you're going to sit back and watch that old man pull the boat all by himself?"

"He's in better shape than I am."

Tracey glared at him for a moment, then folded her arms and looked down. Slowly she softened and tried to be reasonable.

"Phil, washing dishes and cleaning fish is one thing. But no one planned that the shaft should bend."

Phil turned sideways to avoid Tracey's accusing eyes.

"This is a time when we have to work together," she pleaded.

"It's not that serious."

"How do you know? What do you know about boats?"
Phil said nothing.

"Now is just not the time to raise the issue, honey," she continued. "Later, when we've docked at Nassau, we can do anything we want. Even take a plane back home. But right now we must all help."

Phil rubbed his eyes. He looked haggard. "Christ," he muttered. "I'm just not in the mood for boat-pulling!"

"Necessity has nothing to do with one's mood," Tracey gently admonished.

Phil sighed and stepped down into the water. He walked until the sea was chest high and then swam out to the dinghy floating several yards in front of the bow.

McCracken waited in the dinghy until Phil hoisted himself up on its side, then pointed to the stern of the boat lying in the mud. "The tide is going to lift us just off the mud. You're going to have to pull the boat from the front, while the mate and I push. That will turn it into the channel."

"I don't get it. How the hell do you expect three people to budge a boat this size?"

"It's much easier than you might think. Understand, you're not *lifting* the boat. You're sliding it over the surface. If there's no current or obstruction, it will simply glide along. Just don't be deceived by the ease of pulling it. In other words, don't get too close to the boat if it climbs close to rocks or a beach. It still weighs quite a few tons and one wave is all it takes to put an end to you."

Later, while McCracken pushed upward and to the side, standing at the stern, the tide lifted the *Penny Dreadful* into several inches of water. Penny had hauled the anchor onto the deck and stowed it. With a wave of his arm, McCracken signaled to Phil. Phil held a rope over his right shoulder and strained against it. He leaned forward with all his strength until the veins in his forehead knotted and bulged. At the stern, their backs pressed against the hull, their feet finding purchase in the slippery coral, the Mc-

Crackens pushed. Slowly, the bow of the *Penny Dreadful* swung forward into the rising water.

"That's it, darling!" Tracey called.

"We're free!" McCracken called. "Straight out to the first sandbar!"

Phil looked ahead and saw where the tide had not yet covered a sloping field of smooth mud. He realized that by the time he advanced the boat that far, the mud might well be under water. The western sun gleamed off the water, blinding him. Already he felt the burning of the rope against the flesh of his shoulder. His eyes ached from the glare. His feet slipped against the grainy sand below. From time to time he stepped on sharp stones or seashells, and he wondered if stinging anemones were in these waters. Tiny fish darted around his legs, and he swore he felt them nip at his knees.

"Capital, Mr. Williams!" McCracken shouted. "Take a rest!"

Phil lowered the rope and turned around. He dipped down into the water to ease the pain of his shoulders. Tracey waved to him from the aft deck. He was surprised to see McCracken huddled over the instrument panel taking measurements in the wheelhouse. Why the hell wasn't he pushing, Phil thought angrily. Underfoot the surface was unusually rough and full of rocks. Perhaps there were crevices nearby. When the tide rolls it acts as a current. Phil knew he would not be able to hold the boat against that. And if the boat settled badly, who knew what kind of damage the bent shaft might sustain?

"We'd better take her up, Mr. Williams!" McCracken called.

"Pull, darling!" Tracey called. "We're a fourth of the way through!"

Phil turned and pulled the rope taut around his shoulder. He felt the familiar pressure biting into his red flesh, his legs slipping against the sand. The water seemed to have grown colder. Ahead, the ocean gleamed brightly until he shut his eyes against it. Sweat rolled down his forehead. Bit by bit, the *Penny Dreadful* slid forward.

Suddenly there was a bump. The rope jerked Phil painfully backward into the water. He swam after the floating rope end.

"No harm! Keep pulling!" McCracken shouted.

Cursing, Phil strained at the rope. The water remained chest high now and it was nearly impossible to find a way to push his legs with any strength against the bottom. At last he stubbed his foot against a rock. He pushed, using the rock as a support, and felt good progress behind him.

"Terrific, Mr. Williams!" Penny called.

Her voice came from somewhere beside the boat. He glanced behind and saw her sculling the dinghy. He could not see whether she was pulling in a side direction with another rope or just signaling to the Captain how to turn the rudder. It looked almost as though she were observing Phil. Was he pulling the damned thing all by himself, he wondered? His headache grew worse and he closed his eyes and pulled forward, feeling the blood throb in his head. His muscles now trembled unevenly from the fatigue.

"Halfway, Mr. Williams!" Penny called.

Now he felt the bottom slope upward underfoot to form the sandbar. It was easier to get a purchase against the sand, but his arms were weak, flighty, and he let the rope drop. His head drooped and he caught his breath.

"Not here, Mr. Williams!" Penny called. "If the tide goes down we'll roll!"

Phil woke as from a dream. His body felt as though it belonged to another. The water to his side flowed round in vague washes. He wondered if it would help or hurt the passage of the boat. It seemed he had been doing this all his adult life. He lost a sense of time.

Now he was on the downward slope of the sandbar and the boat was clearing the peak. He saw McCracken in the water, dreamlike, and Penny pulling with an additional rope from the dinghy. The sun lay blood-red and cold close to the horizon. His legs were numb from their long immersion in the water.

When he looked back, McCracken was back on deck in the wheelhouse. Penny and Tracey were nowhere to be seen.

The *Penny Dreadful* rested on a foot of water under the keel. Phil saw the shadow of the boat extend almost directly, uncannily, onto the sand below the keel. Now that the whole boat was visible from this peculiar angle, Phil was surprised at how little of a boat sits below the surface. It looked odd, ungainly, and strangely awkward and helpless.

"Pull hard!" McCracken bellowed. "We're almost through."

When Phil picked up the rope again there was no strength in his arms. He made the motions, floundering ahead, his feet pushing up tiny clouds of white sand in the water, but his breathing was spasmodic and his head pounded.

"Harder!"

Phil stumbled forward, falling into the water.

"Are you all right?" McCracken yelled, coming to the railing.

Phil raised a hand to signal that he was, but he found it difficult to stand. The weak currents of the waves around his waist were enough to upset his balance. He floundered again. His arms thrashed against the water. McCracken went back to the wheelhouse.

Slowly Phil learned not to pull with his arms and shoulder, but simply to fall forward against the rope until the boat moved, drawn by the pull of his hundred and eighty pounds of human weight. Then he walked forward, hauled up the slack and fell slowly into the rope once again. In this way he moved semiconsciously through the water, dimly aware of the white shape that he neither loved nor hated, but which followed him silently, everpresent, ambiguous.

"You can come aboard!" McCracken shouted. "We're through!"

Like a prisoner blinking at the sunshine upon his release, Phil gazed with surprise at the boat. The shadow fell away into water and did not flatten at an acute angle on the seafloor. The sea floor itself was darker. Five feet of water extended from the keel to the bottom.

"You'll have to come here," Phil cried hoarsely.

"What?"

"I can't walk anymore."

"But I can't move the boat, Mr. Williams. Not to where you are."

"I can't walk anymore," Phil repeated dazedly.

He was unable to speak again. Dimly he saw Penny sculling out in the dinghy. He shivered as he washed his face in the cool water. The sea was really warm, but exhaustion made him cold. When the dinghy came he leaned forward and fell half into the seat. Penny laughed and pulled him by an arm into the boat. Where she pulled along his biceps the pain was excruciating. He maneuvered his way to sit up in the boat. His legs hung limply in front of him. Penny watched him oddly, almost with satisfaction, but said nothing as she worked the tiny boat forward to the *Penny Dreadful*.

"You will do very well," she finally said.

"Thanks," Phil moaned. "But I've never felt so sore in my life."

She chuckled softly. "You'll get used to it."

"I hope you'll wake me in time for August."

"You have an amusing sense of humor, Mr. Williams."

"I know. I'm going to pretend that I can't climb that ladder. And you're going to have to help me."

Phil was aware of a strong grip on his arm. McCracken was pulling him up the ladder.

"Excellent, Mr. Williams!" McCracken praised. "Even a seven or an eight would have been proud to do what you have done this day!"

Phil stared at McCracken and blinked his salt-encrusted eyes. He wiped his thick, raw lips. Penny handed him a glass of wine. After drinking, he could speak again.

"Why didn't you help me?" he croaked.

"We were working at the sandbar."

"The sandbar?"

McCracken tilted his hand slowly over. "We would have been at a very nasty angle," he said, "if we had gotten stuck there."

Phil sighed. His breath came out unevenly. The trembling in his arms and shoulders increased. His back was aflame with sunburn. The McCrackens watched him as he sat on the edge of a deck chair. He tried to speak but found he needed more wine to lubricate his throat.

"Where's Tracey?" he asked.

"She's in the galley," Penny said. "She was kind enough to begin supper when she realized we were both busy at the sandbar."

Phil nodded, though it all made no sense. He stood uncertainly. McCracken held out a steadying arm. Then he felt himself going backward and realized that the Mc-Crackens were laying him down in a lounge chair. They spread a wool blanket over his chilled arms and maneuvered an umbrella in front of the sinking sun. Phil's irritation against them evaporated. Instead he had become mechanical. Scattered, disconnected thoughts and odd phrases of the McCrackens' voices surged through the bleary corridors of his brain.

"Now you ought to rest," Penny said softly. Phil nodded. The sinking sun glared over the water. In his delirium, Phil thought the sun was rising. It was as though the razor-sharp horizon, now deep blue and gold, had brought on an epiphany and yet, the meaning of it all eluded him. The McCrackens went back to a small table at the railing. Dimly Phil saw Tracey dutifully serve them a tray of cocktails and then retire toward the galley.

Much later he awoke with a chill. It was dark. The

McCrackens were finished with supper. The stars were out. The *Penny Dreadful* moved slowly, barely at quarter speed. Phil sat up. Every muscle in his body sent pain shooting along his limbs. He wrapped the blanket over his shoulders and struggled down the hatch stairs to the galley. Everything was freshly washed and put away. He found Tracey in their stateroom. Her hands were red from hot water.

"Oh, darling," she whispered, "you're up. . . . I was afraid to wake you . . ."

"I feel like one of the walking dead."

"You worked so damned hard!"

Phil sat down heavily on the bed. "You look like you've been working, too."

"It was nothing. They were both busy when the boat got near the sandbar. It was the least I could do."

Tracey stroked the back of Phil's neck. He moaned softly. Heat radiated from his face and pain spread from his shoulders into his arms. Visions of glaring water and the sun hanging on the sharp horizon danced in front of his eyes. He felt, like an ancient curse, the weight of the boat behind him.

"Your back is so red. Oh, dear God."

Tracey took a small yellow bottle from the suitcase and squeezed the contents into her hands. She slowly applied the cream to Phil's back. He started at her touch, then gradually relaxed.

"Some vacation," he snorted. "Are we going to Nassau now?"

"Yes. He's going to try to nurse it in. I told him to wake us when we get there."

Phil started dozing. He awoke to find Tracey by his side and the bottle of lotion on the bureau. He awoke a second time with pain shooting into his side until he moved off his arm. Again he saw the sun, neither rising nor sinking, but hanging in front of him, crystalline pure and bright, sharp and alien, blinding his eyes.

"Can I do anything?" Tracey whispered.

Phil shook his head. Tracey snuggled into his side.

"I . . . think we should," Phil said.

"Should what?"

"Take a plane back when we get to Nassau."

For a long time Tracey said nothing, but Phil sensed her disappointment.

"Why don't we see how you feel in the morning?" she asked.

Phil drifted back into an unpleasant sleep. Nightmares of red and yellow seas bit at his legs. He had to get somewhere but could not maneuver through the high water. Then there was a knock on the door. Tracey pulled the sheet up to her chin. Phil could tell from the bobbing silence outside, and the lack of human voices, that they had not come to Nassau.

SIX

Phil could not raise his head without pains shooting through his neck and shoulders. He tried to roll himself to a sitting position. Every muscle crossing his skeletal structure was stiff with pain. He was immobilized, ludicrously paralyzed. There was a sharp rap on the door.

"What is it?" Phil mumbled.

"Eight-thirty," McCracken called crisply.

Phil moaned.

"Too late for breakfast," McCracken said. "There is some coffee left."

"Forget it!" Phil shouted.

"Come now, Mr. Williams! There's something on deck we'd like to share with you."

When McCracken left, Tracey climbed from bed, tiptoed to the door, and peeked out to make certain McCracken was gone.

"This *is* getting out of hand," she said softly. "You were right. We should have asserted outselves from the beginning."

"We'll leave them in Nassau. We'll hide out a few days in Nassau and fly back." Phil moved his arm to the side of the bed and pulled himself forward. "Christ! I'm in knots. Help me sit up, will you?"

Tracey helped him to the chair at the foot of the bed and massaged his legs.

"This is really crazy. You can't even walk. Please, honey, get back to bed."

"No," Phil panted. "If some other damned thing has gone wrong, I want to know about it."

Tracey's gentle hands massaged Phil's hips where the sun had spared him. She helped him dress. Like an aged man, knees stiffly unbending, he made his way with her help out into the corridor that led to the galley and the stairs.

"How am I going to get up the stairs?" he muttered.

"Lean on my arm."

Making his way laboriously to the deck, Phil spotted the McCrackens at the far end of the boat. Faint wisps of clouds hung over the horizon, delicate feathers in the blue. The cool smell of the open sea blew over the open deck.

"Good morning!" McCracken called, waving. "How are you feeling?"

"Terrible."

McCracken laughed. His big, booming, irresistible laugh reverberated over the deck. "You'll get used to it."

Phil hobbled with Tracey to where McCracken sat at a folding table. The large black logbook lay open before him. Phil's muscles rebelled as Tracey helped him into a deck chair.

"So," Penny said, folding her hands on the table, "down to business."

"Right." McCracken cleared his throat. "For his efficient assistance in repairing a faulty davit line, and in the procurement of food from the sea, and for his yeoman effort in hauling the boat through dangerous coral beds, the proper execution of all services thereunto appertaining, it is proposed that Mr. Williams be herein designated as second mate."

Tracey burst out laughing. Phil coughed and turned his head away to clear his throat. It hurt him to laugh.

"You find this amusing?" McCracken asked.

"I think it's utterly charming," Tracey said.

"I'm pleased . . . naturally," Phil said. "Who wouldn't be?"

McCracken looked at them both. A shadow cut across his nose and lip. McCracken looked at Penny, pen poised in the air.

"I will support that motion," Penny said.

McCracken turned to Tracey. "Mrs. Williams?"

"I'll have to think about it."

"You have an objection?"

Tracey leaned forward. "Well, formerly I was the only second mate. Mr. Williams was third mate. I really would like more of an opportunity to exercise responsibility over him."

"I see."

"Nevertheless," Penny said, "he performed very well."

Tracey stepped on Phil's toe, pressing it.

"He performed *very* well," Tracey agreed. "However, I would like to propose a probationary period for Mr. Williams. Should he continue to perform such obligations as are required of him, correctly and efficiently, I would have no objection to his immediate promotion."

McCracken slowly lowered his fountain pen. He fingered his lip, perplexed.

"What do you propose we do?" he asked Penny.

"I think we'd better close the book until we are all in agreement."

"Then the matter is postponed," McCracken concluded, gazing at the logbook carefully. "For now," he added for Phil's benefit.

Phil leaned forward to whisper into Tracey's ear. "Is this on the level?"

"Of course," she whispered back. "How do you think I got to be second mate?"

Phil smiled, then settled painfully back in his chair.

"Don't worry, Mr. Williams," McCracken said. "Your case will come up for review very soon."

"Good. I'm glad to hear it."

McCracken made several notations in the ship's log with the black fountain pen.

"You're writing this down, Captain?" Phil asked.

McCracken winked at him. The shadow hit the other eye as though it were a black hole in the socket. Without a word he closed the logbook.

The sea was flat, blue, and empty. Something uneasy floated through Phil's consciousness.

"Why aren't we moving?"

"Couldn't chance it."

"You mean the shaft? . . ."

"Hanging by a thread."

McCracken spat into the sea and wiped his mouth.

"God," Tracey said. "What'll we do?"

"Wait," McCracken said. "And drift."

"Drift?" Phil said uncertainly.

"About two miles. We're drifting with a current."

Phil's face visibly brightened. "I get it. The current will take us into Nassau."

"Not to Nassau. Close by."

"And you can fix the shaft there?"

"Don't worry, Mr. Williams. It's all been thought out. Come!"

McCracken, ignoring Phil's injured muscles, rose and rapidly escorted his guest to the wheelhouse. There, by the maps and ancient sea instruments kept on brass pegs near the radar, McCracken brought forward a large chart. Phil and Tracey leaned forward to examine it. Several wavy concentric lines made patterns in various shades of blue.

"The port is roughly fifteen miles south and five miles east of where we are," McCracken said.

On the chart a black dot appeared at the bottom of McCracken's pen.

"The *Penny Dreadful* sits here."

A second black dot was inked about three inches away.

"The current in which we ride will curve to within two

miles of this basin." McCracken indicated a series of concentric lines circling the point of a small landmass.

"That would sweep us past the island," Phil observed.

"Except that at this point, at the curve where the current veers away from the basin, I will start the engines and cross over to the other side and take the tide into the shore."

"Will the shaft hold?"

"It better."

McCracken rolled the chart and placed it on the shelf over the radar.

Phil lowered his voice. "What if we miss the basin?"

"Then we suffer the ignominy of being towed into port like a sick whale."

"Jesus."

McCracken laughed. "Don't worry. The finest coast guard in the world is less than a hundred miles away. I recommend that you enjoy the sun. We should reach the point close to the basin a little after sundown."

Phil and Tracey retired to the foredeck. Tracey stripped down to her bathing suit and lay, eyes closed, on the warm boards next to Phil. Not having eaten, they felt themselves drifting in and out of dreams, dizzily, almost pleasantly.

"Mrs. McCracken is bringing lunch," Tracey whispered.

Phil looked up and saw Penny carrying a small tray to a table that had been set up only a few feet away. When he stood, his head grew light.

"Mrs. McCracken," Phil said, sitting down painfully, "I'd like to get something off my chest."

"Yes, Mr. Williams?"

"The situation is that for the last few days Tracey and I have felt overly supervised. If you know what I mean."

"No, Mr. Williams, I do not know what you mean."

"Well, breakfast this morning, for example. We are used to having breakfast whenever we get up."

"On board the *Penny Dreadful* breakfast is served at six o'clock, Mr. Williams."

"That's an ungodly hour, Mrs. McCracken."

"That's the hour of sunrise."

"That's beside the point," Phil persisted. "We are trying to say that this sort of rigid structure goes against our grain."

"It's so hard to relax this way," Tracey added softly.

Penny turned to Phil and smiled warmly. "Of course, many of our guests do object. But in the end, it works out so much better."

"We would prefer things a bit more casual," Phil said with a touch of irritation.

"It may not be possible now."

"What do you mean?"

"We are in a difficult situation."

"You mean the shaft?"

"Certainly. Don't you think that's a cause for discipline? We must make some decisions for the safety of the boat," Penny said. "It's for your sake as well."

"What's that got to do with letting us sleep late? With not having breakfast at a civilized hour? After all, we paid a luxury rate for these conveniences."

"Under the circumstances, what you paid is irrelevant, Mr. Williams. The Captain must decide on the best manner of handling the ship's affairs."

"Well, it makes no sense to us."

"It will."

Phil felt Tracey's foot gently touch his leg. Without looking at her, he knew what it meant; they would leave the boat in Nassau. Phil settled back in his chair. He saw McCracken bent over the console in the wheelhouse, presumably taking a location fix over the radio.

For the rest of the afternoon the boat drifted slowly, bobbed and swayed on the azure sea. The atmosphere of anxiety on deck was palpable. Phil could stand it no longer.

"How long is this going to take?" he asked.

"If you didn't know the shaft was damaged, you'd enjoy

the tranquillity," Penny said, smiling. "In this way our minds dictate over our sensations."

Exasperated, Phil lay down again on his long green towel next to Tracey. He dreamed. In his dream there was a fleet of sailing vessels on the Gulf Stream and the sinking sun shone through their transparent hulls. Suddenly he was awake.

"What's the matter, darling?" Tracey put her hand on his arm. "You jerked right out of sleep."

"Did I? Phil shrugged. "Weird dream, I guess."

"I'm having them, too. Last night I dreamed I was a big fish and they chased me across the deck with an ax. It was terrifying."

Tracey's face had taken on a tanned glow in the late afternoon sun. Her hair was more blonde. Her hazel eyes looked sharper, more green.

"How about a drink?" Phil suggested.

"Can you get up?"

"I think so. If you give me a hand."

When they got to the liquor cabinet below, however, the latch was locked with a large padlock.

"Christ!" Phil sputtered. "I can't figure them out at all!"

"They're afraid we'll steal their liquor. Remember when we helped outselves to tea and toast, and Captain Jack implied that Penny would be upset about it?"

Phil fingered, to no avail, the bolt, the rusted wheel of the combination lock, and the chipped numbers around the edge.

"Well, so much for our cocktails."

The sun, a perfect red ball, slipped slowly through the yellow haze at the edge of the sea. On deck the overhead lights came on. The McCrackens served a light meal—a creamy bisque, toast points, and fish fillets poached in wine. McCracken appeared nervous and frequently checked his watch. After dinner they drank a light whiskey in a thick fruit punch.

"To Davy Jones' locker," McCracken said. "And whatever's locked inside." He winked at Tracey. "Unfortunately, it requires no intelligence to open Davy Jones' locker. Just two quarts of seawater in the lungs."

A chill raced up Phil's spine.

"Is it about time?" Penny asked McCracken.

"Yes."

McCracken blew into his hands as though to warm them, a habit he had picked up of late. He walked to the wheelhouse. Penny excused herself and joined him.

Phil and Tracey felt deserted and isolated, alone at the white table. Their fate rested on the skill of McCracken and his wife. It was a bit like surgery. The world of navigation remained an ungodly mystery.

There was a slow churning below half an hour later. Phil looked from the railing. The *Penny Dreadful* was pulling powerfully forward through the water. The engines grew louder and the clean, darkening water, lit only by a vague and distant rim of red light in the west, rolled faster and faster underneath. Ahead lay the limitless basin of the Atlantic.

The long, gleaming wake of the *Penny Dreadful* arched slowly and grandly to the east.

McCracken cut the engines and lit his pipe. Slowly the boat lost its forward momentum and bobbed pleasantly on the black water. He exchanged a few words with Penny, then looked up at Phil and Tracey.

"What do you think happened?" Tracey whispered.

"I don't know. But you can bet it's not good."

McCracken stepped forward across the deck and sat down beside them. He shook his massive head slowly.

"As you saw, the shaft is irreparably damaged."

"Yes," Phil said. "I thought we were going in circles."

"A very large circle. The shaft has worked itself off its supporting plates and perhaps has buckled somewhere."

"I take it we missed the tide."

"Yes. I steered almost due west, but . . ."

Both men were silent. McCracken puffed on his pipe.

Phil leaned forward in concentration. Tracey watched them both, trying not to reveal her mounting anxiety.

"Well," Phil sighed, "what's our next step?"

"I expect we may need to radio for help. Much as I regret that."

"Isn't there some way to maneuver? Some trick of navigation?"

McCracken abruptly scratched his head in frustration. "I've wracked my brains, Mr. Williams, but nothing comes to mind. If we had sails . . . but we don't."

The overhead lights cast green and red auras over their heads. Tracey nervously lit a cigarette and covered her shoulders with a sweater.

"I would like to try one thing, Mr. Williams."

"What's that?"

"I have a feeling that with some ingenuity and a few long bolts we can get going again."

"You're going to try to repair the shaft under water?"

"Absolutely not. I couldn't get to it. But I believe—though I'm not certain—that the angle of deviation is steady. As long as the shaft remains stable . . . well, I may be able to tilt the propeller to compensate. The only problem, Mr. Williams, is light. I would have to wait until daylight."

"Well, we have no objection."

"Then we're agreed. Operations should begin shortly after breakfast. About seven."

Phil said nothing. It hardly seemed fair to request the Captain to attend to a thing so mundane as a later breakfast when he was going to work on the boat in mid-sea. They felt the night close around them. It was oddly intimate, but unpleasant. The darkness was like a presence.

In the morning Phil and Tracey were roused from bed at five-thirty. They washed, dressed, and came to breakfast before six. Penny served a homemade marmalade of pineapple and orange which they spread on thick, flat crackers.

"Fresh fruits," Penny confided, biting into the marmalade. "That's the secret."

Phil felt the sleep slowly evaporate from his mind. His body was a dull ache, a uniform stiffness. Tracey had been unable to sleep well. Rings showed under her eyes. She seemed distracted and unable to concentrate.

"How do you feel, Captain?" Phil asked.

"Jolly damn good. And you?"

"Good enough."

"Glad to hear that. Who's on clean-up duty this morning?"

"I am," Penny said.

Tracey's spirits lifted. She and Phil went up on deck. To Phil's surprise, the water bounced erratically, like an unco-ordinated disorder of waves with neither wind nor current visible.

"Can you work in water like this?" Phil asked.

"I'll be fine. Just tie my rope securely to the rail."

McCracken stripped to his bathing shorts and lowered himself down the ladder. In his hand, tied to his wrist with a short length of twine, was a flashlight, a wrench, and a small bag of bolts and washers. He lowered himself into the water.

"Life is full of risks, Mr. Williams," McCracken said, smiling up at Phil.

Phil tied one end of a rope around the rail. The other encircled McCracken's waist. McCracken bobbed under the water, surfaced again at the stern, then bobbed under again. Surfacing periodically, he worked with wrench and bolts on the unseen propeller for more than half an hour. Surfacing, he spewed water from his mouth.

"What does it look like down there?" Phil called.

"It looks very stable," McCracken called back. "All we can do is try."

McCracken climbed on board, sputtered like an old dog, shaking the water from his ears. Penny draped a huge bath towel over his shoulders.

"With luck," he beamed, "we'll be in Nassau before evening."

"Wonderful," Tracey said brightly.

McCracken rubbed his hands nervously. "Well, then, shall we try her?"

McCracken disappeared eagerly into the wheelhouse. After preliminary gestures over the console, he turned the ignition key. The engines sputtered, caught, and then ran smoothly. McCracken kept his eye on the compass and his hand lightly on the wheel. The *Penny Dreadful* ran forward smoothly, overcame the bobbing mass of undirected waves, and cut cleanly into the south.

Then there was a slight bump, and the white foam trailed from the stern in a great arch to the east. McCracken whirled the wheel around with his hand. The boat purred serenely still, curving slowly around in a vast circumference.

It was strangely silent on the deck when McCracken cut the engines. Phil realized he was perspiring, but not from heat. It would be damned embarrassing to be towed into port. Unaware of his concerns, Penny went down into the galley to make some chowder.

McCracken wrote a small entry into his black logbook, checked his watch, and closed the book. He started the engine. The boat continued on its enormous curve away from Nassau. McCracken turned the key and the boat drifted silently, slower and slower, until it bobbed on the waves.

At lunch McCracken wore a white captain's cap, decorated along the top with gold braid. It made him look distinguished. No one spoke over the soup. At the end of the meal McCracken lifted his eyes upward.

"Shall we pray?" he said.

Phil exchanged a glance with Tracey. They bowed their heads. It was silent, intimate, and perfunctory, although Phil noticed Tracey's lips in motion.

"A bit of a mess, I'm afraid," McCracken said, adding

sadly, "the shaft has worked itself from one of its retaining plates. I probably shouldn't have run the engines."

"It worked for a few seconds," Tracey said.

"Yes, but there can be no question of using the shaft again."

"Why not?"

"It runs from the engine chamber, through the entire hull, to the propellers where it emerges into the water. It's at that juncture that the problem exists. If it should ever rupture—"

"Then what?"

"Then seawater is admitted into the boat."

"We'll sink?" Tracey blurted incredulously.

"No," McCracken said reassuringly. "Our pumps would easily handle it. But the repairs would be quite expensive."

"All right," Phil said. "What do we do?"

"With your permission," McCracken said, "I'm going to radio a friend of mine. He is an excellent mechanic and perhaps can advise us. You see," McCracken added, his face reddening, "it is much less, well, embarrassing to steam in under your own power without the help of the Coast Guard. I'm sure you understand."

Phil nodded vigorously in agreement.

In the wheelhouse McCracken bent over a small microphone at the radio console. He wore earphones. The transmitter was wedged into a side of the wheelhouse on a small ledge. Phil sighed audibly when McCracken said his friend had passed out of receiving range.

"So that leaves us no choice," Phil said.

McCracken faced him squarely. "No choice at all."

"How long does it take for the Coast Guard to arrive?"

"Well, I suspect the Bahamian authorities are closer. About four hours. Since we are not in an emergency situation, we may have slightly less priority if traffic is heavy. All this has to be spelled out over the radio."

Phil's expression conveyed his concern.

"The weather is fine, Mr. Williams. All is not a disaster.

Why don't you have a swim? Good therapy for sore muscles."

As Tracey and Phil floated, looking up, on the rolling waves, their eyes closed against the bright sun, they could see the feathery outlines of interlocked clouds against the blue. As they circled lazily into the shadow of the boat, Phil heard his name called.

"Mr. Williams!" McCracken called. "Would you come here, please?"

Shakily, Phil climbed the ladder. Tracey floated into the sun again. Then she heard loud voices on the deck. She climbed the ladder and for a moment felt vertigo and clung to the side railings. Phil's voice, strident and protesting, came to her ears. She hurried over the edge onto the deck and swung the towel over her shoulders.

"What's wrong, Phil?"

Phil turned, his face twisted by despair, anger, and confusion.

"The radio won't work!" he expostulated. "They think *I* did it!"

"That's absurd!"

Tracey shivered. An unaccountable, cold presentiment ran through her veins. She shook the hair from her forehead. Everything seemed to be happening very far away.

"Well *I* certainly didn't!" McCracken roared.

"Why the hell would *I* do such a thing?" Phil shouted.

"Your reasons are your own, Mr. Williams. I have no way of fathoming them!"

"I don't even know the first thing about this stuff!"

"Everybody!" Tracey shouted. "Please calm down!"

McCracken gazed blankly at her, then at Penny, who stood angrily at the steps leading into the wheelhouse. McCracken slumped abruptly into his chair, the picture of despondency.

"I beg your forgiveness, Mr. Williams. I utterly lost my composure."

McCracken gazed out at the sea, then at Penny. Finally, embarrassed, he stood up in front of Phil.

"You see, my boat is part of me. When it doesn't function, I feel the pain. I . . . I lost perspective."

"Is there a way to fix it?" Tracey asked.

"It's rather odd," McCracken replied. "It's as though there were a bad connection. Listen."

Turning the dials, McCracken leaned forward, cocked his ear. He turned the volume to its maximum. A disagreeable low static emerged from the loudspeaker.

"I just don't understand," McCracken murmured over the static, which now audibly fluctuated, dying slowly.

"Could it be the battery?" Phil suggested.

"It runs off the main generator."

"Maybe one of the tubes."

"I suppose I should take a look."

McCracken quickly unscrewed the case over the interior wiring of the radio. He pulled boxes of spare parts from the lower shelves. It was as though neither Phil nor Tracey were there. From time to time Penny reached down and handed him another tool. They worked in unison, quickly and perfectly.

"A radio is a very simple device," Penny said, discouraged. "There should be no reason why it's not working."

The rest of the day was devoted to replacing tubes and studying the complex diagrams in the radio manual.

As the sun set, McCracken soberly paced the deck. The radio was still not working. Phil and Tracey stood at the stern railing. Tracey often cast probing glances at Phil.

"Did you?" she finally whispered.

Phil turned to her, puzzled. "Did I what?"

"Break the radio?"

For a second Phil was speechless. "Now what the hell are you talking about? Why the hell would I do anything like that?"

Tracey shrugged. "You know . . . afraid of being discovered."

Phil spluttered, seeking words of defense, when Mc-Cracken stepped out of the shadows.

"It *is* the generator," he solemnly intoned. "You remember what I said about the shaft? As I feared, seawater has gotten into the hull and flooded the generator housing. I'm afraid we have no lights as well."

He flicked the switch to the hatch corridor. Down below, the salon was swallowed in darkness. Penny produced three alcohol lamps. One brightened the main salon, another the aft corridor. She carried the third before her. Shadows undulated when she walked. Phil and Tracey followed McCracken down the hatch steps.

"It's like being shut up in a floating tomb," Phil said.

"Hush, Mr. Williams. You're giving way to panic."

"I'm being realistic."

"There's more to navigation than a bit of water in the generator. I warrant you'll be our guests for lobster in Nassau at noon tomorrow."

Somewhat mollified, Phil allowed McCracken to lead him to the dining table. Tracey nervously lit a cigarette. The long shadows frightened her. Penny brought another lamp to the table.

"Please be reassured," McCracken began, "we are no more than twenty miles from a port. We have not one but two spare battery cases with which to resuscitate the radio and call for assistance."

Tracey dug compulsively into the tiny cakes that Penny served them. As she ground them to pieces with the edge of her fork, Phil put a reassuring hand on her thigh.

"Just damned bad luck," McCracken said. "I can't imagine what this will all cost to repair."

"Let's not burden Mr. and Mrs. Williams with that," Penny said. "They've gone through enough."

McCracken raised a glass of liqueur. Phil found his heart racing.

"You're right, mate," McCracken said. "To lobster in Nassau!"

Phil and Tracey raised their glasses in a halfhearted toast. The liqueur was stronger than anticipated. Tracey coughed.

"Everyone will watch us, like a sick turtle at Sea World," McCracken said to himself. "No matter."

They drank. Phil and Tracey retired for the evening.

The single lamp was pure, white, and steady. Overhead they heard the sound of brisk, metallic tools. Tracey was nervous. When they made love, she was unable to respond and fell asleep on Phil's shoulder while he softly stroked her neck and arm.

McCracken banged at something heavy and metal above them. Something else was dragged over the deck. Tracey jerked in her sleep and her arm went dreamily over Phil's chest. Suddenly there was an angry pounding on the door.

"Who—? What—?" Phil stammered, and bolted upright in bed.

"The batteries are corroded!" McCracken roared. "Do you hear me? *Corroded!*"

SEVEN

Two battery cases, black with powder, stood on a bench in the main salon. Their sides had been pulled apart, revealing the caps of the interior cells and, in one case, the small, still-wet metallic grid. Like two sinister dead blocks the battery cases seemed to have a gravitation of their own, weighing down the bench with the abnormal weight of decay.

"Christ!" Phil exhaled, approaching them slowly.

At his touch more powder fell onto the bench. He drew back his hand as though stung. He whirled to face Mc-Cracken. "What happened?"

McCracken licked his lips, shuffled closer to Phil, and roughly nudged the nearest casing with his foot. The water inside an open cell glistened darkly in the undulating lamp-light.

"Casings cracked, Mr. Williams. There must have been a flaw in them. They, too, were stored below. Seawater got in. Perfect electrolyte."

McCracken heavily sat down opposite the dead batteries. He passed his hands over his face and exhaled roughly. He looked tired, worn down. His hair was unkempt.

"You can't recharge them?" Phil asked.

McCracken hit the batteries angrily. "There's nothing to recharge! Look at them!"

Phil turned away from the bench. The sight of the

ruined battery cases nauseated and frightened him. Arms folded, he leaned against the wall. At the far end of the salon, Tracey watched quietly. Behind her, watching them all, Penny stood, starkly silent.

Looking at the battery and McCracken's capable, oily hands, Phil felt mistrustful. But then why should Mc-Cracken defraud him here on the open sea? It was equally to *his* advantage to get the boat home.

"What the hell is going on here?" Phil said softly. "What's going to happen to us?"

"Don't worry. I have a pulse, operated by its own small battery, that sends out a continual signal," McCracken said. "It transmits for fifteen miles."

"Fifteen miles? We must be forty miles from land."

"Not that far. Besides, ships pass frequently through here. They'll know what it means."

"But how long will that little battery last?"

"Not long," McCracken admitted. "With intermittent use, maybe a few weeks."

"Oh, well. A few weeks."

"*If* anything passes within fifteen miles," McCracken said.

Tracey, though she had heard everything, stepped through the salon door, avoiding the batteries as though they were emblems of death itself, and went to Phil.

"What is it, Phil?" she said in a tiny voice.

Phil extended a hand in the direction of the batteries. McCracken turned away from them in disgust. He started to put tobacco into his pipe.

"The batteries. They cracked and seawater got into them. They're ruined."

"It's all my fault," McCracken said. "I stored them down below. Never, never do a thing like that."

"What does that mean?" Tracey asked. Her hand rose slowly to her neck.

"It means," Phil said simply, "that we're floating. No engine, no radio. No way out of here."

Tracey turned to McCracken. "Is that true, Captain? Are we shipwrecked?"

McCracken paused, licked his lips, started to light his pipe, paused again, and put down his unlit pipe. "We are disabled, not wrecked. Disabled."

"What's the difference?" Tracey demanded. Her voice rose slightly.

"A wrecked ship is in danger of sinking. People are starving, have nothing to drink. Life-and-death situation. But for us, the main problem is different."

"And what exactly is our main problem?" Phil asked, still leaning against the wall, speaking quietly.

"Waiting," McCracken said, finally lighting his pipe.

"Waiting?"

"Just that, Mr. Williams. For another ship. A passing plane. It's not enjoyable, but we're not in extreme danger either. There *is* the pulse. We stow a half dozen emergency flares. We'll be found. We'll make it to Nassau, never fear."

Phil perspired heavily. An unpleasant, heavy heat weighed down his body. Tracey had been right about one thing. He *was* afraid of being discovered. If the *Penny Dreadful* were towed to the repair dock of the Nassau marina, she would be lifted out of the water, turned over, and local crews would set to work on her. It meant that the marina would soon know all about them. And who frolicked at Nassau this time of year? New York people. Should word eventually circulate back to New York, it meant that his wife would have witnesses, maybe even legal entry forms that he had been in Nassau with Tracey. Barbara would have the mechanisms to dispose of him. Phil wiped the perspiration from his lip.

And what about the design center? Would she take that away? Nothing was in his name. His status was little better than a hired hand. Could she take his sons away? Was there no limit to the abyss? Phil awoke as from a nightmare. Could they possibly slip incognito into Nassau?

Tracey's voice brought him back from his thoughts.

"Then we're not so bad off, are we?" she said, a bit too quickly. "I mean, we're not sinking. Just drifting. Isn't that true?"

McCracken said nothing, only inhaled deeply from his pipe. Then he stood up slowly, turned his back on the batteries, and raised an eyebrow.

"Drifting," he repeated. "Yes, we're drifting."

"But we'll be all right?" Tracey asked anxiously.

"We have stores for several days," Penny said. "With what the sea can provide, we can stretch that to weeks if we have to. There is emergency drinking water. No reason to be anxious."

McCracken nodded. "It's just the waiting that's going to get on your nerves," he said softly. "That's the one thing you'll have to get used to."

"How long do you think it will take?" Phil asked.

"Two days. Three. Depends on the shipping out there."

After a few moments Phil gave up. If there was waiting to do, there seemed no point in doing it in front of the salon door. The wall clock showed the time to be a bit after four. Unable to sleep, he and Tracey went to the stairs and slowly climbed toward the deck. What was strange was the manner in which the McCrackens merely sat and observed them walk away. It was as though they were waiting for further reaction from their guests.

Up on deck Phil and Tracey strolled to the wheelhouse, then to the flagpole, then to the deck chairs where they sat down. The night had turned cooler. The moon, full and bright, rapidly descended in the heavens.

Phil held Tracey's hand but she sensed something more bothered him.

"What are you thinking?" she asked.

Phil released her hand. After a moment, he measuredly spoke. "I did not break the radio. But I *am* worried about what happens when we get rescued." He turned to her.

"Nassau is filled with New York people. Word of this is going to get around."

Tracey looked at him, unable to conceal her bitterness. "I'd say that's a small price to pay for getting to shore, isn't it?"

Phil sighed. "For you maybe, but not for me."

Tracey leaned back, and stretched out her legs. She strove to remain calm, yet her voice trembled. "Terrific! At a time like this all you can think about is her."

Phil searched for a cigarette, found one, and took a lighter from Tracey's pocket.

"I'm not thinking about her—at least not the way you implied. Hell, let's be serious. She knows I'm not on a business trip."

Tracey turned to him with a look of genuine surprise.

"She knows about us, you mean?"

"Sort of. Not all the details."

"I see."

It meant that this was not the first time for Phil. His wife apparently chose to look the other way. Tracey had guessed as much but it had never been out in the open. It demeaned her.

"If this gets out, she'll ruin me." Phil's face was ashen. "Barbara is paranoid about scandal. I'd be worth as much divorced as in the flesh. She'd take everything from me. The business, the kids—Christ, what a mess!"

There was not a sound of the ocean, not even wavelets against the hull. Briny and unpleasant, a strange lassitude settled over the decks. Tracey shifted her weight on the hard deck chair.

"Well, you may be lucky and no one will find out." Her voice took on a noticeably hard tone, which Phil ignored.

"Of course they will. A disabled cruiser, a luxury yacht, pulled backwards into the marina? Gossip flies, local newspaper, hell. They've got nothing else to talk about. Sooner or later, it'll get back to New York. And when it does, my head goes on the block."

Tracey snapped, "What about *my* head! What about my marriage! I have something at stake here, too!"

"Don't get sore."

"What do you want me to do? Throw myself overboard?"

"I was just communicating my worry to you, Tracey. Don't take it wrong."

Even in the cool of the night, the perspiration trickled from Tracey's neck. She reached for a towel and dried herself. She was too despondent to return to the stateroom.

The moonlight bathed their legs. The railings glittered in its lambent glow. And thus they remained, sitting in silence, as the moon gradually relinquished its priority in the heavens to the red ball rising hotly in the east.

"I'm thirsty," Phil said. He rose, leaving a small damp spot where the backs of his knees had lain against the chair. "Let's go and see if there's anything cool to drink."

In the salon McCracken and his wife were taking notes, earnestly talking, from time to time referring to pages from the ship's log, the black ledger. When Phil and Tracey entered, they gathered up their notes.

"Could you unlock the padlock?" Phil asked.

Penny glanced up at him. "The combination is written on the back."

"It is?"

"Certainly. We just use it to keep the handle latched. I hope you didn't think we were locking you out?" Penny chuckled.

Phil flushed. He mixed a mild whiskey and soda for Tracey and a tall scotch and water for himself. They picked up magazines from the rack next to the liquor cabinet and idly paged through them.

"We have divided the tasks of the next few days into segments," McCracken said. "Your suggestions will be taken into account."

"Thanks," Phil said dryly. "There is one thing . . ."

"Yes?"

"If a freighter or a patrol boat picks us up, what actually happens? I mean, do we need to present passports and identification?"

McCracken tapped his pencil against his lip.

"I must present my papers, state the nature of the cruise, and the cause of disablement. Insurance. My own nationality. Registration. Why?"

"Just curious."

McCracken turned back to making notes with Penny. Phil shot a glance at them, but they made no sign of understanding his motives in asking. Phil turned the pages of his magazine and sipped his drink. The hours passed relatively cool, quiet, undisturbed.

Penny and Tracey went to the galley to prepare breakfast. McCracken gathered up his log and notes to take them to his stateroom. At the door, he turned to Phil.

"Mr. Williams. If it turns out that the repairs will be lengthy . . ."

"Yes?"

"We really ought to come to an understanding about the remainder of the cruise. Nearly seven days, I think."

"And?"

"The first mate and I have discussed it. Whatever suits you will be just fine with us. You can spend the several days on shore while the shaft is repaired. Or, if you like, you can consider yourselves free to engage another boat."

"I'll speak to Tracey. I really don't know our plans at this point."

"As you like. The unused days would be refunded, of course, if it came to that.

"That's very fair."

McCracken smiled paternally and excused himself. While he was taking his material into his stateroom, Penny laid the table in the aft salon. Since the fans no longer worked, it was growing warm below, stuffy, though the portholes were wide open.

Breakfast was light. Soft-boiled eggs, water biscuits, and

sliced oranges. Phil picked at his food. His intestines troubled him, and he suspected he would have to see his doctor when he returned. After coffee, McCracken brought a morning bracer to the table.

"Damn luck but good liquor," he said genially. "Here's to you both."

"To the *Penny Dreadful*," Penny said, raising her glass.

The boat's silence was unnerving. It was as though they were waiting for something, like thunder after viewing the lightning flash. Tracey helped herself to a second small glass of the liqueur but could not drink it.

"Excuse me," she said nervously and hurried off to the stateroom.

Phil excused himself and followed her.

"Are you ill?" he asked, opening he door.

Tracey lay on the bed, staring starkly at the ceiling. Her voice, when she spoke, was as pale as her face and devoid of emotion. "Isn't it strange?" she whispered.

"What?"

"Drifting like this."

"Well, certainly nobody planned it."

"First the shaft, then the generator, then the batteries . . ."

"What are you trying to say?"

Tracey stirred on the pillow. Phil sat despondently on the chair by the bureau.

"This is the first time—the only time, really—that I . . ."

"That you what?"

"That I've done anything wrong. Really wrong. And here we are. Stuck on the open sea."

Phil did not like the tone in her voice. It was as if she were alone in the room, talking to herself.

"Get some sleep, honey," he said.

"It's the first time," she repeated to herself. "And the only time."

Phil went to her, stroked the side of her face. Gradually she became tired and closed her eyes. Phil ambled up to the wheelhouse, where McCracken sighted the sun through his ancient brass sextant.

"How is Mrs. Williams?" McCracken asked.

"Not holding up well, I'm afraid. Nor am I, for that matter."

"Relax, Mr. Williams. This ELT unit is sending out a continuous distress signal. Someone is bound to pick it up."

"We hope," Phil said, and walked away. He felt useless. The waiting was getting on his nerves. Penny was at the stern of the boat busily swabbing down the deck. Why, Phil wondered, couldn't he follow their example? They were the acknowledged leaders, if not the high priests, in this society of four. And if the society were to survive, its dependent members would have to absorb the discipline and values of the Captain and his wife. Why couldn't Phil try to think as the Captain thought? Why did he resist such an obvious mechanism? Why did he feel violated? Was it simply the breaking of the last illusion that he, Phil, was master of his fate, an individual with his own rights and destiny? Why did he feel that he was now on the point of a monstrous defeat?

The day passed in a boring progression of minutes. Lunch was skipped by unanimous vote. Tracey remained in her room through a simple, delicious dinner—beef fillets on crusty sourdough followed by fruit and cheese and a spicy wine cooler.

Later, as the sun swiftly settled into the horizon, McCracken appeared with an alcohol lamp, which he lighted and affixed to the stern railing. Apparently, he was worried about being hit by another vessel, for he put a second lamp at the bow. That left four lamps for the deck below, one in each stateroom and two for the midsection of the boat. Penny had turned down the flame to a dull glow and left a note for Phil to be sparing in his use of the fuel.

Phil went to bed. Tracey still slept uneasily, tossing and turning. He held her head against his chest. It seemed to calm her and she slept more peacefully. The darkness never really dissipated, and Phil could not see his feet at the end of the bed. He remained awake for what seemed hours, thinking about his home, his children, his business, and his wife. In that order.

Whenever Phil thought of home, it always began with the vision of his lovely Cape Cod house built in 1788, a tall white structure that had undergone three restorations and two expansions. It was located in Ossining, within a few minutes' drive of the Hudson River. It had been bequeathed to his wife by her grandfather, the founder of the business that Phil had assumed after marriage and which, by now, included leather and suede design for women's fashion. It was a noble house, utterly out of keeping with his or Barbara's ancestry. Phil loved it. It gave him a powerful sense of his own validity to see the dew form on the trees and hedges that bounded his property. He loved to see his two sons play football among the red and golden leaves.

Barbara Sobel wore white blouses and tweed skirts, expensive suede and leather from Phil's design centers. Her taste ran toward pewter and silver, and she kept the house dark with oak and mahogany. She required that the live-in servants be dutiful and unattractive. What Phil did in New York was his own business, but the house in Ossining was her cloister. From it she worked to extend her social connections to those families higher in the river valley. She gave Phil two sons, somewhat against her will, and now she demanded that not the slightest breach of decorum, much less hint of scandal, ruin the life her forebears had entrusted to her for safekeeping.

At the design center, Phil was regarded as a pace-setting competitor. His talent was to catch wind of tiny, almost unnoticed advantages in Europe or in the New York supply and distribution network, then drive hard until he had them. He paid his designers extraordinarily well and kept them circulating in Europe on a seasonal basis. By this

method he had an underground channel of information on
the fashion centers and he was able to anticipate them
rapidly in New York. From time to time he went on a
buying trip himself, generally to Europe but lately also to
the Mideast. Barbara demanded only that he leave and
arrive alone and that he be discreet.

Tracey had not been the first wife of a partner or a
friend that Phil had seduced. Unlike the others, she had
been very difficult. There were dimensions to Tracey that
led away to refined areas. She was elusive, like quicksilver.
She was almost virginal, in that her husband was timid.
Though hesitant and shy at first, she grew under Phil's
training. Her warmth enveloped him until he felt like a
small boy again, secure in the arms of a woman who
responded to him.

A cold snow turned to rain when Tracey's husband,
tapping his black glasses against his teeth, told Phil about
the Arctic assignment. The Air Force was working on a
network of portable guidance systems for missiles along the
Alaskan-Siberian frontier. It involved heat-seeking missiles
from both submarines and motorized launchers. Larry was
sworn to secrecy but he confided that for three weeks no
one in the world would know exactly where he was, nor
would he be permitted to write or telephone home. Phil
saw his chance.

In a dentist's office, paging through a dilapidated copy of
Sun 'n' Fun, he came across a boxed advertisement on the
back page.

Phil telegrammed an expression of interest. He received
a typed reply, asking him about his interests, his wife, his
business, his proposed itinerary. The letterhead was "Caribbean Cruises, Inc." The signature was nearly illegible.
Phil could tell it was probably a husband-wife team. That
they had included photographs of the boat, the islands, but
not themselves amused him. There was something low-
pressured, almost familial about the approach, and they
obviously wanted to please him. He wrote, subtly com-

municating his desire to be discreet and their reply, an invitation for the first two weeks in January, was sent, like the first letter, to his post office box.

Over a lobster dinner Phil and Tracey agreed to go. They agreed not to see each other upon their return.

The Christmas season seemed to pass with unprecedented slowness. Phil instructed his wife not to seek him out for two weeks after New Year's. He said nothing more about it, nor did she. Christmas was a lovely snowfall, glittering Christmas trees, and dark, immense nights. All was correct, Phil thought. Overcome with tenderness, he watched his sons romp in their pajamas over the braided carpet and hardwood floor by the stone fireplace.

The day after New Year's Phil instructed the office that, due to the pressures of the holiday work schedule, he was going to leave for two weeks' vacation. He left no address, delegated his responsibilities to his associates and took off. Somehow the idea circulated that he was going to Morocco. He did nothing to correct the rumor.

His one concession to Barbara was to insure that there be no chance his activities were discovered. It was, he supposed, the one thing he owed her.

Like a little boy before his birthday, Phil imagined the next few weeks and he was distratced. He daydreamed and became aroused easily. On the flight to Coral Gables he was suddenly worried that Tracey might not come. It was not, he knew, the kind of thing she normally did. He alternated between elation and depression, pacing the walkway at their designated meeting place, a restaurant on the marina.

Tracey moaned lightly, wresting Phil's mind back to the present. Drawing her close to him, he stroked her gently. He closed his own eyes, expecting not to sleep, but, oddly, did.

EIGHT

Phil woke with no memory of having gone to bed. A repugnant odor drifted into the stateroom. Tracey dressed silently. When they went out into the corridor a thick, sweet aroma suffocated them.

"Pork!" Phil muttered. "At five-thirty in the morning?"

Penny looked up from the salon table, neatly set in white.

"Since the generator is out, the food is spoiling," she said brightly. "We'd better eat it while we can." She cast a sympathetic glance at Tracey, "I hope you're feeling better, dear. You slept the day away."

"Yes," Tracey said listlessly.

Phil sat politely, but the sight of the roast, its sides gleaming in gravy, carrots floating in grease, turned his stomach.

"Better stuff yourself," McCracken said gruffly. "Hell of a lot where that came from."

Phil jabbed at the roast and gingerly ate a small section. Nevertheless, he felt his stomach rebel.

Studying the pork in her plate, Tracey's eyes suddenly brightened as a thought struck her. Her voice held the tone of a master detective carefully sifting through clues. "If the food is spoiling, Captain, we will not have three or four days' supply. It will all be rotten by the end of the day."

"No," McCracken said. "The meat locker is cool. We

are going to suspend a few tins into the sea, just to see if fruits will keep that way. I see no reason to revise our estimate."

"Why haven't we been picked up?" Tracey went on suspiciously. "I thought we were in a shipping lane."

"There may have been a storm. That would slow the freighters."

Tracey picked at her roast, drained her coffee cup, and lit a cigarette.

"Maybe they can't pick up our pulse. Maybe the battery is dead."

"No, the pulse is transmitted by its own battery and is functioning properly. It is limited, as I tried to explain, to about fifteen miles."

"I just know the battery is dead."

McCracken and Penny exchanged glances. Phil knew Tracey was falling apart.

"In the old days," McCracken said in a relaxed tone, "a becalmed ship was a fearful thing. Fights broke out. Thirst drove the crew crazy. The passengers saw visions. But most survived. As much as you might criticize the European navies, their officers were top rank. I think, Mrs. Williams, that much of that sea lore, while true in its day, is a bit sensationalized. On the whole, sailing was just a hard, rough business. If the captain knew his area, if the crew obeyed, it was a rare ship that did not reach its dock."

"I don't know anything about the old days," Tracey shrilled. "All I know is we're crippled. We're like a cork on the water."

"Let me finish, Mrs. Williams. Add to what I just said all the difference that a hundred years has brought—the Coast Guard, the communications, the perfect sea charts, improved methods of keeping locations, superior boat design—and you must agree that the situation is not so bleak. Not so romantic, but not so bleak."

Tracey studied the Captain intently. "All right," she said finally. "I'll trust you."

"Please do. It'll make things so much easier. Now, who's on cleanup?"

"Penny handled it yesterday," Tracey said glumly.

"Would you mind doing the chores in the galley?" Mc-Cracken asked.

"No, I guess not."

"Be sure to use the water in the gray pail," Penny said.

Tracey nodded. McCracken excused himself and went to the wheelhouse. Penny finished shoving all the fruit into the meat locker, and then she set to scrubbing out the refrigerator. She had a few tiny tins in which she put cream and a bit of butter, some juice and jam. She suspended the tins from twine through the porthole in the galley down into the water. Tracey peeked into the meat locker. It seemed to her that a copious amount of fruit, vegetables, and pork remained.

On deck, McCracken set Phil into the fishing chair. Tracey replaced Phil in an hour for the second shift.

"This is ridiculous," Tracey whispered. "They've got us fishing while we sit like dying ducks."

"Nobody's dying," Phil said patiently. "Besides, we need the food."

"Why hasn't the Captain talked to us all day?"

"He's busy. Making calculations." Phil glanced toward the wheelhouse. "Look at him. He's using those old instruments. That's a sextant, I think. It measures the height of the sun or something like that."

Tracey looked down with disgust at the single, black fish that flopped desperately on the hot deck. She reeled in her empty line and cast down again.

"I'll bet we're picked up today," Phil said. "I'd like to spend a few days in a fancy hotel. One with swimming pools and tennis courts and nightclubs. Wouldn't you like that?"

"I'd like to visit a church," Tracey said.

"Why not? Isn't Nassau British? I'm sure there are some beautiful cathedrals nearby."

"I haven't prayed since I was a girl."

Phil frowned slightly and leaned forward to kiss Tracey as she stared into space. Her mouth was slightly open, her thoughts far away.

By midday they had caught three small fish, which Penny placed into the recesses of the meat locker. The galley had grown warm and humid. McCracken did not appear at lunch. At three-thirty a tiny speck of a plane flew over the horizon. McCracken fired off four of his six flares toward it, but apparently it was too far away to notice.

The main salon was the coolest spot on the *Penny Dreadful* and Tracey spent the afternoon tensely looking through the novels in the bookcase and at the facsimile maps on the wall. McCracken remained silently brooding in the wheelhouse.

"More problems?" Phil whispered to Penny, out of Tracey's earshot.

"The Captain will let us know as soon as he knows."

Phil looked out at the horizon. They stood in the doorway of the salon so all he could see was the white-hot ocean. Suddenly he turned back to Penny.

"You don't suppose we're drifting to Cuba?" he asked.

"If anything, we're moving the other way."

"I mean, they'd seize the boat and lock us up, wouldn't they?"

Penny shrugged ambiguously and laughed softly.

"There's no possibility of winding up in Cuba, Mr. Williams."

"Yeah, well, I guess I get a little paranoid. I didn't know it, but I guess that's how I react to danger."

Penny fixed a porthole glass that had rolled slightly shut. She turned, facing the minimal sea breeze that lifted the few loose strands of hair under her red kerchief.

"Danger galvanizes the Captain," she said.

"Well, he's a professional."

"I suppose, on balance, that people either sink within

themselves or reach out even to the point of recklessness. There doesn't seem to be much of a middle ground."

"No, I guess not. Extreme situations sort of burn out the middle ground, don't they?"

The afternoon remained hot. Even when the afternoon sky had taken on a yellow glow in the west, Phil's face ran freely with perspiration. Due to the finite supply of water, they were limited to dips in the ocean for their baths.

McCracken did not appear in the salon for supper. He spoke only to Penny. The wheelhouse was cluttered with instruments, charts, and compass readings. Phil avoided the wheelhouse but paced the deck from time to time, studying McCracken at a distance.

"Why haven't we seen a ship?" Tracey whispered.

Phil shrugged.

"Shouldn't we be looking for ships?" she asked. "Why didn't they think of that? The Captain has a telescope."

"You're right. Let's go ask him."

McCracken did not look up when they approached, nor did he respond when spoken to. They sought out Penny, cleaning fish at the stern railing, next to the flagpole.

"Shouldn't we be looking out for passing ships with the spyglass?" Phil said.

"If you would like to," Penny replied laconically.

"Well, I mean, would it help?"

"Passing ships will pick us up on radar before you can see them."

"Oh, I didn't know that." Phil sighed and shrugged his shoulders.

"We're depending on the pulse, then," Tracey said, "which only operates for fifteen miles in an ocean that's thousands of miles wide."

"Not where we are. Freighters and sailing ships converge as they come to the islands. Keep your perspective, Mrs. Williams."

Tracey's flushed face suddenly stiffened. McCracken had banged three clear notes on the ship's ornamental bell.

"The Captain's decided," Penny said, taking off her apron. "He wants us to assemble in the main salon."

McCracken spread out an enormous sea chart, weighting the corners with ceramics from nearby shelves. Phil observed a small circle drawn where three pencil lines intersected. A cool breeze at long last stirred the curtains at the portholes. McCracken jabbed lightly at a series of light blue bands, curving around a landmass.

"You will recall this current, Mr. Williams," McCracken said crisply. "It is the one we missed the other day."

"Yes."

"Apparently we curved father out from it than I had thought. That is why we saw no freighters."

Another cool breeze circled into the salon. Penny fanned herself with a Japanese fan. The Captain went on. "In short, we are quite a bit to the north of where I had hoped we'd be."

"What does that mean in practical terms?"

"It means—you see this second current here?—it means we are slowly drifting out to sea."

An awesome silence filled the room. The curtains rustled as far away as the galley. What frightened Phil was Tracey's calm acceptance of the news. She only nodded to herself, as though slowly digesting the information.

"I don't get it," Phil protested. "There's no wind. We're not being blown out to sea."

McCracken cleared his throat. "I explained it to you, Mr. Williams. A current is like a river. Anything in it flows with the water."

"Well, that's—I mean, how far is this thing going to take us?"

McCracken's compass point scratched out to where the concentric lines gradually curved back to the south.

"By the time it curves down—two hundred miles."

"Jesus, this is a disaster," Phil blurted.

"Yes, Mr. and Mrs. Williams. Things have become serious. We can no longer pretend."

Phil leaned back in his chair. He threw a crumpled, soiled napkin to the floor, looked up at the ceiling, and whistled. Tracey nodded bleakly. The McCrackens observed their guests' demeanor.

"I knew it," Tracey said hollowly. "I knew it the moment I woke up."

"Okay, Tracey, keep calm. We all have to keep calm and listen to what the Captain says. This is just going to take a little more time and we're just going to have to work a little harder, that's all."

"He's right, Mrs. Williams," Penny said. "You must be realistic. It's no longer a pleasure cruise."

Penny stopped fanning herself. She studied Tracey, who wiped her face with her hand and brought her trembling under control.

"You're right," she murmured. "It's not for pleasure."

Phil kissed Tracey on the back of the neck, trying to be casual. She stiffened when he kissed her.

"What are your orders, Captain?" Penny said briskly.

"The first is that Mrs. Williams should return to her room and try to sleep. We may need her assistance, and I want her to keep in good spirits."

Phil patted Tracey on the thigh.

"The second we have already begun," McCracken continued, "and that involves certain procedures relative to the remaining stores of foodstuffs and drinking water. It may well mean some rationing." Phil's eyes narrowed. "Since we had anticipated being at dockside several days ago, and since most of our stores are fresh fruit, meat, and vegetables, all of which are subject to spoilage, our stores are quite low."

"How low?" Tracey asked softly.

"As I said before, three or four days. But now we must entertain the possibility of a longer period."

McCracken gazed at Phil who found nothing to say. McCracken fingered the chart, tapped on the table, then cleared his throat again.

"As for the most urgent matter," he concluded, "that of establishing contact, I have some ideas, but they require just a bit more calculation."

"You've got something in mind?" Phil asked.

"Yes, Mr. Williams. When I'm certain, you'll be told."

McCracken abruptly stood. He rolled up the chart and disappeared into the wheelhouse once again. Penny went to the galley to make an inventory of the foodstuffs and prepare the menus for several days.

"Well," Phil sighed, "I guess this is for real."

When Tracey made no reply, Phil turned to her. Her eyes were pinpoints of intensity. A knowing smile played at her lips.

"First the storm, then the generator," she said in the measured tone she had used at breakfast. "Then the batteries, and now the Captain has miscalculated where we are."

Phil remained silent, but watchful. Tracey pressed on, Miss Marple closing in on the villain. "If you had a manager who made this many mistakes, what would you do?"

Phil's finger traced a pattern on the tablecloth. "I know what you're saying, but—"

"Just tell me that. If you had a manager whose machinery was damaged, who didn't have an auxiliary engine or whatever, who couldn't tell you where he was in the schedule, what would you do?"

"That's different."

"You're afraid to look at this objectively."

"In the first place, I know more than any of my managers. I can tell if they're competent, if their schedules are realistic, or where any of the problems lie. I know what's easy and what's difficult. God knows about out here. Do you know how to navigate? Everything on a boat is so goddam complicated. Who can tell if McCracken should have done something differently?"

"Phil. In your heart you know better," Tracey shot back loudly, firmly.

"Not so loud. In the second place, just like in a battle, you don't remove a general if something small goes wrong. Accidents happen. There is such a thing as bad luck. Besides, what do you expect me to do? Fire the Captain in the middle of the sea?" His voice lowered. "Here comes the mate. Change the subject."

Penny came to the salon table where Phil and Tracey still sat.

"I've devised a crude sort of schedule," Penny said. "Alternating fishing shifts, cleanup shifts. It's a good idea to keep things very shipshape, and our morale high." She handed Phil a sheet of paper with hand printing on it. "This is not written in iron," she continued, smiling. "It's just to structure the duties a little. I think that makes it easier."

Phil accepted the paper from Penny. He perused it carefully, then showed it to Tracey. "There. You see? Everything's under control."

"Yes," breathed Tracey in a strangely calm voice. "Everything's under control."

A clanging bell at five-thirty sharp in the morning tore Phil and Tracey from their sleep. After a breakfast of fruit, crackers, jam, and coffee Tracey was strapped into the fishing chair. The small chunks of fish on the hook revolted her. When she reeled in a flapping black fish, she smashed it ten times with a pliers until it was still. At first she had to ask Phil to unhook it. Later, when she was sweaty, dirty with the guts of fish, smelling of decay and entrails, it did not seem to matter. She violently pulled the hooks out with the special hook pliers.

Phil scrubbed out the meat locker. Some of the vegetables were going bad. The tomatoes were soft. As he leaned into the maw of the cabinet, the smell of leafy decay increased. He poured baking soda on his sponge and vigorously scrubbed the wire shelves. The meat still looked good. On the inside of the door was Penny's menu schedule, a careful combination of fruits, starches, fish or meat, for the next week if need be. Phil counted up the remaining foodstuffs. There seemed to be nothing left over after seven or eight days.

Phil's head jerked backward, banging painfully against the meat locker door. An echo of the ship's bell reverberated strangely among the shelves. He took off his apron, wiped his hands, stepped over the bucket of soapy water, and rapidly climbed the stairs. On the deck Tracey washed grime from her trousers with a bucket of seawater. She looked defeated, her hands bruised and chapped from fish scales, sunburn, saltwater, and from wrestling with the three-pronged hooks.

"Where are we meeting?" Phil asked her.

"She's setting up a table in front of the wheelhouse."

McCracken, not seeing Phil and Tracey, vigorously slammed the knotted rope against the inside of the bell. When he saw them, he stopped. He wore a white shirt with brass buttons, black stripes at the cuffs, and his white captain's hat.

"Two small freighters were spotted," McCracken said. "Coffee freighters, as far as I could tell. They did not respond to our flare." His voice lowered. "We've only one left."

"*I* didn't see any flare," Tracey said.

"That's because you were too busy beating the fish to death," Penny scolded.

McCracken abruptly rapped for silence. His demeanor changed. Penny sat down, expectantly. With a raised eyebrow and slight gesture of his head, McCracken indicated that Phil and Tracey also sit down.

"We continue to drift east, away from the shipping."

On the chart, a revised intersection of lines was circled nearly an inch and a half to the right of the previous circle. Suddenly the chart took on meaning for Phil. Ominously, it verified their drift into the open sea. It was like the medical chart of a dying patient. He could not bear to look at it.

"We're still in the current," the Captain went on. "We have to get out of it."

"God help us," Tracey whimpered.

McCracken rapped on the table. "I've warned you about that attitude, Mrs. Williams," he said sternly, then turned back to the business at hand. "We must get out of the current because it is taking us to a place where the ship traffic is much less dense. Is that understood?"

Phil nodded. At a signal, Penny adjusted the table umbrella so that the shadow fell on the chart, eliminating the blinding glare.

"In about two hours we will have the best opportunity." McCracken pointed down at the map. "Here, where our current loops close to the one we missed not so long ago. It may be we can even enter the second current which is westbound, taking us closer to the islands. I've tried to be simple. Have you understood?"

"I think so," Phil said.

"Good. It's not fast travel. Not exciting, but it should prevent our being stranded in a deplorable wasteland far beyond the continental shelf."

Phil and Tracey waited for further instructions. But McCracken and Penny remained silent, waiting for them to comprehend.

"Yes, go on," Phil said at last.

"Is there nothing that excites your curiosity?"

"I don't know what you mean."

McCracken seemed disappointed at Phil's obtuseness. "We have no sails."

"Yes, I know."

"We dare not, cannot, operate the engine."

There was a silence. McCracken waited for Phil to understand. Perplexed, Phil scratched his head in embarrassment. "I don't get it. We can't pull the boat like we did before."

"You can. You will."

"The water's half a mile deep out there!"

"You'll row."

Phil turned to Tracey. Tracey was pale, her expression indecipherable.

Penny, like an owl or sphinx, watched Phil. Her lips moved subtly in a smile or perhaps only a nervous gesture.

"I can't row," Phil said. "I don't know how."

"You'll learn," Penny said. "Necessity will be your teacher."

"We'll work in shifts," McCracken said.

"It's not fair," Tracey said, almost inaudibly. "Just not fair."

"The Captain and I will row for six hours, you and your wife for two. Isn't that fair?" Penny said. "Any little bit you can do to help will be so much appreciated."

"You can't pull a boat this size!" Phil objected. "Not by rowing."

"It's the same principle as before," McCracken said. "The boat glides horizontally along the surface. If a tug can move the *Queen Mary* we can move the *Penny Dreadful*."

"Have you ever done this before?" Phil asked.

Strangely, there was a pause.

"I have, in my time, pulled a boat. The principle remains the same. Let inertia work for you."

"Once you find the rhythm," Penny added, "the rowing becomes mechanical."

"It's like being punished," Tracey blurted, her voice breaking.

"Of course not," Penny said. "Why should you be punished? What have you done wrong?"

"If there were any other way," McCracken began, "but—"

"All right, damn it!" Phil shouted. "We'll row!"

There was a momentous silence. The tension dissipated. The McCrackens looked at Tracey. She was tearing apart a paper napkin. Her moving lips made no audible words.

NINE

Phil sighted along the dripping cable that led from the dinghy, then through thirty feet of water; up to the *Penny Dreadful*. He raised his oar and set it into the water, about halfway to the bow of the dinghy. Tracey followed suit. Their oars pulled simultaneously through the water. The rope tightened but the sleek white hull seemed fixed and impervious to their efforts.

"Watch your oar blade," Phil said. "Keep it pointed up and down."

After twelve strokes they exchanged sitting positions. Thirty feet away, the *Penny Dreadful* loomed over them. The portholes glittered, blank and pitiless against the sun. After twelve more strokes, Tracey's hands bled. Phil took off his shirt and wrapped it around her hands. After another dozen strokes Tracey began rowing sideways to lessen the strain on her back. From the bow McCracken signaled them to correct to the right. They paused to rub the backs of their legs. Each stroke soon forced the air from them in quick exhalations.

"The salt . . . in my hands . . ." Tracey said. "It burns . . ."

"Wipe them on my shirt."

"Oh, Phil, it burns."

"All right. Let's go back. I mean it."

"No. They'll be furious. A little bit more . . ."

"Honey—"

"Really, I want to. We have to."

After twenty more strokes, the oars slipped regularly out of the water. They stopped, exhausted. The *Penny Dreadful* seemed to observe them sardonically, its eyes open on their weakness.

"Our rhythm is wrong," Phil said. "Let's start again."

They eased their oars into the water. They pulled slowly. Phil cursed the aching of his back. He thought he heard Tracey call on the Virgin Mary, but when he looked she said nothing.

After twelve more strokes, McCracken appeared at the bow and raised a yellow cloth up and down.

"What the hell does that mean?" Phil asked.

"He's beckoning us back. It's our shift! Two hours! We're all done!"

Phil turned to Tracey. "Hell, that wasn't so bad. How are your hands?"

"I have some lotion in my suitcase."

"There, you see? Now you know where that expression, pulling your own weight, comes from."

Phil wound in the rope, drawing them toward the *Penny Dreadful*. The sea had taken on different personalities as they had rowed, malevolent, indifferent, awesome, and yet intimate. Now it appeared more friendly. All tricks of the mind, Phil thought.

They climbed the accommodation ladder. Their muscles fluttered from fatigue.

"How did we do?" Phil asked.

"A good stroke takes practice," McCracken said.

"A little rest and you'll feel fit as a fiddle," Penny added.

A glass of wine appeared in Phil's hand. Things passed in and out of his awareness like a madcap montage. The McCrackens lowered Tracey down onto a deck chair.

"I'm all right," she protested too loudly. "I just saw red stars."

The McCrackens ordered them to their stateroom. Sandwiches and fresh towels waited on the bureau. They gobbled the sandwiches to the last crumbs. Fully dressed, they fell into bed and slept the peaceful sleep of those who have given their destinies to a superior authority.

Tracey sprang upright in bed. In the darkness the metallic bang of the bell reverberated down through the stateroom.

"Larry, I'm frightened—what is that sound?"

Phil struggled to his feet, then sat clumsily down on the bed. He pushed his hand through his hair. His body felt like lead. He yawned. The bell rang again, strident, harsh, stinging their nerves with every strike.

"Christ," Phil mumbled, covering his ears.

"We have to get up," Tracey whispered. "We have to row again."

"No. I can't. I'm done in. Tell the Captain I'm sick."

Tracey shook him by the arm. Pain shot like a spider, rippling up into his shoulder. He put his hand on hers.

"You had another bad dream, didn't you?" he said sympathetically.

"I . . . I don't remember."

"You called me Larry."

"Did I?"

"It doesn't matter. Let's get dressed."

They dressed fitfully in the dark. Phil slipped Tracey's sweater over her head and helped her put on her shoes. She limped after him into the dark corridor. Only a single lamp burned, very low, from the McCrackens' stateroom in the far distance, a blue glow that formed no shadows. On deck, the McCrackens waited for them at table. Bottles of wine glimmered in front of a small lamp.

"You slept like the dead," Penny said.

"I feel like the dead," Phil answered.

They sat despondently. Tracey could not find a way to keep her left leg from tightening.

"It was a marvellous row, Captain," Penny said.

"It was," McCracken agreed. "I wanted to row to Mexico!"

"It gets in your blood. You feel you could row forever."

Tracey sipped. As the alcohol slowly took effect, her leg relaxed. She felt unwashed, cramped, her mind unclear.

"And the sunset!" Penny said to Phil. "It streamed out against the sky like orange banners!"

"And the storms," McCracken added, lifting the casserole dish to her. "Sheer Götterdämmerung!"

"You must try to imagine this," Penny said, her eyes sparkling. "In the twilight we saw, far against the northern horizon, a stream of black clouds, each spitting lightning. Crooked shafts of white light. It was indescribable."

"Sometimes the air heats rapidly, gets pushed out to sea where it rises," McCracken explained. "Then, if it gets pushed back it cools very quickly and you get these characteristic black clouds and lightning."

"Sounds better than what we got," Phil said. "Just flat, hot infinity."

Penny dished a reheated pork casserole onto their plates. The bread was crusty at the edges. The last of the butter had turned. The fruit, however, was succulent. The wine pleasantly inebriated them.

"Not so fast, Mr. Williams. You'll fall asleep," Penny laughed, her face radiant in the glow of the lamp. The exertion of rowing had fanned a deep, almost rosy hue into her cheeks, apparent through the suntan.

"You should be able to line up the rope with the alcohol lamp that's set on the bow," McCracken said. "Don't be frightened."

"You must promise to wear your life jackets," Penny said.

"I have a whistle here." McCracken put a shiny whistle around Phil's neck. "If you fall in or need assistance, let us know."

"Tomorrow is going to be another long day," Penny said. "We must pace our progress. That's why we'll be asleep."

"I don't blame you," Phil said. "Six hours of rowing. Jesus!"

After a final quick drink of white wine McCracken helped Phil and Tracey into the dinghy. He watched to make sure that their life jackets were secure. They rowed into the inky blackness vaguely perceiving McCracken on the ladder. He consulted his compass and shouted to them.

"The prow of the *Penny Dreadful* is dead on course! Keep the line taut and steady as she goes!"

"I can't even see the end of my arm!" Phil shouted back.

Silently, they rowed. The ocean had no demarcation. No horizon was visible. Only the nearest waves were discernible. Thirty feet behind them, over fifteen feet in the air, a single alcohol lamp burned in the night. The splash of their oars, the enormous pull at their shoulders frightened them. The pain proved the reality of the ocean, made the fear larger.

"The McCrackens seem to be enjoying this," Tracey muttered.

"I can't talk when I row!"

"Never seen them so happy, have you?"

Phil did not answer. Tracey gritted her teeth. Cold sweat appeared at the back of her neck and dampened her hair. Salt formed on their lips. The blackness seemed to roll side to side underneath them.

"Turn to the left," Tracey said.

After half an hour their strokes had diminished to noisy paddling. They rested. The sea was utterly silent. The night played tricks.

"Let's go!" Tracey said shortly.

Phil thought he heard a splash. It was Tracey's oar. He matched her stroke. After twenty more strokes a fresh breeze chilled them. Mist collected on their clothes, their skin, and the seat. Tracey wrapped her hands in Phil's handkerchief.

"I can't go any farther," she panted, and sank down on the bench.

"All right. That's fine. Enough is enough. We did what we could."

Phil maneuvered Tracey to the rear seat where she slumped over. She breathed regularly. Her hands flopped onto her knees, the blood trickled up from torn blisters. Phil took her oar and turned the boat back in line with the prow of the *Penny Dreadful.*

"You shouldn't have to row alone," Tracey protested.

"Rest where you are. If the Captain can do it, I can do it, too."

Phil could not coordinate the two oars. He tried pulling one, then the other. The dinghy turned from side to side, but did not move forward. There was no more strength in his biceps. He blew the whistle. No sound emerged.

"Goddam!" he spat out, splashing at the oars.

After several good strokes, a wrenching pain climbed into his neck. Phil grabbed the rope at the stern and carefully pulled the dinghy back to the boat. They rested nearly five minutes, then slowly climbed up the ladder. McCracken was waiting for them when they got to the deck.

"An hour fifteen," he said, checking his watch. "Fair. Very fair."

"Your goddam whistle won't blow!"

McCracken took the whistle and blew into it. A shrill blast shocked them all. "You have to blow hard, that's all." Phil groaned in pain. "You'll be all right. Your body has told you to quit, and you must obey."

"I can't even raise my arm."

"Relative to your rating, you've actually done well, Mr. Williams."

Phil covered Tracey's shoulders with a blanket. McCracken helped ease her down the stairs. Two lamps glowed against the salon walls.

"I'm so hungry," she murmured. "Is it possible to have a sandwich?"

McCracken checked his watch. "We'll have breakfast in

only four hours. It would be better to keep to our schedule."

In bed, Phil flexed Tracey's knees, pulling and pushing her legs. He slowly rolled her head from side to side. He rubbed her lower back. Phil found a cold capsule, hoping it would help her sleep.

"I have sleeping pills," she said.

"You do?"

"I was nervous before I came to meet you. I thought they might help."

"Where are they?"

"In my suitcase."

Phil cut a pill in half, brought it to her with a glass of water, and watched her drink. She held the glass with two trembling hands. Her eyes filled with tears. "Oh, Phil. Are we ever going to get home?"

"Of course we'll get home. In a few days we'll be in Nassau laughing at all this."

Tracey undressed. Phil helped her. They slipped into the sheets. As the sleeping pill relaxed her, her breathing became smoother. A flush came to her forehead. She put her head on his chest, favoring her sore shoulder.

"Make love to me," she whispered desperately.

As in a kind of dream, fatigue and pain turning his limbs to worn putty, his head swimming with the taste of the black ocean, Phil embraced her. But in that position they both sank into sleep.

When they awoke, Phil was embarrassed, though he could not remember why. Tracey did not appear to have slept well, despite the half sleeping pill. After they sponge-bathed, they still felt light-headed.

Dawn crept into the salon. Toast was piled high on a plate next to a thick broth. McCracken wore his well-starched white captain's shirt and his cap. With a gesture he indicated for them to be seated.

"How are you this morning, Mrs. Williams?" McCracken asked.

"All right, I guess," Tracey replied wearily.

"And you, Mr. Williams?"

"Sore. All over."

McCracken chuckled. "It'll pass. Simply dormant muscles being awakened after years of slumber." His smile faded. "The first mate will bring down the charts. We can explain the situation to you after you've eaten."

After breakfast Phil and Tracey remained hungry. Penny brought the rolled chart down from the wheelhouse along with several small pages of notes. She wore a small white cap.

"Crew present and accounted for," McCracken said as Penny cleared the plates, carefully dusted the crumbs into her hand, and threw the crumbs out the porthole. "We are going to be strict with water," McCracken said. "Our morning washups have been freshwater ones. Now that luxury must be suspended.

"All right," Phil said.

"Secondly, the first mate is drying fish and the remaining pork to preserve them. After your rowing shift she will instruct Mrs. Williams on how to perform this duty." Phil put a hand on Tracey's shoulder. "The third order of business refers to the rowing. Our progress is satisfactory, but no more than that. I would like to be encouraging but, in plain truth, we have not cleared the current."

Phil became unutterably depressed. "How much farther must we row?"

"Four miles. Quite a distance, I'm afraid. We're drifting around the loop, away from the neighboring current."

"God in heaven," Tracey sighed.

McCracken pointed to the third circle drawn on the chart. In fact, the circles, describing their slow drift, indicated a northeast direction now.

"Will you give us your best effort?" McCracken said.

"We'll try."

"Good. Let's get started."

On the deck the morning heat prickled their skin. Phil

hated the sight of the sea. The immense band of brightness reflected the sun. It hurt his eyes. Already his throat and lips felt like dried cardboard.

"Here is a thermos of water," McCracken said. "And bandages. I trust you can apply them yourselves. Don't let a blister get aggravated."

They climbed down the ladder. Tracey's bandaged hands reached for the oars. An involuntary cry escaped her lips as her fingers closed around the handle. Phil pushed off from the *Penny Dreadful*.

The heat desiccated their flesh. Small blisters formed over their hands, even on their feet where they pushed against the bottom of the dinghy. Stinging sweat rolled into their eyes. Tracey's bra was clearly visible through the wet, white blouse.

"Only twenty-five strokes," Phil said.

"I know, but I'm done. I'm starving. I'm going to die."

They rested. Phil gave her the thermos from which she drank. Her legs were limp, rubbery. Nevertheless, she grabbed the oar again.

"We *must* go on," she said in a plaintive, obsessed voice.

Twelve strokes afterward, Tracey's oar fell overboard. Phil grabbed it. Tracey began to cry.

"Why can't I row anymore? Why am I so weak?"

"You're not made for this. Nobody is. Let's get back."

As they climbed the ladder McCracken appeared disappointed. He put his watch into his pocket and said nothing.

"I think this is the end, as far as my wife is concerned," Phil whispered to him.

McCracken put a hand on his shoulder.

"We'll talk about it later. Put hot compresses on her legs and back. Keep her from stiffening."

After Tracey fell asleep, Phil went to the meat locker. He took one of the grapefruit and a small slice of pork back to the stateroom. He fed Tracey, who awoke with a start at the sound of the door opening. Then he cleansed her neck and arms with a damp cloth and kissed her eyes closed.

"Relax," he said softly. "No more rowing for you."

Tracey mumbled something, turned over, her arm across Phil's lap, and fell asleep again.

Phil went on deck and attempted to slice, salt, and hang pork and fish in the sun. The sun was blistering, and the briny water burned his hands. Out in front of the *Penny Dreadful* rowed the McCrackens, dark silhouettes against the mirrorlike brightness.

The tedium weighed on Phil. He had never experienced such a vast weight. There was nothing he could do. Their fates were insignificant. Eternity opened up all around them, indifferent as the salt sea.

Perspiring freely, McCracken came up the ladder after six hours. He rubbed himself down with seawater and dried himself, then put on his white shirt and cap. His bearing was regal, official. He wore white shoes.

"How are you doing, Mr. Williams?"

"This is a stinking mess. A damned, stinking mess."

"Eight, nine, ten fair-sized fillets. Good work. This will keep a long time."

"I don't ever want to see a fish again."

McCracken moved back to the wheelhouse where he took up his brass instruments. He was the picture of a sea captain, Phil thought, except that his trousers were not white, but light blue.

For dinner Tracey had changed into a delicate pink blouse with ruffled sleeves. A patterned silk scarf was around her neck, and her hair was freshly combed. She looked exhausted, but her complexion was again creamy.

Penny served grapefruit sections with cherries. She flashed Phil a look which seemed to him accusatory.

"The matter of rationing is not trivial," she said.

Soon clouds appeared in the west, tiny puff balls slowly turning orange against the sun.

"Mrs. Williams," McCracken suddenly said. "We understand that you are unable to continue."

"That is correct," Phil said.

"It's possible to work around that. If Mr. Williams will consent to row with one of us, alternating in three-hour shifts."

"I'll do what I can, Captain."

McCracken considered for a moment, then fell to eating the pork on his dish. It was dry, smothered in a sweet syrup. The bread was hard and had to be toasted. Red wine had not yet turned, but neither was it pleasant anymore.

"Eat well, Mr. Williams," McCracken said.

Phil forced himself to eat the pork, though his expression betrayed his repugnance. Penny noticed.

"At this point, eating is no longer for pleasure," she said. "It only maintains the body's strength."

"So our rationing will be selective," McCracken added.

The pork was several inches from Phil's mouth when he lowered his fork, then raised it again. Again he paused.

"Say that again," Phil said.

"Selective," Penny said rapidly, "to those who work."

Phil lowered his fork. "I still don't understand."

McCracken leaned forward, looking into Phil's face. "Basic, Mr. Williams. Those who row dehydrate. They need vast amounts of water. They burn up a terrific amount of calories. They need fish, pork, fruit. Those who lie in the cool of a stateroom are conserving their energy."

"I don't think you can punish me for not working," Tracey said shakily.

"Nobody is punishing anyone, Mrs. Williams," Penny said. "We—"

McCracken stopped her with a gentle hand on her arm. "It's the only method of conserving. Otherwise we'll not get free of the current."

Phil stopped chewing. "Are you saying that my wife will not be fed unless she works?"

McCracken chewed, swallowed, and looked from Phil to Tracey and back again. "Not at all, Mr. Williams. Your wife won't starve. She will simply receive a ration commensurate with the energy she expends."

"That's not so bad," Penny soothed. "She won't have the appetite we'll have anyway."

Phil and Tracey exchanged quick looks but said nothing, which McCracken took for compliance.

"I'm glad we're agreed," he said jovially.

After supper no one moved. The empty dishes, remnants of an insufficient meal, remained glittering by the brass lamp. As the sun set, Penny lit the lamp. The salon was silent, restful. Phil felt no desire to move his weary body. His eyes found a spot beyond the porthole to dwell upon. The sea had a phosphorescent glow in the south and east. It was an eerie, greenish patch off the port rail, glowing so faintly it was easier to see with side vision. McCracken spoke several minutes on diatoms, plankton, and photosynthesis on the surface of the water.

"Amazing, isn't it?" Penny said. "Here we are, floating like a piece of driftwood. No home in sight. Just like little tiny sea animals."

"A difference, mate. We are unable to produce our own energy. The sea and our dwindling stores must supply that." McCracken turned to Phil. "What say, Mr. Williams? Which is reality? The elements out here? Or selling leather coats in New York?"

"It's all goddam unreal to me," Phil grumbled.

McCracken smiled, accepting the answer. Tracey bit her lip and pretended to read a magazine.

Later, when they were alone, Tracey turned to Phil tensely. "I'm so hungry, I'm going to faint."

"Relax. When they go to bed I'll bring you something."

There was a splash out the window. Wafting into the salon was a smell of rotting fruit mixed with the distant smell of the sea.

"There goes the last of the fruit," Phil observed, looking down into the bobbing water.

McCracken slept in the wheelhouse. A blanket lay over his shoulders. The most recent computations were on a notepad by his table. Penny cleaned out the meat locker, then bade them good-night.

Tracey went to bed. Phil opened the meat locker, removed several tomatoes, dried carrot cake, and tore a slice of fish from a plate. He presented thi to Tracey, placing it over a towel on the bureau

In the morning, the breakfast was fish and carrot cake. "We've lost most of the tomatoes and some of the unsalted fish," Penny said, dishing out bountiful portions of fish and bread to herself and the two men. A tureen of reheated chowder was positioned between them.

Tracey nibbled at dried cereal without milk, toasted bread, and two thin strips of pork in tomatoes.

Phil helped himself to soup, crackers, and white wine. McCracken's burly and tanned arms rested on the tabletop. His eyes held a steely glint. He waited for Phil to finish.

"Do you have any question about the rationing?" McCracken asked.

"No," Phil said. "Should we?"

"Does it seem fair?"

"It seems logical."

"Good. Then there's no reason to speak of it further."

Under a cloud of silence they finished. It was Phil's turn to man the dinghy with McCracken. Tracey washed the dishes. A foul odor came from the drain in the floor of the center bathroom. Water was seeping up through the drain. It had a gristly, oily scum. The odor permeated the boat.

"We're sinking!" she called, waving her arms frantically.

Penny woke, rose from the deck chair.

"Good heavens, Mrs. Williams, calm down! What is it?"

"Water—in the bathroom—coming up from the floor!"

"From the floor?" Penny's expression hardened. "Did you take a shower?"

"No—the other bathroom—near the salon—nobody uses it—"

Penny stepped down into the corridor, went into the center bathroom. On the blue tile floor a small puddle had formed, its outer edge dark and viscous.

"Bilge," Penny said. "I suspected it would happen."

"We're not sinking?"

"Not at all. Water collects at the low point of the hull. Electric pumps drive it out. Now, of course, we have no electricity."

"Then we *are* sinking!"

"No. There's not that much open volume for the water to fill. The problem is the smell of what is coming up."

Penny stepped around the puddle. She examined it for several more seconds. "We shall have to add it to our roster of duties—bailing out below."

Penny grabbed a small bucket. Tracey watched her as she lifted up the floor hatch, partly disappeared, found her footing, bent down, and picked up a bucket of dirty water. She took it up the stairs and heaved it over the rail. While she was gone, Tracey opened the door to the meat locker and ate two strips of unsalted fish and a handful of crackers.

It was now the McCrackens' turn to row together. Phil slept uneasily, turning over and over, craning his neck. Tracey pored, nonseeing, through magazines, articles of which she knew now by heart. She wandered to the Captain's table, gazed intently at all the charts and instruments laid there, then went back to the salon and waited for Phil to awaken.

"Did you steal food?" he asked, rubbing sleep from his eyes.

"No. Why?"

"There's a lock on the meat locker."

"I don't understand. Why would they do that?"

By the time the McCrackens returned, Tracey was filled with anxiety. She felt further and further estranged from the land of the living. She was isolated because she had sinned.

For supper, Tracey ate string beans in syrup, a small slice of pork, a gluey corn starch gravy, and hot tea. Afterward, Phil and McCracken examined the charts in the wheelhouse. They were on the south border of the current. One more day would swing them into motionless water. The skin peeled in large, white flakes from Phil's forehead. McCracken decided it was safe to suspend rowing till morning. A drag anchor was lowered into the water.

During the long night Tracey played cards with Phil. She was unable to concentrate. Under the table he gently rubbed her aching legs. Her stomach growled. She rose and went topside.

Tracey wandered the deck, looking for the moon or passing airplanes. The silence mocked her. Phil joined her.

"Come to bed," he whispered into her ear.

But sleep did not come to Tracey. She sat upright, listening for the faint musical sound of the chain from the flag pole. There was not a wave, not a sea gull, not a radio to interrupt the silence.

"We're being tested," she said. "It's because of what we've done."

Phil leaned from the bed, turned up the flame. Tracey's face was white, drawn, and her eyes strangely black.

"You know what?" Phil said. "You're hungry. That's what's wrong with you."

"Phil, I . . . I *did* steal food. I couldn't help it . . ."

Phil laughed. "I thought so."

"It's like being in hell here," she whispered.

"Stay put. I'll get you a little something."

"No . . . don't—"

"Why not? They're not going to do anything."

"I'm afraid."

"Of what? Relax. I'll be right back."

Phil went down the corridor. There was not a glimmer of light. He smelled the faint, nauseating odor of bilge

water at the side. He walked through the main salon, banging his knee against the desk. Cursing, he found his way
through the door. The stars shone overhead beyond the
open hatch.

On the meat locker a small combination lock had been
fastened. Phil tugged at it with frustration but it did not
give. He listened for sounds of Penny and McCracken. Phil
took a knife and pried at the hasp.

"Christ almighty," he swore to himself, "*give!*"

Fumbling in the drawer, Phil felt among the knives. A
multiple-bladed knife had a small file next to the handle.
He sawed quickly and lightly through the hasp, pulled the
latch, and reached inside the locker.

The fish were clammy in the humid coolness. Phil
grabbed a dish of cake and two cucumbers.

"I owe you a lock, Captain Jack," he whispered.

Tracey ate the cake and a cucumber. She hid the second
cucumber under her lingerie in the bureau. Phil nibbled the
crumbs from her nightgown. He ardently kissed her breasts.

"Please," she whispered, "no. I don't feel—"

Phil kissed her on the mouth. His kisses ranged all over
her body. She cried out softly, then bit her lip. She was
sharply, violently satisfied. Phil drew himself up to her.
Then he, too, was through. They lay, spent.

She stroked his hair, slightly damp.

"Am I a bad girl?" she whispered.

"No. Of course not."

"But look what we do. Why do I love it? Isn't that
bad?"

"Shhhhh."

"Hold me, Phil. I want to sleep with you forever."

They held one another through the darkness. At dawn
the bell reverberated painfully. Phil felt as though he had
been struck over the head.

"I wish he would just knock on the door," Phil mumbled
sleepily.

The aft salon was set for breakfast. Coffee steamed in four cups, a shining pot on a trivet over the white tablecloth. Potato fries and dried cereal waited. Pineapple juice filled three tall glasses. McCracken distributed the potatoes. Hanging from his belt was a *.38 caliber revolver.*

TEN

McCracken apportioned the salt for the gritty potatoes. Small fans lay at their places, since the humidity seemed to mount daily. Tracey fanned herself as she ate her reduced portion in silence. Phil sneaked a look at McCracken's hip. The black and gleaming revolver lay in a small canvas holster.

"You see what we have," McCracken said, reaching for words. "A few potatoes, something to drink, a bit of, well, you have failed to grasp the situation, Mr. Williams."

"I—"

"The pilfering of food stores must cease,'" McCracken said.

Phil thought of many things to say, all of which seemed selfish, even to himself. McCracken's hands spread expansively. He nearly knocked over the glass of juice.

"It is, in fact, an emergent situation. Hasn't that dawned upon you? The ship is sound, of course, but it floats daily into greater and greater tests of its seaworthiness. As the Captain, I must rack my body and brain to the core, to the very inward core, Mr. Williams, just to get us back again. And it is only by observing such measures as I impose, Mr. Williams, that you will see your leather factory again."

"Of course, I—"

"In short, there can be but one brain on board, Mr. Williams. It is I who have the greater experience, the su-

155

perior knowledge. When I make an order, it serves only one purpose, and that is to return us to shore. You certainly are cognizant of that."

McCracken, carried away, soared into oratory.

"You are no longer paid guests aboard a pleasure cruise. The storm and the corrosion of the batteries have altered everything, everything. You are now members of the crew, with duties and responsibilities. And it is of no importance that you understand every minute thing, only that you obey. If there are no rules, we are four horses pulling in opposite directions."

McCracken suddenly ceased, bent forward, looked Phil in the eye.

"You agree, Mr. Williams?" he said matter-of-factly.

Phil nodded.

"It's our survival."

"We were overcome by hunger."

"Hunger! You have no idea what hunger can be! It drives strong men insane! That, Mr. Williams, is why we ration!"

McCracken leaned back, helped himself to the last of the potatoes, and sprinkled them liberally with salt. The top of the pepper shaker had fallen off. Tracey scraped pepper from her plate. She broke into a fit of sneezing. Phil shoveled the remaining bits of crisp potatoes onto his fork. McCracken, out of the corner of his eye, observed Phil's hunger.

"That" McCracken repeated, "is why we ration."

Inwardly shamed, Phil recalled the days in the army, when he had had to swallow orders, the reasons for none of which were apparent. Survival still seemed an abstract notion, just as the concept of being cut down by enemy bullets had seemed farfetched. Like most men who have not been wounded, stricken with disease, or suffered physical disaster, Phil could not understand his own mortality. Nevertheless, he grudgingly accepted the notion of authority.

"Will that be all for now?" Phil asked, barely concealing his embarrassment and irritation.

McCracken ostenatiously took out his large watch and studied the face. "First shift, twenty minutes. Mr. Williams and the first mate."

Phil took the opportunity to do stretching exercises in the stateroom. He limbered up his back, legs, arms, and twisted his torso from side to side. He did several deep knee bends. He breathed deeply, already perspiring. Penny waited for him on the deck. At her gesture he went down first into the dinghy.

It had become a dream. The hot sheet of the ocean everywhere blinded him. He had developed a diminished capacity to understand what was happening. All his body bent to the task of rowing, rowing mechanically, pulling the weight of the *Penny Dreadful* against the even greater weight of the sea, and he felt crushed. He sank into a daze, burned under the direct rays, and washed his face with seawater when instructed by Penny.

On board McCracken cast long lines, baited with the fish Tracey had caught the previous day. He stood patiently, braced, casting out again and again. From time to time he threw scraps of spoiled food into the water. Unmindful of the heat of the day, McCracken stood and made no sign of fatigue nor thirst.

The meat locker was refitted with another larger lock. Tracey was surprised to be trusted to prepare lunch from the stores set out on the galley counter. She followed the recipe and made a fish bouillon. The bread had grown so hard it had to be soaked in oil, making a kind of garlic bread. The salad was composed of leafy greens grown dark around the edges. Hunger gnawed at the foundation of Tracey's composure, still she resisted the temptation to pilfer.

As instructed, she set her own plate with the smallest portion. She felt a ringing headache when she saw Phil help himself to a second portion of soup and salad. She became dizzy. In her mind she saw the nun who, twenty years earlier, had found her lost in the schoolyard. She was taken by the hand, down the long corridors. . . .

"Jesus Christ," Phil murmured. "How long? How long do we keep on?"

"As long as we have to," Penny said.

"There is no way that we can make it," Phil lamented.

McCracken looked up sharply. "Is that an attitude? What if the men of the *Bounty* had given up? What if Magellan's crew had lost hope? Remember, Columbus' crew was on the point of mutiny. The body is only a slave to the mind. And the mind, Mr. Williams, dreams great dreams. It does not surrender."

Phil turned away. The sun's reflection in a hot band of light gleamed hostilely at him. White speckles of brightness danced on the deep blue. It was a vision of things greater than himself. Suddenly he grasped the physical possibility of his death.

"I've had such thoughts," Phil explained. "It's when I wake up after rowing. I feel it's all useless, that we'll never get out of here. Never."

McCracken pointed his soup spoon at Phil. "You shall look back on this as your finest moment, Mr. Williams."

"Look at you," Penny said. "Your biceps, your shoulders. You've lost weight at your waist and put it into muscle."

Phil lapsed into silence and stared at the sea. At the far horizon a haze of small clouds rose into lighter blue air. There was only the small tinkling of the food tins in the water below the galley.

"The fishing is poor," McCracken announced. "Who will take the shift this afternoon?"

Penny drew out her work schedule and perused it quickly. "I have Mr. Williams scheduled for the first shift.

"All right. Nail that schedule to the cabin wall so everyone can see it."

Phil strapped himself into the chair. McCracken used

three-pronged hooks, dug well into large chunks of the black fish. Phil could barely imagine the size of the fish that would swallow such a large bait. He braced his feet, sipped fresh water from a warm thermos, and cast off. Nothing struck.

Tracey scrubbed out the bathrooms, especially at the drain, where the odor was foul. Then she washed their clothes in seawater and detergent and hung them on a rope stretched from the hatch to the wheelhouse. Phil observed her through eyes dimmed by sweat and vision scorched from the brilliant glare of the sea.

He thought, once her body seemed so elusive, so subtle, even evanescent, a thousand soft mysteries and a bed of dreams. Now look at her, with her blouse missing two buttons and trousers torn at the knee, stretching to reach the rope. A body was such a functional thing, with moving parts and unmoving parts, whose sole purpose in life was survival. And for what? To procreate another such body? For pleasure? For nothing at all? Was life nothing but a complete accident, an arbitrary conglomeration of stupidities? Phil felt the line tug, but it was only caught on the twine hanging out of the galley porthole. Cursing and sweating, he leaned forward and pulled in both lines, gradually disentangling them. Somehow, the twine had picked up a trace of blood and, when released, slapped a thin red line down the side of the boat.

Tracey had slept most of the afternoon to ease the dizziness. She was losing weight. Taking salt tablets, she avoided the heat of the sun. In the late afternoon she took down the laundry, already stiff and dry. She folded everything into two piles, then delivered them to appropriate staterooms.

"No fish, Mr. Williams?" McCracken asked when he returned.

"No, sir."

"Are you casting deeply?"

"Yes, sir."

McCracken looked at his nautical wristwatch. A thin edge showed where the sunburn stopped at the leather strap.

"Rest," he proclaimed. "Thirty-five minutes. Out of the sun."

Phil stumbled below. Tracey was sponging her nude body in the bedroom with a damp rag. She did not look up as he came in. When she was through he took the rag and dampened the back of his neck.

"Another two miles, the Captain says," Phil muttered.

Tracey lay down, her face flushed.

Phil could not stop himself from talking. "The problem is that every day we don't clear the current it brings us back to the north. In order not to fight against it, Mc-Cracken has to keep changing our direction."

"I don't understand any of it."

"Instead of south, we're slowly turning to the east."

"That means nothing to me."

"It means that the loop of the current is going to be between us and the westbound current."

A heat rash had developed along Tracey's elbows. Phil handed her back the cloth.

"We may have to row down around the loop," Phil said, shaking his head. "I don't know if I can do that. It means days of this rowing."

Tracey groaned softly and stretched her weary arms and legs. "I keep looking at the sky, wishing I could fly. Why can't we fly? Why weren't people made with wings?"

Phil shrugged in his chair. He observed that Tracey's nudity no longer excited him so wildly, but she had become a detached, pretty object to view. She was utterly unselfconscious, and no longer shy.

"Why were we made without fins?" Phil said. "Then we could just swim out of here."

There was no answer. Tracey rested, head on her arms. Phil looked out the porthole, at the belaying pin on the wall, or the capstan pieces in the corner. How pitiable all the elements of decor looked. Good intentions gone for nothing, Phil thought.

Outside, he vaguely heard the splash of the fishing bait being cast into the water. He knew that McCracken was attempting to construct a primitive water desalinizer out of glass, wire mesh, and clean cloth. Phil had acquired the ability of drifting into a sleeplike trance with his eyes open and his hearing muffled but receptive. Instinct had taken over.

During the night Tracey wrote a letter to her husband, to be mailed when they arrived in Nassau. It was addressed to New York. In it, she explained everything she had done and her reasons for doing them. She begged his forgiveness and asked for him to meet her at the airport. Phil discovered the letter. She did not protest when he tore it to pieces.

During the morning shift, Tracey punctured her thumb on the multiple-pronged hooks imbedded in the fish bait. She shrieked as bits of entrails sank into the flesh. Disgorging blood and slime, she squeezed her thumb and wrapped it in a clean cloth. Later that morning two pieces of bait fell off the hook. Once there was a strong pull on the line, but no fish were caught.

The heat had become a factor in their lives. It was no longer possible, by a trick of the imagination, to banish it. During the twilight spontaneity was revived, and small talk reappeared at the white table before the wheelhouse. During the day the oppressive net that bound them closer and closer sapped their vitality, and drank their spirits dry.

Tracey did not protest the lock on the latch of the meat locker. She knew she could not control temptation. It was the best for all of them, she agreed, to keep the hasp closed and the combination a mystery. Phil took from his plate and gave to her, but she also recognized that he needed strength. When they made love, it was as though his body, too, rationed its energy.

During the long night Phil sat on a bench on the deck. As though deep in thought he rested his chin on his folded hands. In fact, all that came to him was the rowing, the endless, backbreaking work through the glittering heat. Now he tried to calculate how much farther they had to go. McCracken kept changing his estimates. One day he said they were nearly out of the loop; the next morning he said the loop had taken them farther to the north, and they would have to row eastward to escape it. Phil sat, his arms akimbo. Out of the corner of his eye he saw Penny approach, a bandana around her hair.

Penny set a chair on the deck and placed a small music stand in front of her. Tracey came up, escorted by McCracken. McCracken carried a dog-eared red leather case. Tracey carried two small chairs. A breeze wafted through the deck. Phil became aware of the smell of the human animal, a peculiar, by no means unpleasant odor, sharply at odds with the briny bleakness of the ocean.

Out of the case McCracken pulled a concertina, the straps pebbled and cracked with wear.

"A bit of old Jamaica!" he said jovially.

Penny placed her ocarina against her lips, and together they tried a note. He nodded at her, and with a vigorous stomp of his right foot, they began. Fast-twirling dance music filled the air in a shocking disruption of the moody silence of the night. Phil involuntarily looked up at the musicians.

In the glare of the alcohol lamps McCracken and his wife played hornpipes, jigs, and a Spanish fandango. Penny's notes were clearly incorrect but it made no difference. They shouted, stamping their feet heavily to the beat, and played with gusto.

"Dance, Mrs. Williams! Dance!" McCracken shouted.

"Oh, no. I—"

"Dance!" he ordered.

Selfconsciously, Tracey stood up and made a few steps

like a one-person fox trot, shuffling on the deck with her cracked sandals.

"Take off your shoes," McCracken sang, stomping his feet against the deck.

Tracey shook off her sandals and sent them flying against the cabin wall. McCracken roared his approval and the concertina trembled, his arms flailing, elbows flying, and where he forgot the melody he pounded out the rhythm in major chords. Tracey twisted her knees from side to side and clapped her hands.

"Not like that!" McCracken shouted. "That's disco! That's nightclub! You must do the hornpipe!"

While McCracken played, Penny abruptly leaped to her feet and cut her steps, cross-pointed, toes up behind the knees, twirled and toe-touch into the deck. Tracey followed suit, improvising, kicking her feet violently, slapping her ankles, and bobbing and weaving, too.

"Now you, Mr. Williams!" Penny shouted.

"Me?"

"*Everybody* must dance!" McCracken ordered.

Laughing somewhat hysterically, Tracey pulled Phil to his feet. Obediently, he shuffled without enthusiasm through several steps. McCracken changed the tune without a pause. Strange harmonies filled the air. Penny's shadow mingled with theirs against the deck. The hours passed. Exhausted, Tracey slumped to the deck.

"Are you all right?" Phil whispered. Perspiration drenched his hair and flowed down in rivulets from his forehead.

"I twisted my ankle . . ."

"Are you laughing or crying?"

"I'm not sure."

Laughing, McCracken wiped the sweat from his brow. He breathed with labor. They played a slower tune, then lapsed into silence, and McCracken leaned on his instrument as though to keep from falling. The silence of the night now seemed dreadful, echoing inaudibly with fine harmonies. Tracey, breathing hard, fell asleep next to a deck chair.

Through the night they all slept on the deck. In the morning a cold dew had formed on the railings.

Tracey awoke, stiff and sore. She looked around for her sandals, and then found that one of them had broken in two when flung against the cabin wall. Her thumb throbbed painfully from the hook the day before. Slowly the light grew over the deck. Phil woke. The McCrackens were already down in the salon, going over the charts.

"Today must be the final effort," McCracken said, when they went down. "If we continue to be swept northward we will, to be sure, never escape the current by rowing. We will be too far from the westbound current. Therefore, we shall commence two six-hour rowing shifts."

Phil sank beside the table as though already broken from the heat of the day. Only the thought that it might be the last day kept him from wilting with despair.

"Double rations for Mr. Williams," McCracken ordered. "I'm afraid he wore himself out dancing." McCracken leaned forward. "In retrospect, we should have, perhaps, conserved our energy. But what a fine time that was, eh, Mr. Williams?"

McCracken's geniality was in marked contrast to the black revolver still strapped to his waist. It was a subject no one mentioned.

Penny made pancakes out of flour and even found thick syrup made of genuine molasses, and as a result they ate without leaving the table feeling empty for the first time in days. Tracey asked the Captain to rebandage her thumb.

By now the Captain had taken to tacking the chart to the wall of the salon. On it he had marked the approximate delineation of the current and, fighting to extricate itself, the erratic, sharp-angled, day-to-day progress of the *Penny Dreadful*. Like a fly in the water, they skirted the southern boundary of the current, always on the verge of breaking out of it, always carried farther to the north, contained within it.

After the heavy meal, McCracken ordered a rest for twenty minutes before rowing. Penny wrapped small pieces of fish inside dried pancakes and this, with fresh water, would be their lunch out in the dinghy. Tracey was ordered to wash down the deck with seawater. Bits of fish entrails and blood spotted the gleaming white wood around the fishing chair. She handled the hooks very carefully now, but it was too late. The throb in her thumb was a constant reminder of the weakness of flesh against iron.

Like an oiled, mindless machine, Phil had long ago forgotten why he was rowing, only that soon he would row no more. His arm and shoulder muscles grew hard, his neck and cheeks reddened. Strips of flesh hung from his sunburned skin. Through a haze he saw his own knees flexing, disembodied, alien. He could not bear the sight of the oar. Dirty water sloshed at the bottom of the dinghy.

"It was not our intention to get lost," McCracken said during rest period. "But since we have, you must, finally, have learned something."

Phil said nothing. He reached for the thermos of tepid water.

"Do you understand, Mr. Williams? We are a mile from . . . from disaster. If we don't clear the current, and clear it soon . . . who will find us? Out here? Who?"

Phil handed back the thermos. He looked out over the flat sea. Today it looked bluer than usual. Up above there were no clouds. He washed his arms in seawater. McCracken tapped him on the knee.

"Have you ever been so close?" McCracken whispered.

Phil gazed blankly at him.

"Speak, Mr. Williams. It's better for you."

Vague, seemingly insignificant, thoughts crossed Phil's mind. No thought was worth the monumental effort of opening parched lips and forcing the tongue to utter them. Phil feebly gestured, then wiped the sweat from his lips.

"You are . . . *this* far," McCracken said suddenly, holding up his thumb spread an inch from his index finger, "from extinction. We all are. Just a few mistakes, my dear guest and now my crewman, and it will be . . . how? As though we had never been at all." McCracken's shoulders slumped. He tossed seawater over his midriff. "As though we had never been at all," he repeated softly, watching drops of water collect on the dinghy seat. "Absurd, isn't it?"

McCracken stretched his neck. The bull neck, a conglomeration of muscles, revolved, and now he rolled his shoulders, relieving them of the strain of four hours' rowing. Again, he slumped on the seat. He looked up pleasantly at Phil and studied him curiously with a twinkle in his eye.

"And this means nothing to you?" he asked.

Phil looked up from examining a blister on his foot. He shrugged.

"You disappoint me," McCracken said. "I thought a New Yorker, like you, a sophisticated person—I thought you would see what I am trying to explain. You are passing through fire, Mr. Williams. Can you ever be the same, again?"

Phil picked up his oar. Its weight felt like a leaden extension of his own hands. In his sleep now he felt the sea's resistance to his long pulls.

"Row!" Phil croaked.

Through the afternoon their oars dipped and pulled through the sea. The *Penny Dreadful*, tied by the rope cable, remained thirty feet behind. To Phil they might have been stationary. Nothing looked different. Only the chart on the salon wall daily picked up new markings, new circles, different notations along the margins. Reduced to an unthinking, doll-like mechanism, he tried to remember where he was, who he was, and what he was doing here. But later, after the scanty dinner and some fresh water, when he slumped on the deck chair and watched the cruel sun sink like a globule of blood into the horizon, a different sensation came over him.

Yes, the fat around his ribs had fallen away, and his arms and legs had grown taut. All his organs seemed to work in harmony, his circulation and breathing an almost pleasurable feeling. His mind was nevertheless acutely aware of the sea, the boat, the shifting values of the people on board. He seemed to share with McCracken a secret understanding, his intelligence of the body. By comparison Tracey was an undeveloped, merely potential human being.

Tracey's thumb now had a puffy look. Under the bandage Phil saw the begininning of darkness. McCracken boiled water and stuck her thumb into it. Phil turned away as the white pus shot into the water, then rolled to the top.

"That should do it," McCracken muttered. "We'll bandage it better this time."

Nevertheless, Tracey favored her other hand and, while she fished, the left hand hung down at her side.

Covered with a towel for protection against the sun, Phil slept on the deck. Dimly he was aware that the McCrackens rowed only thirty feet in front of the boat. It was a fact that had no particular meaning. Reality and fantasy commingled in his mind. Pictures of his sons came to him. He saw them being pulled over the snow in a double sled. They were going over a hill on a long winter night toward lights, and yet the snow was glittering and bright. Like a dream, the sound of the McCrackens' rowing came, muffled, to his ear.

When the McCrackens climbed up to the deck at the end of their shift, they looked spent. McCracken joked about his age, clapped Phil on the shoulder, examined Tracey's thumb, and then, uncharacteristically, slept in his stateroom until dark, when he roused himself and worked on his charts. Later, Penny, smiling, whispered to Phil that according to the Captain's calculations they had cleared the current and no longer drifted.

The new position was circled in red on the chart, and a relaxation of mood pervaded the boat at the sight. They stood in front of the chart, admiring it pleasantly.

"No mistake?" Phil asked.

McCracken shook his head. "'Accurate to ten yards."

"Then we're no longer drifting?"

"It took a long time, didn't it?"

"Yes. But we're here and we're going to stay here. Right?"

"Right."

Phil stood and stared at the chart. It was documentation of his liberation from slave labor, too good to be true. Tracey could garner no solace from the news; her concentration was devoted entirely to her thumb.

"It throbs up to my wrists," she lamented.

"Let me see," McCracken said.

A red bulge distorted the flesh. It had an angry flared look that had worked its way under the fingernail. In fact, a shooting sensation had developed along the vein that led past her wristbones. Tracey's body had become sensitive to pain as a result of her malnourishment. Her gums ached and she sensed the drumming of blood and nerves in her ears.

"Well," McCracken said, turning her hand over, "let's try again. We didn't get it all out last time."

Penny boiled a small pot of water. The Captain dampened his medi⌐¹ cloth in it with a pair of tongs and wrapped it around her thumb. After several seconds the small wound again burst and relieved the pressure. He threw the cotton cloth overboard. A small pad of cotton covered the puncture. Adhesive tape pinned it to the flesh.

"There," he said softly. "Christ's hands should only have been bandaged so well. I told you we'd make it out of here. Of course, we still have to row into the westbound current."

Phil blanched.

"At least we won't be fighting it," McCracken quickly

added. "A day, maybe two of easy paddling. Then we'll coast."

Phil remained mute. His once dignified bearing abruptly gave way.

McCracken fed him extra portions of fish and induced him to drink more cognac. Phil fell asleep at the dinner table as the sun set.

"Perhaps he was overextended," McCracken said to Penny.

"He seemed to bear up so well."

"A relapse. And yet, he had reserves even he did not know."

Tracey picked up the cognac glass Phil had knocked to the deck.

"Let's not talk about him as though he were dead," she protested. "Let's get him to bed."

"Right. We'll put him on the donkey's breakfast. That's the bench mattress in the wheelhouse."

They laid him near the chart table, covered his shoulders with an extra blanket, and set an alcohol lamp not far from his head. The light gleamed among the brass instruments and crinkled shadows over his pallid face. He did not stir. Tracey became frightened. McCracken led her away.

"Now, now," McCracken reassured her. "That's the sleep of the angels. He depleted his reserves. A good thing we're no longer inside the current."

Phil woke late at night. Dreamily, he observed the cold, still stars in vast formations through the wheelhouse windows. He smelled the ocean breeze. There was no hint of decay, only the freshness of thousands of miles without land. He scarcely knew where he was. He was disembodied, heavy and weightless at the same time, as though etherized after surgery. Content in his immobility, he stared upward and the majesty of the heavens seemed to have been spread for him personally. No longer were the ocean, stars, and darkness agents of indifferent mechanical systems. His destiny was unfolding. Now he could only watch the immobility of the constellations. There was time. Stars had infinite amounts of time. He closed his eyes and, without moving, sank immediately into unconsciousness again.

Tracey sat, wrapped in her blanket, on a bench next to the wheelhouse. It was like being married. She could not sleep alone so she had moved up to the deck to be near Phil. She was bone tired, blood tired, sick of the entire cruise and everything connected with it. She felt herself physically wasted and fantasized that she was rapidly growing transparent. Like a chilling film, images returned to her. Larry met her at the airport. He demanded an explanation. The darkened, bereft apartment, a picture of emptiness, floated into her mind.

The ship's bell echoed softly. McCracken smiled down on Phil who shot awake and sat up with an immediate headache.

"No rowing, Mr. Williams," McCracken said kindly. "Only I do want you to have some breakfast."

"Breakfast? Okay. Christ, my head!"

Phil pulled himself up slowly. With Tracey he went down below, washed, shaved, and found a clean shirt and a pair of Bermuda shorts. On the outside he appeared the carefree traveler. His body, though trim, remained broken, debilitated, suffering from exhaustion and malnutrition.

"If I may make an observation," Penny said cautiously, "your thumb is terribly infected, Mrs. Williams."

Tracey held up her hand. A dark bluish area extended outward from the thumbnail.

McCracken put on a pair of small wire-rimmed glasses, unwrapped the bandage, and peered down at Tracey's thumb. "I believe it will be necessary to open it entirely."

"It looks horrible," Tracey said, frightened.

"It's a first-rate infection, all right," McCracken said softly.

After breakfast, he had Tracey lie down on a deck chair, and had her drink two small cognacs. He sent Penny to the galley to boil water. In the cabinet that adjoined the entrance to the master stateroom was a small medical box. Opening it, McCracken removed two small lances and a razor-sharp needle. Penny carried clean bandages up to the deck.

Phil took McCracken out of Tracey's earshot.

"What are you going to do?"

"It must be lanced. It will turn to poison if I don't."

"What about the pain?"

"What's happening?" Tracey demanded.

"They have to dig under the thumbnail," Phil said directly, walking to her and kneeling beside her.

"Do they know what they're doing?" she asked in a trembling voice.

"I'll be watching, honey."

"Phil—"

"Listen to me, Tracey. Infection spreads like poison. We have to get the poison out."

"It's going to hurt, isn't it?"

"It's like going to the dentist."

Tracey looked apprehensively at the McCrackens. Phil gently turned her head away. He sat down, holding her arm. She felt a tightening on her wrist. A sharp jab went up into her thumbnail. She fainted.

"Mr. Williams," McCracken said quickly. "There is a small plastic packet in the medicine cabinet. Will you bring it, please?"

Phil went down below and found a gray plastic bag with a snap. He brought it up to the deck. McCracken twisted open a small glass bottle and sniffed it. It knocked his head back.

"Ammonia salts," he coughed. "All right, let's continue. You may leave if you feel ill, Mr. Williams."

"I'll stay."

Phil was nauseated by the sight of the blood and pus dribbling very slowly over Tracey's white skin and onto the deck. The rich red blood brutally pulsated, dropping heavily to the deck. Phil had a physical sensation in the pit of his stomach. After five minutes he was forced to walk away. The whole voyage had turned into ungodly horror, he pondered, as he hunched over the railing and gazed out to sea. He allowed enough time to pass before returning.

The McCrackens were putting away their instruments. Their shadows elongated around him. Phil went over to Tracey. The hand was thickly bandaged in clean white cotton. McCracken cleaned up bits of blood from the back of the chair. Tracey slept a deep, deep sleep, her nostrils flaring slightly as she breathed. Phil put a comforting hand on her clammy forehead.

"Think you got it all?" he asked worriedly.

There was no answer.

Penny took away a small pot of hot water with soiled cloth and instruments in it. An object, small and light-colored fell to the deck. Phil stared at it.

"What's that?" he stammered.

"We had to amputate," McCracken said weakly.

Penny rapidly cleaned everything that had fallen and took it all downstairs. Phil stared at McCracken.

"You what?" he shouted.

"The infection was clear below the skin," McCracken said. "It was seeping into the veins."

"But . . . how could you—what have you done?"

"We've saved her life, Mr. Williams."

Phil slumped at Tracey's side. Still asleep, she lay awkwardly in the deck chair. As of their own volition, his eyes turned to the mass of bandages around her hand. To be sure, the form of the hand was sheared at the thumb line.

"Oh, God!" Phil cried out, reeling dizzily, clutching the chair arm for support.

"Mr. Williams—"

The bottle of ammonia salts was opened under his nose. Phil felt a sharp wave knock into his nostrils, penetrating into the core of his brain. McCracken helped him to his feet.

"Be strong, Mr. Williams," McCracken counseled. "She will need your encouragement."

"But how could you . . . without asking me—the pain alone?"

"We had morphine."

"Morphine?"

"Of course. Small injections. Disposable needles."

Phil shook himself free, once again sobered. He caught his breath. He leaned down over Tracey again. He mumbled several phrases. Realizing he made no sense, he stopped. There was nothing to be done. The ease and quickness with which the makeshift operation had taken place was horrific. It made no sense. Wasn't the human body inviolable?

"Help me carry her to her bed," McCracken said to Penny. "We'll alternate a watch over her. She may become ill."

Phil mechanically followed them.

Down in the stateroom they undressed her and lay the sheet over her. Slowly Phil became aware of passing time. The voyage had turned an invisible corner, though he could not define the difference. He asked McCracken to leave him alone with Tracey. He felt unutterably humiliated and violated, as though he should have been there to defend her.

Slowly, Tracey surfaced from the drugged sleep. Phil sank into a deeper depression. After this, how could her life return to normal? Tracey moaned, rolled toward Phil, and became ill. He tenderly cleansed her face. Slowly she opened her eyes.

ELEVEN

"Where am I?"

"In our stateroom."

"I keep . . . phasing out . . ."

"Don't talk."

"Is my thumb gone?"

Shocked, Phil did not at first reply. His body was caught, motionless.

"Yes," he finally answered softly.

"I thought so," Tracey said without looking at her hand.

"It's not so bad," he said quickly. "It doesn't change the person you are."

"I knew it," she said, as though it had nothing to do with her own being. "I could hear them. It sounded like a piece of metal grating under the ocean."

With a chill Phil realized that that must have been the sound of a ligament torn, perhaps even a bone.

"You see," Phil said, still speaking quickly, "it had to be done."

Phil spoke rapidly because of his guilt. He had been an accomplice to a tiny murder, a mutilation. Inwardly he begged forgiveness.

"Yes, you're right," she murmured, wincing sharply. "It had to be done."

Phil kissed her all over her forehead. Tears came to his eyes.

174

"Oh, honey, you must believe they saved your life!"

She gently patted his hands. He wiped his eyes. A stillness, a quiet light, tranquil, yet imbued with fear, came in through the portholes, cast bright areas over the blanket and sheet. Absurdly, it was she who comforted him.

"Poor Phil," she said. "How you must have worried."

"I was beside myself when they told me."

"How will we ever tell poor Larry?"

Phil instinctively flinched, then quickly covered himself.

"Let's not think about that now," he said gently, though his mind was racing.

"We'll have to face it, sooner or later."

"Maybe there's a doctor with whom you can be . . . who is discreet . . . who would help us."

Tracey looked at Phil and smiled sadly. A certain mild fatalism had softened her features. Now she winced again as the painkiller continued to wear away. She finally turned to look at her bandaged hand, which was sheathed cleanly in white. No blood showed, but its profile was unnatural. Tracey's face turned white. She stared at it fixedly and began to tremble in revulsion and fear.

"No," she blurted, tears welling out of her eyes. "There's no doctor. Nobody who would write me a false medical report. And where would I get a surgeon, a hospital, and an anesthesiologist to also write phony bills, phony medical records, phony—oh God, Phil, don't you see? There's nothing phony anymore. Nothing. This is my sign for adultery."

"Take it easy," Phil said. "It'll be all right. We'll think of a way. We have to be strong. We have to think together."

Tracey cried softly, without rancor or fear, only a total and purifying release of her soul.

"Dear Mother of God . . ." she whispered through her tears.

Phil comforted her. He swallowed heavily. He cursed himself for trying to think of a way out at a time like this. His mind seemed to race ahead down vicious alleys looking for a way to save his own reputation, his marriage, the sturdy world of his sons and their future. Could he sacrifice this for Tracey?

"We'll think of something," Phil repeated over and over. His litany slowly calmed her.

He placed the sheet over her hand.

"Don't leave me," she begged.

"All right. We'll sleep together."

Fully clothed, Phil lay next to her. Neither slept. They heard sounds of the McCrackens in the salon. Christ, he thought, what is this? What is going on? It's like a prelude to hell.

Much later, neither having slept, they went out into the salon. McCracken was obviously startled by her whiteness, though he tried to check himself. They sat Tracey down and fed her thick fish soup. McCracken's eyes often went to her bandaged hand.

"You must believe," McCracken whispered hoarsely, "how dreadfully sorry—"

"Please don't speak of it," Tracey said.

"But I must. We were completely taken by surprise. The vein was punctured and the surrounding—"

"I beg you, Captain, I have adjusted to it. Now you must do the same."

McCracken leaned so close that the pleasant aroma of his warmth came to her face. His eyes expressed great weariness, yet a deep curiosity, the same curiosity, Tracey realized, that had appeared in Phil's eyes.

"Nothing has happened to us like this . . ." McCracken said. "We feel not only responsible but . . . we can't even believe it . . . like a bad dream."

"Why? Because I was stupid enough to hook myself instead of the fish?

"Are you in pain?" Penny asked. Finally stirring from the desk, she was pale and, for once, without her habitual elegant manner.

"Yes. Do you have some aspirin?"

Throughout the afternoon Tracey swallowed nearly a dozen aspirin. Phil cut half a sleeping pill for her shortly before supper. A grim quietude permeated the decks of the boat. It was, Phil thought, the first undeniable sign that they would not survive.

No one rowed. McCracken shot up his last flare at what seemed like something tangible on the horizon. The white smoke trail twisted out, the bright central spark arched slowly, then steeply, down into the ocean. The twilight darkened. They were low on alcohol. According to the marks on the sea chart, they were in the position they held that morning. Phil studied the map. It would take three days' rowing to cross into the westbound current, McCracken told him.

Darkness settled. Phil no longer thought about the lock on the meat locker door. He no longer thought about the revolver on McCracken's belt. He only followed orders, waited for the next rowing shift, and tried to fight the guilt that assaulted him from all sides. Beyond that was the darker premonition that if they were rescued his world and Tracey's would fly apart, never to come back together.

McCracken tried to be jovial or to issue crisp orders. Neither attempts altered the mood on board. Phil dully comprehended what he was to do and, according to instructions, fished from the deck, cleaned the galley, or rowed. Tracey sat, agitated yet unmoving, avoiding the sight of her hand and the glances of the McCrackens. It was as though she tried to avoid thinking. The hours passed. No boat appeared. Only the subtle sounds of the ocean were heard. Once McCracken came into the salon to mark the position of the *Penny Dreadful*. They had traveled a miniscule distance, and it was clear that their rowing efforts would require more than the "easy paddling" of McCracken's prediction.

Unable to keep her dinner down, Tracey retired, ill and shaking, to the stateroom. A lamp next to the bed kept the darkness away. From time to time McCracken came in to speak with her. He told her stories of the Indians off the Venezuelan coast and tales of the Spanish who had fought the British in the waters they now drifted over. When he was gone, Phil read to her from a book of sea romances. They held hands while he read. She took the other half of the sleeping pill and gradually fell asleep. Phil put the book on the bureau, kissed her, tucked her in tightly, and walked alone on the deck.

In despair, Phil wondered how the McCrackens maintained their vigor while he and Tracey were worn down to the point that their thoughts were unmanageable. Perhaps they sneaked into the galley, late at night, opened the meat locker, and devoured the fruits and vegetables. Perhaps they had a secret cache in their stateroom?

"Are you all right, Mr. Williams?" Penny asked.

Phil turned.

"I'm just wondering about all that's happened to us. What does it all mean?"

"What does anything mean?"

"Surely there must be *some* sense in all this."

Penny shook her head and smiled; her eyes betrayed worry.

"An accident, Mr. Williams. A series of accidents. Nothing more."

"It seems so hard to believe."

"Until you've suffered you believe that life owes you something. You believe in your personal destiny. Then you see it isn't so. Life owes you nothing."

Phil looked at her, mostly to avoid the endless depression of looking out into the darkness.

"Do you still believe that we'll return?" he asked softly.

Penny's eyes flashed peculiarly in a dark glimmer, and she answered thoughtfully. "We will return. But after today one must think of the physical cost. I will be honest, Mr. Williams. It has been and it will be difficult."

"Do you really think they'll find us, all of us, crippled and helpless as we are?"

"Mr. Williams. You must, by now, have learned the secret to the Captain's strength?"

"No. What is that?"

"Positive thinking. You must not dwell on the negative. There is no room for such luxury—not here."

"It seems beyond hope now. I know that I am disintegrating. I feel it, physically and mentally."

"Nonsense. You're not accustomed to trials."

Phil did not know whether to believe her or not, but he decided he must if he were going to be lowered in the dinghy even one more time.

"Tomorrow?" he asked. "What happens tomorrow?"

"We shall row in four-hour shifts. The Captain will give us a new course."

"And after that?"

"After that we shall be very close to the islands. I beg you to maintain your sense of discipline throughout everything."

After Penny left, Phil found it difficult to go down to the stateroom. Like an eternal, infinite reproach he would see Tracey's bandaged hand, yet his duty to her required that he comfort her. He went down. She was sleeping. Phil saw she had taken another half sleeping pill. Illuminated by the bright alcohol lamp, she was angelic. Her hair was spread out on the pillow. He turned off the lamp. For a while in the darkness it seemed everything would be all right. Things would work out. Holding her close to comfort himself, Phil slowly fell asleep.

The days melded together. The seawater at the bottom of the dinghy irritated the blisters on his feet. A small thermos of fresh water bumped and rolled underfoot. Overhead the sun burned through shirts, hair, and even the skin, it seemed, reddening the interior flesh, dehydrating the body, beating the head into oblivion. Occasionally, Phil looked up at the sea. Implacable, it rolled for miles around him, oblivious of his need to exist. His spirit was diminishing, drying up, just as his body was breaking under the rowing.

"Come, come, Mr. Williams," McCracken grunted. "Row."

"I can't. I don't care anymore."

"If not for yourself then for Mrs. Williams."

Phil lowered his head and began to scoop seawater to drink. McCracken slapped the water from his hand and deftly opened the thermos.

"That's it," McCracken encouraged. "Your wife is injured. She's counting on you. She needs you to row."

"She's not my wife."

"Of course she is. The sun is making you irrational. Now row, Mr. Williams! Make yourself! Back, down, now pull. That's it!"

Phil rowed and looked at the deck of the boat. The *Penny Dreadful* would survive them all, he thought. He wondered how many people it might have survived already. Tracey sat on the deck in the fishing seat. Her black pole angled down into the water, a wide-brimmed hat obscuring her face. She slumped, waiting for the fish that never bit.

"Row, Mr. Williams. Don't think."

"How do you do it, McCracken? You sneak food at night?"

McCracken laughed. "Superior training, Mr. Williams. Pull hard. That's it."

"I don't believe you. How come you keep the meat locker locked? Are you keeping food from us?"

"Row harder, please. Our strength must be productive."

"And what about that stupid gun, Captain Jack? You going to shoot me if I don't row? You'd just let me starve if it came to that, wouldn't you?"

Rowing all the while, Phil railed against McCracken and against the ill luck that stranded them in the hot Atlantic. In mid-afternoon he complained about a business associate who had ill-advisedly closed down the Hartford plant while maintaining the facilities in New Jersey. McCracken said nothing except when Phil stopped to explain the details of the transaction.

"Row, Mr. Williams. Row while you speak."

Phil picked up the oar and spoke at length about the difficulties of finding good leather. Foreign competition was extraordinary, particularly from Switzerland. Tariff laws were no longer sufficient. Phil lapsed into silence. He turned to McCracken, who offered him the thermos.

"Have I been babbling?" Phil inquired, dazedly.

McCracken smiled, wiping the perspiration from his bushy brows.

"It's been very informative."

"Nothing too intimate, I hope."

"Alas, not."

"I don't know how much longer I can continue, Captain."

"I see that. Can you row another half hour?"

"I don't think so. There's nothing left in me."

"Will you try? With me?"

"Yes. All right. I'll try."

The strokes became shorter, little pulls. Phil slid from the seat. McCracken picked him up, washed his face in salt water, rubbed fresh water over Phil's bruised, chapped lips. Phil was rubbery. He tried to take his place on the seat.

"No, Mr. Williams. That's all for today."

"I'll try. I can do it. Let's go."

"We have several more miles. You can't deplete yourself totally."

"Several more miles? No, I must do it, Captain, or we're all going to die."

McCracken took both oars and turned the dinghy toward the *Penny Dreadful*. In his blurred vision Phil saw the tiny white trail of the oars, the bulging green ocean, the bubbles that floated slowly away. He felt like a patient on a table. It was the end. It was coming to a conclusion. There was only water and distance. Phil tried to call on his father but he could picture nothing at all. It was as though he was already dead, and in front of him was a vision of the earth without Phil Sobel—bleak, endless, a beautiful, seductive world with deceptive sunshine.

"Give me your hand, Mr. Williams," he heard over his shoulder.

McCracken helped him up the accommodation ladder. The ladder seemed to have grown ten feet in height, and all the rungs were monstrously far apart. It was like scaling a great cliff. When Penny helped him to the deck, he noticed her smooth shoulders and full breasts. By comparison, the younger Tracey had withered away. When they first entered upon the cruise, Phil had thought of Penny as an older woman. Now there was something, if not more youthful, more robust about her.

"How are you, darling?" Phil asked Tracey.

"I caught a fish," Tracey said solemnly. "A small one."

"You're a brave girl."

"No, it is you who are brave. You work so terribly hard."

Phil slumped next to the fishing chair. He sat on the entrails of bait. His head rested in Tracey's lap. From time to time he felt her move as she reeled in the line. He watched the slender line of her legs. Her feet were sunburned and the nails badly chipped. A deep scratch angled up around her right ankle. He put a hand on her thigh and took comfort from her warmth.

"You're a brave girl," he repeated, almost inaudibly.

Lunch was an indecipherable mixture of potatoes, spices, pork bits, and fish. Wine made them sleepy. Now Phil knew the meaning of hunger. He jealously consumed the very last specks on his plate. He stared at the serving bowl, still containing bits of potato in the bottom.

"I am ordering one hour of rest," McCracken said. "You shall find a spot of shade and not move from it until the direct heat of the sun passes. I shall signal you from the wheelhouse."

Phil lay in the shade. Lying quietly diminished the hunger. Tricks of the eye, bright spots hovered over the horizon. Tracey sprawled under a deck chair. Her arms were stretched out. The bandage had been changed by Penny. A clean, white bulge at the end of her arm, Phil thought. When it came off she would look like a cripple. People would notice, blanch, stare, then take pity on her. Her whole future life would alter. But there was no future, Phil reflected easily. It didn't matter.

The sharp bang of the bell shot through his consciousness. The McCrackens went out to row. Phil was ordered to fish. Tracey continued to sleep in the shade of the deck chair. A mad compulsion to ravish her came to Phil but there was no desire, only violence in him. By the time he had unstrapped the belt of the chair, he fell back, depressed, all desire gone. Did the mere absence of the McCrackens ignite his body? Or was it a signal that something deep down had broken loose, a spasm of instinct, a biological mechanism to survive? It occurred to Phil, as he calmly reeled up the empty hook, the bait having fallen into the deep, that the human ego was a pitiful, fragile island. He was shocked at his own animality. A cold chill raced up his spine. He had heard stories of cannibalism.

Supper was a thin soup made from the fish and potatoes, some dark leafy greens and more wine. Hard biscuits, cooked in the soup, were filling. After the meal Phil was still hungry. Tracey showed signs of extreme nervousness, even trembling, and had to lie down. No one spoke. Even fear was routine.

In the salon another circle on the chart showed minimal progress. McCracken showed them card tricks on a table. A white tablecloth and candlesticks had been set, with dried seaweed attractively arranged in bowls as a centerpiece. Phil stared dully at McCracken's fleet hands. The cards fanned out, appearing mysteriously behind Tracey's ears. The ten of diamonds floated miraculously to the top of the deck. Two hours had passed before he knew it. He was too jittery to sleep. Unconsciously, Phil and Tracey feared sleep.

Hot tea and two soaked biscuits were served at breakfast to Phil. For Tracey it was only hot tea with plenty of sugar. A moderate series of swells had forced the smell of the bilge up through the bathroom drains. It was like an accompaniment of decay, and it made the taste of breakfast nauseating. For the first time the dinghy set down in rolling water.

"A storm," McCracken observed, pushing off from the *Penny Dreadful.* "By-products of a distant storm to the north. We're lucky it missed us."

Silently Phil began to row. He pulled until the rope took up its slack. He braced his legs and felt the small shock as the *Penny Dreadful* slowly began to budge. Had the dinghy been larger they could leave the *Penny Dreadful* to the mercy of the sea and just row, taking all their remaining stores with them. Penny waved to McCracken from the deck of the bow.

Phil peered at Penny. There was a kind of undecipherable signal. It looked like an emergency, though he quickly spotted Tracey ineffectually drying a small fish on a line over the deck.

"What is it?" Phil asked.

"I'm not sure. It looks serious. I don't see anything wrong."

"Maybe the boat's sprung a leak?"

"Listen to me, Mr. Williams. I'm going to go back. I don't like the looks of this. I wnat you to stay here. You needn't row. Relax."

Phil nodded. McCracken tucked his revolver securely beneath his cap and slipped into the water. Phil was again surprised at the man's burly strength. If anything, he grew stronger daily. McCracken swam leisurely, with powerful, sure strokes, and climbed the accommodation ladder.

On the deck Penny gesticulated to McCracken to a point behind the boat obstructed from view.

Phil touched the oars into the water, stabilizing the
dinghy, and waited. Now Tracey became excited. Yelling,
she ran to the side railing and pointed behind the boat. Her
shouts stirred the McCrackens into action. They ran
toward the stern deck.

Phil rowed with difficulty at an angle, parallel to the
boat. Tracey ran the length of the deck opposite him. As
he cleared the bow of the *Penny Dreadful* he saw, star-
tlingly close, a huge black freighter. Two enormous yard-
arms were painted deep yellow and a red flag was affixed to
her stern, rippling in the breeze. It was less than a mile
away, Phil judged, and even at that distance its mottled
letters were clearly visible across the bow. They spelled
out: *Murmansk II*.

Laughing and weeping absurdly, Phil raised his arms
and waved.

On the foredeck Tracey jumped up and down, waving
her blouse. The freighter did not bear down on them but
came at a forward angle that promised to come within a
few hundred yards of the *Penny Dreadful*. No one was
visible on the freighter, but the plume of black smoke
trailed luxuriantly away into the sky.

"It's here! They've come!" he heard Tracey shout happily.

Phil shook his head, scarcely daring to believe it was not
a dream. He rowed to the stern of the *Penny Dreadful*. In
the shadow of the boat he saw the cursed propeller gleaming motionless down below. When he looked up he saw a
figure on the deck of the freighter, a tiny silhouette walking, then disappearing down a ladder. Soon other figures
were visible. By squinting, Phil made out the rough, gray
shirts and sweaters of the crew. Several waved back.

The freighter turned parallel to the *Penny Dreadful*. Its
great wake rolled into the smaller boat, rocking it. Phil
dizzily held onto the *Penny Dreadful*. His feet were un-
steady, as the dinghy violently shook and banged against
the boat. Then the freighter passed to the other side of the

Penny Dreadful. Phil paddled forward to see it. The freighter's crew waved and passed beyond the *Penny Dreadful.*

"Help! Help!" Phil shouted. "Come back!!"

Phil collapsed from the effort. Overhead Tracey shouted. The freighter steamed onward, its engines echoing powerfully across the still sea. Phil frantically rowed to the rear of the boat, waved his hat, and cursed furiously.

He turned back and looked up on the deck. Dressed in flowery shirts and multicolored swimsuits, the McCrackens were playing volleyball. They wore Panama hats. From time to time they turned and waved cheerfully to the freighter.

In the distance the freighter turned gray, less substantial. Soon its oil slick dispersed over the water. Occasionally a crew member waved back.

TWELVE

When Phil pulled his torso onto the deck, the volleyball net was gone. McCracken had even removed his Hawaiian shirt and shorts. Nevertheless, when he saw Phil he stopped, backed up, and raised an arm in defense.

"Bastard!" Phil screamed, and flung himself at McCracken who slipped, ducked, and tried to twist away, but Phil's fingers, tendons bulging, squeezed around McCracken's throat.

"You sent them away!" Phil yelled, tears welling from his eyes. "You *sent them away!*"

Clutching Phil's wrists, McCracken choked, wheezing against the wheelhouse wall. Suddenly a yellow flash obscured McCracken. Phil's fingers groped in air. Losing consciousness, Phil saw the entire deck glow red, then dark red, then it went black, stinging with a thousand flecks of light.

When he came to, he saw Penny standing over him. She held a belaying pin. McCracken was seated in a canvas deck chair only two feet in front of him. Phil's arms were secured by two lengths of rope to the stern railing. Like two actors waiting for their cue, the McCrackens silently observed him, expressionless. Their eyes, however, were alert.

"Tracey?" Phil muttered thickly.

"I'm here." Her voice came from his left, hollow, distant, dissociated.

Phil craned his head painfully.

Tracey slumped, weeping, against the wheelhouse floor. Disaster had struck. The boat deck looked hideously red in the sunset, bright with sin and evil. The sea was a vast lake of heat and suffering.

McCracken leaned forward with a steaming cup in his hand. "Some tea, Mr. Williams," McCracken said. "It'll cure the dizziness."

Phil pressed backward against the railing, his arms pinned tightly to the center rail and post.

"Get away from me, McCracken!"

McCracken sighed. He handed the cup to Penny who took a crisp step forward to receive it.

"Mr. Williams, I—"

"Why didn't you let that ship pick us up?" Phil yelled.

"There was no way that freighter would have stopped for us. It was Russian, probably on its way to Cuba. I suspect there was something under the tarpaulin nobody is supposed to know about."

Phil mumbled and slumped forward with tears of frustration in his eyes.

"Well, I hope you had a good volleyball game," he croaked.

McCracken looked at Penny in confusion. Penny shrugged.

"Mr. Williams," McCracken began. "What—"

"Fun and games on the *Penny Dreadful*," Phil moaned. "Some pleasure cruise."

McCracken set his chair closer, Penny followed by one step, and the Captain peered closely into Phil's face. Phil looked up, startled to see McCracken so close.

"What volleyball game?" McCracken asked.

Phil turned to Tracey for corroboration.

"I was on the other side of the boat," she lamented. "I didn't see anything."

"They were playing volleyball!" Phil shouted. "They deliberately let the freighter go by!"

McCracken leaned back, perplexed.

"You were very fatigued," McCracken offered. "You made a violent exertion to row back, then to the stern, then to the bow. Your eyes—"

"BULLSHIT!"

Phil cocked his head, his eyes dark and penetrating, as though to fix forever the image of the two criminals before him. Unused to hatred, Phil sensed a strange thrill, overpowering and uncoordinated, in his veins. He was deeply afraid. A cold chill spread along his neck. He wondered if he would die from the blow on his head. Why did he feel no pain? Wasn't that proof that even now, as he accused the McCrackens, he was slipping forever from the world of awareness?

Phil violently shook his head from side to side.

"God help us now!" he bellowed hoarsely at Tracey.

"Your mind altered what you saw," McCracken said sadly. "I've known men adrift on a raft who hallucinated dining salons at sundown."

Hardly articulate in his dark and bitter frustration, Phil could only laugh a sinister laugh. Like a trapped wolf, Phil watched every step McCracken made. His arms flexed at the ropes.

"I don't know what to do with you, Mr. Williams," McCracken said softly.

"Shoot me, McCracken. You'll have to shoot me. Because I promise you, when I get back, the whole Coast Guard will be out looking for you!"

Penny whispered in McCracken's ear.

"Yes," McCracken said, and turned to Tracey.

"Mrs. Williams," McCracken said. "Will you please come with me?"

As Tracey rose unsteadily, a shot of panic went through Phil. He was going to hurt Tracey. He struggled against the ropes, but his wrists were bound thickly. He saw their silhouettes at the stern end of the boat blotting out the stars, but he could not hear what they were saying.

Tracey remained mute, staring, as McCracken paced the deck, arranging and rearranging his thoughts. Penny stood by in supportive silence.

"Never," McCracken mumbled, "never has this happened before."

Then, after several more turns about the deck, "Your husband is suffering from delusions, Mrs. Williams. We have no medicine for this. But I believe we can snap him back to reality."

McCracken paced clear to his stateroom and back, his finger playing against his lips. He reached for his pipe but could not find it in his pockets.

"I detest physical violence," he said ambiguously.

Tracey stepped uneasily back toward the hatch. "What are you talking about?" she asked in a very soft voice.

McCracken made a vague gesture with his hand. "If he were a child, you see, a small sharp slap would bring him to his senses."

McCracken went swiftly into the salon and quickly returned with another pipe, a white long-stemmed pipe, filled with tobacco. Suddenly, his movements became brisk, assured. He fitted his shirt into his trousers and smoothed his hair. He snapped his fingers and Penny came forward.

"Mrs. Williams," McCracken said with authority. "You may not like what we must do." Tracey stepped away, her mutilated hand protected behind her. "But just as we had to resort to strong measures to save your hand, now we have to save your husband's reason."

"You're going to keelhaul him!" Tracey gasped.

"No, no, nothing so drastic. We're going to bring Mr. Williams around," McCracken said patiently. "If you don't support us, it will be all that much harder."

Tracey nodded dumbly.

"That's better. We'll have to prepare. And, please remember why we do this."

Once again McCracken went into the salon, coming

back with a short black-handled whip with several knotted leather strands. It looked like a child's toy.

"Mrs. Williams," McCracken ordered, "when we begin, stand with us. He will see you supporting us and it will lessen his tendency to remain obdurate."

Uncomprehending, Tracey nodded. It was going to be a kind of surgical game, she thought. Nothing was clear.

McCracken snapped the whip purposefully and approached Phil who struggled desperately to free himself. Penny brought a lantern and raised it on McCracken's red, beefy face.

Phil felt his shirt ripped away. A voice screamed. It was his own, disembodied. His back was on fire.

"Christ! Help!" Phil cried out, his hands pulling against the ropes, his knees knocking against the railing joint.

A second blow compounded the first. Stinging fingers of pain shot into the bleeding channels of injury. Phil's breath came short. He heard Tracey whimpering.

A third blow streaked his back. Phil knew he was going to die. His vision was the color of blood. Yellow sparks surrounded the dark ocean. The seawater prepared to receive him.

"Stop!" he shrieked.

A fourth blow sliced into his back. Phil felt bits of skin slaking away. He writhed like an eel, unable to feel his body as an entity, only as an amorphous arena of pain.

"Phil, darling!" Tracey sobbed. Penny's strong embrace restrained her as she lunged forward.

A fifth blow stroked across the welts. Tears flowed down Phil's cheeks. Mucous dropped from his nose. With horror, he saw flecks of blood spattering the railing. Air touched flayed skin. He screamed.

A snap of leather again laced into his wounds.

"That's six, Captain," Penny said matter-of-factly.

McCracken ran his fingers through the thongs. Bits of skin, blood, stuck to his hand. His breathing was labored.

His body trembled. Penny presented a bucket. He washed his hands. Shaking, Phil soiled his trousers.

"Should I wash his back?" Penny asked.

McCracken shook his head. "That's salt water," he panted. "Burns like hell. We'll salve him down below."

McCracken carried Phil, moaning, on his shoulders below deck. His whole body shaking, his vision wavering, Phil felt strong arms lowering him down through the floor trap in the galley.

In the hold McCracken leaned Phil forward, then tied his arms to an overhanging pipe so that in the darkness Phil's lacerated back would not touch the floor or walls.

Penny closed the door. Phil was left in blackness. His back was a sheet of flame. His posture was of torture and crucifixion. His torso leaned forward with his arms pinioned over his head. Furiously, blindly, he gnawed at the rope around his wrists with his aching teeth.

Suddenly the rope gave way, and he fell to the floor. He had no strength to rise. The darkness was relieved only by a soft aura of light seeping through the cracks of the trap door above his head.

He did not know whether he fainted or slept. He became calmer, though the pain was excruciating. The silence weighed on him. He curled, sat up, and tried to reason.

Clearly, he thought, these people were insane. All their eccentricities were but the facade for deep, malevolent disorders. Whether they had snapped under the ordeal of the broken shaft or had always been touched with madness, he could not know. Above all, what were the McCrackens planning now? Were they frightened, fumbling for answers? Or had they formulated a program for him and Tracey?

It was equally clear, Phil continued carefully, that the McCrackens had no intention of being rescued. Probably the pulse transmitter was a fiction. The flares? Nothing but useless fireworks.

Suddenly, Phil began to perspire. The pain that had

turned his back into a single exposed nerve was forgotten as a terrible conviction assailed him. He and Tracey were the McCrackens' playthings. Their fates had been orchestrated from the start. All the dancing attendance, the charm, the gourmet meals, were all part of a program, a subtle fattening of the calves before the slaughter. He wondered if even now it was too late, if Tracey was already dead. Then, to his surprise, a rectangular light shot down from above. The trap door was opening.

"You freed yourself," Penny observed, her silhouette looming before the well of light.

Phil said nothing.

"I've come with some medicine."

"I'm all right." His voice was an animal growl.

"Your back will become infected. Turn around."

Now Phil made out the revolver protruding from the hand that held the small jar of unguent.

"Lean against the wall," Penny ordered, "your weight on your arms."

Phil turned away. Apprehensive, he felt her approach. A cold sensation came to his back, then a soothing, tingling feeling. He felt Penny's breath on his neck.

"What have you done to my wife?" Phil spoke in labored gasps.

"Your wife is just fine, Mr. Williams. She's resting." There was a small pause. More salve eased the burning around his ribs. "Your back will heal. We had hoped it would shock you out of your delusion."

"Delusion?" Phil laughed crudely.

Penny smiled. "I've brought you some pillows, a blanket, a bit to eat. I want you to rest, Mr. Williams. If you can, try to think on what's happened. A delusion is like a chill. The body throws it off, and your mind, likewise, will revive."

Phil saw the blankets dropped at his feet.

"When do I get out of here?"

"The Captain will interview you later. Sleep well, Mr. Williams."

The door closed. In anguish Phil slumped to the floor, racking his brain. What to do? How to escape? How to survive; to get back home? Home? What home, *now*? Bleak phantoms danced before his distorted vision. Barbara's ire-filled countenance. His sons' confused, hurt faces. The judge's steely dictums. These were the joyous prospects awaiting him in Ossining. His feelings of being in hell intensified. Soon, though he fought against it, Phil's eyes fluttered closed, and he sank into a shattered sleep.

In her stateroom, having spoken not a word since the afternoon, Tracey was accosted by inner voices. Phil's, Larry's, and McCracken's, each with a different version of reality. She listened as the McCrackens prepared food in the galley above the hold where Phil was being kept prisoner. Why was he suffering, she wondered. She knew why *she* was suffering. It was to demonstrate to Larry that his sweet Tracey had turned into a cheap, degenerate whore. All their refined life had turned into refuse. What would happen when she returned? Darkness, Tracey thought. I am in hell. All four of us, Larry, Barbara, Phil, and I are in hell, and it's all my fault.

She reached for a sleeping pill. Her left hand hovered over the bottle. Wrapped in white, strangely elliptical in shape, it was an abnormality of flesh. It was a stigmata of desire. Holding the top of the bottle against the bandage, turning the bottle with her right hand, she emptied sixteen capsules onto the bureau. Surprised, she watched them roll on the hard mahogany top, come to rest against the alcohol lamp.

"Dear Mother of God," she whispered, her mutilated hand against her breast.

Drifting like a cloud, she thought there was no purpose in surviving. She walked into the salon, the capsules in her pocket.

"I can't sleep," she said weakly. "Could I have a drink?"

The McCrackens were sitting across from each other playing cards. They looked up from their hands.

"Of course," Penny said. "The cognac is behind the vermouth. Second shelf."

"You might pour us a nightcap, too, if you don't mind," McCracken added genially.

Tracey reached into the liquor cabinet. She took the fat bottle into the galley and looked for glasses. The confusion cleared from her mind. Did not the Church teach that suicide was a sin? Then how could the solution to sin be sin itself? In the void Tracey found no answers. All that was left were voices, conflicting, demanding, oppressive, and a sense of failure. The cognac poured into delicate stemmed glasses was an amber liquid, viscous, gleaming in the wan light of the distant salon lamp.

A peculiar sickness flowed through her and gave a bitter taste to her tongue. Darkness encroached. The tunnel narrowed. It was at that black moment that the solution came to her. Why not give the sleeping pills to the McCrackens? Then she would let out poor, sick Phil. They were both so sick. They had broken together. How much better to drift together, to slowly die together, Tracey thought, neither floating out to sea nor yet floating inward to shore.

The sleeping pills were elongated capsules. Breaking them open, she sifted a dull white powder equally into two glasses of cognac and pocketed the empty bottle.

"A good stiff drink," McCracken said, smiling.

They raised their glasses to toast, but under the circumstances no one found anything to say. Awkwardly, they drank. McCracken emptied his glass in one quick draught. Tracey sat on the couch in the salon. There was a ringing in her ears. Now she was frightened. She had become a naughty little girl.

For some minutes the McCrackens continued to play their game. Then, yawning tiredly, the Captain threw his hand in.

"Let us say good-night. Tomorrow we shall examine the situation. Let's hope for a speedy and just resolution."

McCracken rose, then sat down again, shaking his head. Penny looked at him. She held out a hand to touch him, to see if he was all right. McCracken smiled a sleepy smile. His eyelids fluttered. Then Penny leaned backward in her chair.

"Gas leak," McCracken said. "There must be gas . . ."

With an enormous effort he pulled himself from the salon table, stepped out into the corridor, and dragged himself toward the galley.

Tracey followed McCracken into the corridor.

"Are you all right, Captain?" she asked.

McCracken leaned against the stove. He sank to the floor while in the act of opening the oven door. His feet slipped against the floor, his face contorted.

Tracey remained rooted, watching as McCracken crawled like an enormous infant, his legs rubbery, toward the stairs. On the third stair his head fell low. Soon he was asleep. As Tracey watched, his arm crashed across his side to the floor.

"Captain?" she asked, nudging him with her foot.

There was no answer.

In the salon, Penny had moved to McCracken's seat at the desk. Her head was slumped forward, supported by one hand. She looked sick, as though she had a terrible head-ache, or were recuperating from surgery. She had not fin-ished her drink.

"Here, Mrs. McCracken," Tracey said.

"Thank you . . ."

But the cognac was too sharp. Penny refused it after a single swallow.

"You must," Tracey said.

Penny shook her head.

Tracey held Penny's head back and, with effort, over-came the stiff, closed mouth by inserting the Captain's ruler between the teeth and prying open. She poured the cognac down and saw Penny swallow.

"Mrs. Williams, what have you done? . . ."

"Go to sleep."

Penny stood up, sat down, then slipped from the chair. She sprawled onto the floor, her right hand twitching.

Tracey carried a small tray of what was left of supper, the fish and pork intended for the next day's rowing. She ate some and set the remainder on the galley counter. She opened the trapdoor. A humid, unpleasant smell greeted her out of the darkness below.

"Darling," she called down. "We're free."

THIRTEEN

Like the stirring of a zoo animal, Phil's rustling movements were heard long before his face emerged, blinking in the light.

"Tracey . . . thank God you're alive—!"

"I've brought you food," she said.

"Where are the McCrackens?" Phil's eyes roved about.

"I put them to sleep."

"How?"

"My sleeping pills. I did it with my sleeping pills. Wasn't that clever?"

Phil kissed Tracey over her face. He devoured the food in a few bites, then wiped his hands.

"Come! We've got to tie them up!"

"Tie them up—?"

Only now did Phil realize that Tracey's voice had a little-girl quality, a simplistic flatness. This was not the woman he had brought on board.

"Just follow me," he said softly, "and do exactly as I say."

She nodded. Holding her by the hand, Phil led her into the corridor.

McCracken's prone bulk blocked the way to the deck. Phil bent over the huge man. McCracken's face, pulled at the side by gravity now that the muscles were slack, looked like a rubbery humanoid doll.

"Jesus!" Phil said. "He's really out. How much did you give them?"

"Eight pills each. I put them in the cognac."

Phil looked up, startled. "Cognac? *With* the pills?"

"Yes Eight pills each," she said proudly. "I broke the capsules open."

Phil bent lower, placing his ear on McCracken's chest. The heartbeat was low and heavy, like a whale's far under water. "He isn't breathing right," he said nervously. "Help me lay him on the floor."

Tracey took McCracken's feet, Phil his torso, and together they maneuvered him onto the floor. Phil looked for a blanket. In the salon, he saw Penny, motionless on the floor, her right hand curved peculiarly. Phil turned white. He bit his lip. He nudged Penny with his foot.

"She's sleeping," Tracey said brightly.

Phil held up a hand for silence.

"She's not moving," Phil murmured, listening to her heart. Then, turning to Tracey, "Go into the medicine cabinet. Bring me the first aid kit."

Tracey left. Phil improvised a kind of artificial respiration. He blew hard into Penny's mouth. The perspiration on his neck was cold and frightening. It was as though his body knew what his mind could not accept.

Tracey returned, empty-handed.

"I can't find it," she said.

"We've got to get out of here," he whispered.

"Where are we going to go?"

"I don't know. But we can't stay here."

Phil rubbed his hands over his face. He tried to pretend he was in his office and a subordinate had presented him with the problem outlined on paper. It was a technique that always worked. All that counted now was that they were justified before the law.

Rapidly, Phil explored the possibilities. He had never done anything wrong. His record was clean. That would count in his favor. He would simply tell the truth in a forthright manner. The McCrackens were either insane or had broken under the strain of the disaster.

"Tracey, bring me all the food—no, most of the food in the meat locker. Put it into that bucket there. And there are more buckets in the hold if you need them."

"Water, too?"

"Yes, and wine. But nothing if it has sleeping pills in it."

Phil paused, trying to clear his mind of all but the immediate problem at hand. He heard Tracey call him in a child's frightened voice.

"Yes," Phil shouted back, "a lantern. Bring a lantern!"

Suddenly Phil realized the enormity of his ignorance. He was going to set them out in a dinghy, and he had not the slightest idea of what to take. Tracey, absurdly, like a mother setting out on a picnic, carried two buckets of food and drink, and a lantern in her arms.

"Yes, yes, that's it," Phil approved. "What else—? Blankets! Get blankets!"

Tracey dutifully hurried off to fetch them.

From the table Phil grabbed McCracken's telescope. Then he took rain slickers and life vests from the gear and tackle box and the first aid kit from the galley. His arms full Phil ran up to the deck, deposited his stores into the dinghy, then ran back to the salon.

He gingerly worked the revolver from McCracken's holster. He held it between thumb and forefingers. Its cold metallic weight frightened him. He would tell the police that he had disarmed McCracken. He would explain to them exactly what had happened. After all, *he* was the victim. Phil stared at McCracken and his heart contracted with fear.

McCracken had the devil's gift of speech. Phil mopped his brow. Hadn't the Captain hypnotized them both for days with false stories? Wouldn't he spin out a brilliant argument to the police? Phil and Tracey would end up in jail. Just then there was a sound at the salon doorway.

"You mustn't do it," Tracey whispered simply, like a child.

Phil saw his own hand far away, holding the revolver, trembling, at McCracken's heart.

"No, of course not. My God, let's get out of here!"

Weak from exertion, his shirt soaked through, Phil ran up the stairs. Could he not justify the murder of the McCrackens? Self-defense? But they were drugged. An autopsy would show that, wouldn't it? Phil stopped midway up the stairs. The McCrackens could be dumped over the side—or the boat scuttled with them aboard—lost at sea in a storm. It was the greatest temptation of his life. Breathing heavily, he stumbled into the wheelhouse. He was like a wolf in the canyons. Instinct guided his every move, and that instinct told him to kill the McCrackens, destroy them, efface them, annihilate the threat. His reason had dropped into moral corrosion, and he felt superhumanly powerful. Metal glinted on the wall of the wheelhouse. It was the ignition key. Phil jumped forward, grabbed it, and slid it into the ignition slot next to the radar. He twisted. Nothing happened. He searched for other keys. There were none. He grabbed the pulse transmitter and tucked it under his arm. Taking the revolver from his belt, he put it in his pocket so it could not fall. What else would he need? The desk drawers were locked. He smashed them open. Suddenly his eyes were transfixed by the black shadow in the rear of the large chart drawer. It was the log of the *Penny Dreadful*. The pale, wavering moonlight seemed to guide him hypnotically toward it. He lifted it up. It was strangely and unnaturally heavy. He opened it.

The first pages were nautical maps, traced in various colors of ink. All the lines began and returned to Florida. All had strange marking in the eastern loops, with dates and names, and a kind of code. Phil strained, pressed himself against the wheelhouse window to glean what little light the half-moon afforded.

Turning the page, the Captain's beautiful penmanship swam before his eyes. He read:

Charles M. MacIver, 56, chemical manufacturer, homosexual. Genial, poor physical condition, rating: 3. Mentally alert but requires channeling. Country club social background, hobbies includes carriage collecting, vases, astronomy. Knowledge of constellations, perhaps of navigation. False courses not advised. Despite intellectual level, dependent. Probably unable to provide true combat. Suburb of Detroit.

Henry Ford Ransome, 37, companion to Mr. MacIver. Good physical condition, experience in small sailing craft, engine repair, and manual labor. Most dangerous. Most likely to afford excellent combat. Quickwitted, agile, rating: 8. No experience on high seas. Fatal flaw: fear of higher social classes. Perhaps identity with MacIver can keep him subservient until the crisis.

In a small column, nearly worn through the page, were several brief notations. Phil leaned forward, eyes smarting, growing hazy in the darkness.

Discretion necessity for MacIver. Vice-president administers company in absence, brother in communication to Florida: ominous. Must double-check brother. Ransome appears to have no known relatives. Perhaps is a valet? No communication with Detroit.

Phil turned the page. A similar page division was filled in with McCracken's handwriting.

Herbert Wilson St. Cloud, 44, nightclub owner. Candid, good physical condition, rating: 6. A simple man, despite profession. Suspects nothing. Excellent card-

player, likes off-color jokes, holds drink very well. No knowledge of ocean, forest, rivers, or lakes. Street-wary, but trusting on the high sea. Good judgment of con artists. Care required here. Best to show him equipment, make him feel part of crisis. Can be developed. Boston.

Candy Phillips St. Cloud, 24, dancer. Good physical condition, rating: 7. Natural alertness. Excellent combat material. Knowledge of sea limited to small sailing craft off northeast waters. To be used to swing St. Cloud. Poses as wife to H.W. but first mate's investigation revealed true identity to be Helen Slansky. Flaw: fear of disfigurement. How can this be used? Strong-willed, self-controlled. Perfect material. No known city of origin.

At the side, in the long column, Phil read:

"Mrs. St. Cloud" one sister, Maine, no contact ten years. Keeps no postal address. St. Cloud sole owner of nightclub. Closed for holidays, up to end of February, sited in neighborhood of quick-closing establishments. All seems go.

Several entries on the following pages also filled out short paragraphs. Phil glanced quickly at the next one, absorbed, his heart racing, not yet deciphering the meaning of the cryptic descriptions. What was meant by "combat"? By "crisis"? What was "good material"?

Cornelia French, 33, bookkeeper. Poor physical condition, rating: 4. Unimaginative, docile, undeveloped personality. Trivial sense of humor. Likes bridge game. Easy to please. Utilize many water games. Putty. No knowledge of sea, though relatives in Navy. Examine. Probably without stamina. Pittsburgh.

Steven Sebastian French, 34, owns 3 dry-cleaning es-
tablishments. Jogger, health gym, fad diets, physical
rating: 6. Vanity, dominates wife, no children. Preens
on masculinity. Build up or crush early? Some river
experience, transatlantic crossings on liners. Aggres-
sive. A facade? Not to be lulled. A hard case. Pitts-
burgh.

In the long column was a brief notation.

Relatives throughout Pittsburgh and Harrisburg. Sec-
ond honeymoon, on a whim. Possibly no notice given.
Who runs home stores? No return date. Examine con-
tacts in Jacksonville. Relatives? Christmas date? Why
French's vagueness? Perhaps wants to ignore wife's
relatives. Probe.

Phil paged through over a dozen such entries. In the
center section of the logbook, separated by plastic dividers,
were maps. On each a single loop was drawn with markings that increased as the line moved east. Then, toward
the end of the ledger, were more entries, in different form,
carefully dated, signed.

MacIver, C.M. Complaints of hazing, poor food. Hy-
pochondria, sensitivity to salt, blisters, dehydration.
Assault on first mate, punished severely. Work effec-
tiveness reduced. Personality breakdown, very inter-
esting. Reliving events of the military and sexual at-
tachment to senior officer. Most revolting. Resolved,
December 13, 1973, at position shown, 20 miles south
of crisis point.

Ransome, H.F. Arrested for instigating mutiny, theft
of compass, liquor, sweaters and blankets. No respect
for word of law, unlike MacIver. Understands only
force of arms. Fled from imprisonment in hold. Refused

*medication despite advice of first mate. Refused row-
ing despite good physical condition. Observed robbing
MacIver of small foodstuffs, slapping and verbally
abusing MacIver. Attempt on life of Captain with
astrolabe. Disarmed. Resolved, 12 hours post MacIver,
same location.*

Perspiring, cold, shivering, Phil turned the page. He re-
ferred to a map, then peered down at McCracken's handwriting.

*St. Cloud, H.W. Erratic behavior observed in form of
nervous gesture, then quick leg movements, inability
to sleep, severe digestive disorder. Demand to be put
ashore. Scream for help. Minor disciplinary procedures
invoked, removed to hold, resistance broken. Feeble
opposition. Most disappointing.*

*St. Cloud, C.P. Blisters, arms and legs. Excellent men-
tal condition, but delusions as to nearness of rescue.
Refused to sleep in hold. Threatened suicide. Increasing fixation: face, complexion, and shape of legs. Refused rowing. Denied food and drink. Desperately
malnourished despite force-feeding. Both resolved Jan.
5, 1975, north of Cuba as shown.*

Knowing now what the next page would read, Phil
found his fingers moving as though of their own volition,
turning ahead.

*French, C. Developed stomach disorder. Demanded
physician. Diarrhea, vomiting. No crisis developed,
only seasickness. Fear of open spaces.*

*French, S.S. Uncle in Jacksonville, golf date; post
New Year. Returned on schedule. A miserable voyage.
Perhaps time for another this season?*

Phil tucked the logbook under his shirt, buttoned it, and ran out into the night. The cool air refreshed him. The ledger stuck unpleasantly to his skin. It repulsed him. Nevertheless, it exonerated them from everything. Stumbling blindly, still uncomprehending, Phil found Tracey looking for him. Three heavy blankets were in her arms.

"Where were you?" she wept. "You can't leave me alone!"

Phil took her in his arms and gradually brought her down.

"What else do we need?" he panted. "The hand compass. Where's that?"

They found nothing in their search through the wheelhouse. In the salon were only charts, navigational instruments, notations. Nervously, he turned McCracken over. The compass dangled from a lanyard around the Captain's neck. It was like defiling the dead. Or the soon dead. Phil slipped the compass off McCracken's neck.

"Into the dinghy!" he ordered. "Throw the blankets in!"

One of the blankets fell into the black water, turned slowly, then sank.

"Never mind! Get in!"

Tracey climbed down. Holding on to the ladder, she steadied the dinghy. Phil's foot searched for the dinghy, found it, then stepped down. He pushed off. He rowed desperately into the night. He remembered the compass, then realized he had forgotten a flashlight. There was a lamp, but they had only a single book of matches. Lighting one, he saw that he was rowing almost due east.

"Christ, that's toward the open sea!" he muttered.

The *Penny Dreadful* was a dark indistinguishable bulk between them and the west. Was McCracken's palaver about the currents true? In any case, to the west, sooner or later, were islands, Florida, at least not the open Atlantic. Phil began to row south, then west, giving the *Penny Dreadful* a wide berth. As in a nightmare, the more he

rowed, the less difference it seemed to make. The Mc-
Crackens' boat was still only a few hundred yards away.

What was he going to do, Phil thought. Row the Caribbean? Had he panicked? Had he performed a fool's act?

"Hold me," Tracey whimpered. "Please hold me."

Leaning forward, Phil kissed her.

"Phil," she said softly, "I want to go home. Take me
home."

When the first light of dawn glimmered beyond the
Penny Dreadful, silhouetting it as a nearly rectangular
block, Phil knew that he had rowed less than four hundred
yards. Still, he took a grim satisfaction knowing the
McCrackens were out cold on the floor, hopefully forever,
and no one knew but he and Tracey. The best man had
won after all, Phil reflected. At least that was something.
Come what may.

Tracey dozed against the stern, a blanket wrapped over
her shoulders, making a hood over her head. She woke,
then smiled.

"Poor Phil," she said. "You work so hard."

Phil gritted his teeth, digging the oars into the water.

"I don't get it. I row and row and never seem to get
anywhere. I'll bet all that time we were pulling the boat it
never really moved."

"Do you want me to row?" Tracey asked.

Phil shook his head.

"They were torturing us, that's what," Phil said to himself.

Soon the ocean was light gray, not yet having color.
Several pink clouds were visible high over the small boat in
the distance. Tracey pulled several pices of fish from a
bucket which, with bread and lettuce, made their breakfast. They took small quantities of fresh water. From time
to time Tracey cupped her hands and bailed minute quantities of sea water from the bottom of the dinghy.

"I've got to sleep just a little," Phil said. "Tracey, I want
you to wake me when the sun rises."

Tracey nodded and turned her head.

The sun takes well over an hour to rise, once the false dawn has pinked the morning sky. At length there was a sliver, a warm eye rising over the horizon, just behind the graying black outline of the *Penny Dreadful*. Tracey shook Phil, whose teeth were chattering.

"Time to wake up!"

Phil stretched his arms. By now he was used to rowing. He slipped his blanket from his shoulders, braced his feet and silently rowed. By midmorning the *Penny Dreadful* had diminished to dime-size. Gray currents flowed around it, small flecks where the breeze stirred the water. Beyond that the sea melded into a hard, heavy blue.

"Why don't you sleep?" Phil said. "We must conserve our strength."

"No. I slept. I just wish we were home."

"Tell me about Dostoevski."

"Who?"

"You know so much about literature. Tell me a story while I row."

"Oh, I don't remember any of that. That was so long ago."

"Didn't you study French literature? Tell me about the French Revolution."

"The Revolution? Dickens!" Tracey said, smiling brightly. "You mean *A Tale of Two Cities*. Oh, how does that begin? It's so famous."

Phil wanted Tracey to talk about anything that might bring back elements of her adult life. The child and the woman mixed, melded, and Tracey's face grew troubled. Soon she stopped speaking.

"Go on," he encouraged.

Tracey shook her head, her expression woebegone. "It's all so hopeless. We should never have come."

The heat blistered at high noon. Though they sweated profusely, they kept the blankets over their heads and found that it weakened them less. Tracey rowed for an hour. The *Penny Dreadful* was a black dot on the glare of the distant sea.

As Phil looked, the bleak horizon seemed a gray analogue of the past and future possibilities surrounding his existence. Scenes of New York flitted through his mind. All the facades of Sobel Enterprises, of which the design center was but one, now became transparent. For all his energy, it had remained Barbara's money. The staff was Barbara's. The foreign contacts, the market liaisons, were Barbara's. Even that secret judgment of taste, that mysterious ability to fathom the mind of America's better-dressed women, that, too, was hers. Now, with this betrayal, there would be no forgiveness. Knowing Barbara, she would simply tear the tissue of their relationship apart and throw the pieces away. He was as good as a beggar on the street, a miserable pretender. There were no options anymore. Would he ever see his sons again?

Phil took over the oars from Tracey.

What was the use of rowing, he thought. Why not drink seawater now and sicken and get it over with? Tracey looked at him with soft eyes. Was there the slightest chance Barbara would take him back? Phil tenderly rubbed his calloused hands and began to row.

"How much water do we have?" Phil asked through chapped, puffed lips.

"A bottle and a half. See?"

Phil rested. He stretched, started to rise, then felt his calf knot, so he remained seated. He bent his back until he could see the horizon upside down. He looked for birds and saw none. According to the compass they still moved due west. Phil wondered if he was headed for Florida or into the enormous Atlantic. Or was all that hundreds of miles away?

Suddenly he moaned.

"What's wrong?" Tracey asked.

"The pulse transmitter. It's wet."

Phil angrily reached down and snatched up the small

box. Seawater dripped from the bottom. It was a self-contained unit, and Phil could see through a slit four small batteries and a coil, as well as a mass of metallic wires and several tiny cylinders. A switch on the front plate turned it on. Phil heard nothing. Was it possible, he thought, a frequency was now radiating out over the ocean with them at the epicenter?

"Probably ruined from the seawater," he said.

It frightened him how poorly he was thinking. By mid-afternoon the *Penny Dreadful* was indistinguishable from flecks of light on the horizon. Time was leaden and without meaning. There was only space, the space that lengthened the distance between the dinghy and the *Penny Dreadful* inside of which, as far as Phil knew, two corpses decomposed.

Light changed. It was late in the afternoon. Tracey rowed feebly and erratically, but hopefully. Phil slept, woke, then slept again. Tracey rowed without a word, her hair damp from the salt spray, her shoulders burned through her blouse, her hand throbbing.

Toward evening they ate more fish with bits of pork scraps from the bottom of the bucket. Everything tasted salty. They moistened their lips with warm, fresh water, then gulped four swallows each. After another hour of rowing Phil took over while Tracey slept. A peculiar orange glow glimmered over the waves. Blue and gold roiled around the oars. There were only identical horizons around them. The shadow of the dinghy stretched undulating behind them, like a crippled spider with but two arms, flopping in its death throes through the glistening water.

During a brief rest Phil picked up the black logbook. Idly, he turned the dreaded pages. It was like reading the news report of a morbid disaster, repulsive yet fascinating. All the names that had been so carefully written—where were they now? Murdered? Dismembered? Their bones floating cleanly on the bottom of the Gulf Stream? Or were they buried in some obscure sandbar?

Turning a page, Phil came to what he was searching for.

Williams, Philip, 38, ladies' leather design, family business. Mildly aggressive, trusting, shrewd but friendly. Fair physical condition, rating: 7. Mentally relaxed, interest in new experiences. Questioning mind. Self-assured, weak point: self-image. No knowledge of sea. Enjoys the good life, gourmet dining, fine liqueurs. Learns quickly. Probably can be developed. Sound-out views of life. New York suburb.

Williams, Tracey, approximately 28, poses as wife of P.W. Name on credit cards: Mrs. Lawrence Hansen. Highly literate, a few years college, perhaps refined family background. A new experience, evidently under instruction of P.W. Some guilt, can be developed? Rating: 3. Little stamina, will fold rapidly. How much mental strength? If in consort with P.W., can be formidable opponent. Divide and conquer!

With mounting horror, Phil turned the pages. A giddy sensation overwhelmed him. It was anger, hot and horrible. McCracken deserved to die, Phil thought. Guilt left him, leaving only the residue of fatigue and worry. Without planning it, he and Tracey had cleansed the world.

Turning a page, he found the map with its date, its incomplete voyage line in red, snaking down the Florida coast and out toward the Bahamas, and a further entry:

No contacts with business. Discretion necessity. No information on Tracey contacts. Explore. Likely whereabouts of both are unknown to world. Confirm.

In the last entries at the end of the logbook he peered down at the wrinkled page.

Williams, Philip. Increasing edginess, turned to drone-like acceptance of work. Takes orders well. Completely at loss on the sea, fear of unknown, away from northeast. Unbroken. Ability to recoup? Took crisis quickly, agility of mind. Perhaps more here than meets the eye.

Williams, Tracey. Signs of latent hysteria. Childhood concept of good and evil. Physical condition very poor. Unable to row. Rebuked by diminished food and drink. Accepted without complaint. No questions. Daily grows more subservient. Infected thumb required lancing. Then amputation. Splendid moment. Lovely drama.

Phil read the entries again and again. It seemed incomprehensible to him that he was judged in such minute script as to his qualities of resisting his own murder. Still, there was no clue as to the method of execution. Did they vary? Poison? No doubt drowning was one. Was there torture? Mutilation on the propeller? Keelhauling? Phil's mind ran through grisly possibilities.

"Why are you staring at my hand?" Tracey asked, awakening.

"Sorry. I was just resting my eyes."

"Are you angry at me?"

"No. Of course not, Tracey."

Tracey avoided the black logbook. To her, it was an instrument of the Captain, like the antithesis of legitimate men. It was not for her to peer into its forbidden contents.

"Did I kill them?" Tracey asked.

"I don't know."

"It was all an accident. I just wanted to put them to sleep. I was going to kill myself, and then I thought I would just put them to sleep. Somehow, it all seemed the same thing."

"Dear, sweet Tracey. Don't blame yourself. Nobody else will."

Tracey smiled abstractly. Wearily she buried her face in her hands. Through the night they rowed. A lighted match revealed a slight drift to the south. Would the metal in the console module draw off the compass needle? Was the pulse still transmitting? Phil looked for an antenna but found none.

Toward dawn Tracey spied an airplane high over the horizon. Phil watched it through the telescope.

"It must be going to Africa," she said softly. "I'd love to go to Kenya." Then, "If we had a flare, the pilot might see it and radio for help." Then, "How far do we have to go?"

Phil patted Tracey's knee.

"I don't know if we're in the Atlantic or the Caribbean, honey. It's a real mess. Maybe we should have stayed on the *Penny Dreadful*.

Tracey shuddered. "No. It was too evil."

"You're right. I couldn't take it. We would have had to tie them both up. Day after day, floating there. God, what a horror."

"McCracken is the Devil," Tracey said. "God put us into his power.'

Phil rowed in silence.

"God has wanted us to be punished because we broke His law."

Phil continued rowing.

"It's true. That's why we are going to die."

Dawn came again. A purple haze dissipated over the eastern horizon. There was no sign of the boat. Phil looked wearily out into the light. How long would his body hold? More than pain, he feared fatigue. Fatigue was a constant drain. Sooner or later his strokes would diminish, become feeble splashings, absurd, jerking little movements in the ocean. The dinghy rotated slowly without direction.

Dehydrated, the two would expire, fainting, then falling into a deep sleep. They would decompose rapidly under the direct rays of noon. He worried about the capacity of his mind to stave off hallucination. Already his eyes did not focus well. The dawn clouds assumed strange formations. They seemed to move and mock him.

"Why aren't there any boats?" Tracey asked unexpectedly, as though her instinct for survival had suddenly revitalized.

"I don't know. I don't think this really sends a pulse."

"Then we really are finished."

At noon Tracey dipped into the bucket. Their discipline held. They moistened their lips and ate very slowly, chewing carefully. They held hands briefly. Phil moved back to the center bench and rowed.

Shortly, Tracey replaced him. She rowed for over an hour with feeble strokes as Phil slept. With a start, he woke. Tracey was hunched over, sleeping on the center bench, the oar floating in the water, her left hand trailing beneath the surface. The soiled bandages unraveled, the wound had begun to bleed.

With horror Phil realized that blood attracts sharks. He moved her to the stern bench and rescued the oar from the water. He rebandaged her hand with strips torn from his shirt.

He began to row but he had lost his sense of direction. He no longer believed the compass. Yet he had nothing else to believe in. He turned the pulse transmitter on and off to see whether it changed the direction of the compass needle. It did not. Tracey moaned. Phil covered her head with the damp, stinking blanket.

In the afternoon Phil lost his sense of time. He calculated he had rowed three days away from the *Penny Dreadful* but he remembered only two dawns. The waves rolled higher. If they broke higher they would ship water; it would not be possible to row. If a storm broke, they would drown.

Horrible dreams assailed him during the night.

Phil looked at what he thought was the sunset. He rowed. Then, glancing at the compass, he realized it was dawn. Cursing, his head bursting with pain, he turned the dinghy around and rowed toward the west. The ringing slowly faded from his ears, the headache dissipated, and his eyes searched sharply, over the sea for an interrupting shadow, the tiniest bulk to signify other human life. There was none. What he remembered of civilization was ludicrously artificial, contemptible, and transitory. McCracken was right. It was here, on the brink of annihilation, that a man discovered his true stature.

At midmorning, Phil noticed a dark, jagged line along the horizon. Unwilling to awaken Tracey, for he couldn't be certain it wasn't a mirage, he picked up his rowing pace and, with a racing heart, pulled the dinghy toward what steadily grew into a tiny palm island fringed by foaming breakers. Gentle hillocks, cool and verdant, rose above a gradually dissipating morning mist.

Phil's muscles bulged as he rowed hard toward salvation. Gasping, unable to speak, he shouted hoarsely at the awakening Tracey. Seeing the expression on Phil's face, she quickly rubbed the sleep from her eyes and gazed wildly about.

It was then that they both heard the sound of a boat. Their heads turned, eyes feverishly squinting into the sun. Eventually, a white form emerged out of the brightness. Phil raised the telescope. It was the *Penny Dreadful*.

FOURTEEN

Its gentle hills jutting above the blue-gray waters, the island offered sustenance and salvation five miles ahead of the dinghy. As the *Penny Dreadful* cut its engines and drifted closer, Phil continued to row methodically, looking over his shoulder from time to time at the land.

Tracey gazed wide-eyed, disbelieving, at the sleek, white hull as it approached. "Phil," she whispered, "it's the Captain. He's alive. He fixed the boat. We can all go home now."

"No. He has no interest in taking us home."

Tracey craned her neck. No one was on the deck. The sharp, white prow loomed closer. Silent, rippling, the *Penny Dreadful* cast its shadow over the dinghy.

"Listen to me," Phil said softly. "I want you to do exactly as I say. Tie your life vest on tightly, and lie down on the floor."

"All right."

Phil was thankful to see her quickly comply. He cinched his own life vest snugly around himself, then surreptitiously removed the revolver from his pocket.

"No matter what happens, *don't* go onto the boat!"

Phil squinted at the white shape, growing brighter, throwing a wake as it arched in the distance toward them. The boat personified McCracken. In vain Phil looked for the bulky figure anywhere on deck. Rage shook his hands.

He tucked the revolver deep into the folds of the blanket and continued to row.

"Show yourself, McCracken," Phil whispered. "Just poke your head out. That's all I need."

But the *Penny Dreadful* only escorted the dinghy. Phil rowed. His arms pulled cleanly with his legs and back working in rhythm. Tracey raised herself cautiously upward and peered nervously toward the deck but saw no one.

Finally McCracken appeared at the port railing.

"Climb up the ladder, Mr. Williams!"

"Go to hell, Captain."

Phil continued to row. The island appeared to come no closer. Tracey hunched over, as though to make herself small. McCracken gave the engine a burst of power, then let the boat glide alongside the dinghy.

"I have given you an order, Mr. Williams!"

Phil rowed, looking away from the boat. Tracey stole a quick glance at McCracken hovering above them. Frightened, she looked away. She felt as though she could feel McCracken's breath. It was humid and stinking of chemical substances. Her lips moved feebly in prayer.

"Mr. Williams! By the authority vested in me I shall command you once more to ascend to the deck!"

Phil rowed, neither faltering nor racing, maintaining his pace, keeping the steady rhythm, preserving his energy. A splash emerged at his right. The water delicately plumed, followed by a long rushing sound. A long, thin spear disappeared like a rocket into the depths.

In one motion, Phil brought in the oars, quickly aimed the revolver and fired a shot up at McCracken who seemed to fall away under the impact. The echoing shot reverberated across the calm waters. Tracey shut her eyes tightly and jammed her fists into her ears.

Surprised at the roar, Phil saw with satisfaction, through the thin wisp of smoke from the barrel, that a black hole appeared on the immaculate upper bow, and splinters of wood and fiberglass showered high into the air. Still, there was no McCracken. The wheelhouse was on the opposite side of the deck. A second shot added a gaping oval at the curve of the bow, and the boat continued to speed around the dinghy.

"Come on, McCracken!" Phil yelled. "Show your face!"

A third shot, aimed below the water line, skipped through the top of the water and buried itself in the dark shadow under the boat. Phil turned, aimed at the engine in the rear, and squeezed the trigger. A smoking hole appeared midway to the rudder. A fourth shot, aimed at the rudder, loudly bounced off the metal.

Phil saw the movement of a bushy head of white hair behind the glass of the wheelhouse door. Steadying himself with both legs against opposite sides of the dinghy, Phil looked with his right eye down the top of the black barrel, where the pointed guide neatly bisected McCracken's neck. Slowly his finger squeezed the trigger, an infinitely slow squeeze, in which he felt the life itself pushed out of McCracken's body.

There was a sharp retort, the barrel kicked up, and glass flew out over the deck. The white head of hair disappeared. Did the bullet find its mark? "Please, God," Phil prayed, "let him be dead!"

Soft laughter descended from above.

"It's no use, Mr. Williams."

In a last, desperate gamble, Phil emptied the revolver into where he reasoned the gas tank must be. There was no explosion.

At the railing, a foot braced against the crossbar, McCracken calmly restrung the harpoon rifle and selected a new spear from a quiver attached to his belt.

"You'll die out there!" McCracken said. "That island has not a drop of water! Don't you understand this is for your own good?"

"I read your logbook, Captain."

"Nevertheless, I shall not have you expiring among the snakes and rocks!"

A second shot blasted the harpoon spear into the side of the dinghy. Acrid blue smoke rose from a point above Tracey's head, leaving a hole a half foot in diameter. Every wave breached several inches into the hole. Tracey lifted herself from the water collecting rapidly in the bottom of the dinghy.

"We're sinking," she said softly, trembling.

"Take off your shoes!"

The water rose to their calves. The buckets floated, spilling fish scraps. The pulse transmitter toppled forward into the water. Phil struggled in vain with his shoes. To his dismay, he saw the logbook float out of the dinghy and join the other flotsam bobbing about in the choppy water. The logbook sank below the surface.

"Now listen to me," Phil stammered. "He won't shoot us. I don't think he will shoot us. It's going to take us a very long time to swim to that island, but we'll rest and swim and we'll make it."

Tracey nodded. He squeezed her shoulder and smiled. The oars floated. Abruptly the dinghy shuddered, settling into the water. They stood with their hips under water, floating on their life jackets. Phil paddled slowly away from the *Penny Dreadful* and Tracey followed.

A spear lanced ahead of them, trailing a rushing sound.

"Just swim," Phil said. "Very slowly. No rush."

On their backs, occasionally swallowing salt water, Phil and Tracey swam. The water was warm, the sky above eternal and blue. Stubborn, Phil knew he could make the island. He would drag Tracey if need be. It might take a day and a night, he calculated, but they would stand on ground again.

"I'm not afraid," Tracey said. "See? I'm not afraid."

She matched his strokes carefully, avoiding looking to her right. Her pants rippled white reflections as she swam. The water transmitted a loud, thunderous roar. The

Penny Dreadful had started its engines. Phil and Tracey rocked in the waves. The white hull, shining in the sun, lazily circled them, churning the water.

"Keep swimming," Phil said. "Just keep swimming."

Seawater drenched their faces, worked into their mouths. Tracey coughed and swallowed more warm water. She paused, became vertical, then Phil pulled her back to swim. The engines roared louder. The *Penny Dreadful* careened at steep angles, sending white, rolling wakes over them. Phil sputtered, spit out water. Tracey had been rolled over, face down.

"Mr. Williams!" They heard McCracken's voice through the roar, the sound droning in different tones as the *Penny Dreadful* circled, now near, now farther. "Will you come aboard?"

Phil righted Tracey. She followed him through the roiling water, broken and crossed by opposed wakes, bubbles, eddies, and colliding waves. The *Penny Dreadful* bore down on them. They saw the sharpness of the prow.

"Mary, Mother of God!" Tracey gasped. "Save us for thy name's sake!"

At the last minute the boat shot between them, separating them. The roar thundered around them. Phil caught the sight of gleaming bits of metal—the propeller—spitting through the white foam. Then he shouted for Tracey.

Her hair matted and clumped over her face, she floated twenty yards away, struggling in the violent wake. Her open eyes were glazed.

Now the engines dulled. The *Penny Dreadful* cruised slower and slower until it bobbed several yards behind Tracey. Phil paddled toward her. A splash echoed from behind the boat. A smell of rank flesh drifted to Phil's nostrils.

"Fish slops!" McCracken called. "Shark bait!"

In terror Phil saw Tracey beat the water around her. She was ineffectually trying to swim. She jumped up and down in the rolling water, as though rising on steps, up and down, arms flailing.

More fish and entrails plopped into the water beside her. Suddenly, there was rapid movement below as pieces of fish disappeared into the dark, forbidding world beneath her.

Tracey screamed.

"What say, Mr. Williams?"

"Get on the ladder, Tracey," Phil called in defeat.

The *Penny Dreadful* glided forward, adroitly separating Phil and Tracey from the boiling, snapping waters. Tracey clung with one hand to a rung of the accommodation ladder. Her blouse and pants were saturated, her hair clotted behind her head.

"Come up, Mrs. Williams!" McCracken reached down and assisted Tracey up the ladder. Frightened, she looked down as the *Penny Dreadful* glided over the choppy waters.

"Now you, Mr. Williams!"

The boat was nearly stopped as Phil took hold of the rungs. Dripping, he saw an area of white, thrashing water behind the stern now. The engines had started. They were cruising toward the island. Fighting the wind in his face and finding it difficult to breathe, Phil climbed the ladder.

Stepping down from the wheelhouse, McCracken stood wearing white pants and a white jacket with black epaulets. In his arms he cradled the harpoon gun.

Phil pulled himself up to the deck, where he stood uncertainly, panting. His heart pounding with fear, he reverted to impotent anger. "You're lucky I'm such a lousy shot," he hissed.

"Why? Would killing me have given you satisfaction?"

"Damn right!"

McCracken smiled softly without warmth.

"Good," he said quietly.

Phil moved toward McCracken who quickly brought up the gun and took aim at Phil's legs.

"I'll cripple you if I have to," McCracken warned. "Now, lie down. Next to your wife."

Phil lay down on the deck. Tracey's head was turned away, her eyes shut tightly. Her hand throbbed painfully. McCracken rolled Phil roughly onto his stomach. Then his hands were tied behind him. A black cloth was wrapped tightly over his eyes.

"Sit up," McCracken said. "Both of you."

Phil rolled sideways, then performed a sit-up. He waited for a blow, the stunning smash into his breastbone. He listened for Tracey, whose warmth he felt next to him. Instead there was an eternity of silence.

"I, John McCracken, owner and Captain of the *Penny Dreadful*, registered the State of Florida, do arrest and confine Philip and Tracey Williams, both of New York, for the crime of mutiny and attempted murder, as well as armed robbery."

After a moment, the engines of the boat were brought back to idle. The stillness, after the churning of the sea, was ominous. For a long time they waited. Phil did not know where McCracken stood. They heard sounds below deck and a heavy tread on the steps.

"Now stand up," McCracken said.

Bumping into one another, they stood, their legs uncertain after days in the dinghy.

"Come, Mrs. Williams."

Phil sensed McCracken lead her away. After a few minutes McCracken returned, took him by the arm, and led him down into the interior. Even blindfolded, Phil knew where he was. He even remembered to watch for the shallow step leading off the main salon. Down the corridor McCracken hustled him, then threw him into the guest stateroom.

"Are you all right?" Tracey asked.

"Yes. I'm all right. Did he hurt you?"

"No."

Feeling their way together, back to back, Phil untied

Tracey. She slipped off her ropes, drew the cloth from her eyes, and untied Phil. They embraced. Tracey dressed, finding trousers laid out for her on the bed. The room was stripped. Only a few changes of clothes remained. The lamps, cutlass, even the antique wooden pegs had all been removed. Phil rattled the door. Now he appreciated its firm construction. The hinges were set with a cap, not unlike a molly bolt, but welded.

Phil sat apart from Tracey on the bed. He hunched up tightly to make himself warmer and ease the chill radiating from deep inside. Cold waves rose from the marrow of his trembling body. Slowly his personality returned. Warmth flooded his face and he felt feverish. Like a broken film, the image of the *Penny Dreadful* came back again and again, and once more he felt the cold black barrel of the revolver and the tight, eager squeeze of his fingers on the trigger. It was like an hallucination he could not block from returning. He almost saw why McCracken had become addicted to such things. For himself, weak as a patient after surgery, pale and trembling, Phil wondered if he had not been victim of an obscene delusion. Was it possible? Could it be that he, Philip Sobel, president of Sobel Industries, husband to Barbara, father to Philip, Jr. and Mark, had shot six times at a human being, praying each time to see brains flying?

The *Penny Dreadful* picked up speed.

"Where is he taking us?" Tracey nervously asked.

Craning his neck through the porthole, Phil saw the island in front of them. Its blue contour revealed brown areas now, birds flying overhead.

"Plenty of trees, wildlife," Phil grunted. "Another one of his lies."

White lines of surf silently cascaded onto the land. Red flowers dangled in the verdure under pure blue skies. It was unreal.

This, Phil thought, was where his destiny would be revealed. Adrenaline flowed again into his bloodstream, his eyes dilated, and he paced almost eagerly, waiting for Mc-Cracken to reach the island. For one of them, it would be the final arena.

Tracey, like a child finding peace, drifted into a light sleep, while Phil remained at the porthole looking out at the approaching island.

The *Penny Dreadful* found its way into a small inlet which led to a tiny cave. Palm trees emerged from dense ferns, grass, thick undergrowth of yellow stalks, and clumps of mud-rich roots with dense clods of fibers. The boat glided to a stop. The engines shut down. Bird calls echoed from the nearby hills.

There was a knock at the door. Phil and Tracey looked up. It did not open.

"The trial will begin in one hour," McCracken's voice came through crisply.

They heard his footsteps retreating toward the salon.

"Trial?" Phil said.

"It's for what I did," Tracey whispered. "For trying to kill them."

Tracey washed her face. Her rapid movements were nervous, and her breathing was agitated. Phil waited, lying on the bed. Now the dread invaded his bones. He knew that certain murder awaited them. His heart pounded. The monstrous injustice of it all overwhelmed him. There was so much in life he had wanted to accomplish, and he had frittered it away in business, in his many little pleasures. He wanted to reach out to his sons, tell them some last things, lest his memory be obliterated. The hour droned on.

The bolt was unlatched. Phil jumped from the bed. Dressed not only in white jacket and trousers, but also in dress black shoes and white cap, McCracken stood. The harpoon gun was aimed at Phil's thighs. In McCracken's belt was a long dagger with a mother-of-pearl handle.

"Come!" McCracken ordered, backing way slowly.

Phil held Tracey's hand. They walked into the corridor. The sunlight glittered on the three prongs of the harpoon. The metal band arched above the trigger, hundreds of pounds of pressure causing the firing mechanism to tremble in front of him. McCracken gestured to the salon where, under his instruction, they were ordered to handcuff one another. The handcuffs were curious double-ring affairs, requiring old-fashioned keys, and it took some time to fit them around their wrists. Phil was gentle with Tracey's bandaged hand.

As McCracken went up the hatch stairs, Tracey looked anxiously over her shoulder.

"He's going to kill us, isn't he?"

"I don't know."

After nearly half an hour McCracken descended to the salon. He took Tracey up the stairs, then returned.

"The court is waiting," he intoned.

A three-pronged blade prodded Phil's flayed back. An involuntary wince and a groan shuddered through him. Phil walked up the steps at the point of the harpoon.

On the deck Penny sat motionless at a small white table. She was covered in a navy blue blanket, and the table was covered with a white cloth. An ink bottle with a curved top held a feather pen. McCracken shoved Phil toward the table. It was the longest step Phil ever took. Penny's eyes were glazed.

"She's all right!" Tracey blurted. "She's alive!"

A few wisps of hair floated in a breeze across Penny's forehead. McCracken reached down and carefully straightened her hair. He readjusted several small pillows behind her. Tracey and Phil were cuffed to the legs of the chairs which, in turn, were bolted to the deck.

McCracken cleared his throat. Before him was a massive book, open on the tablecloth. In reference, his finger pointed to various sections. He wrote on a sheet of large paper with a flourish.

Bits of wood and brown grass floated past the *Penny*

Dreadful. The shadows of the palm trees elongated over the deck, merging with the shade of the wheelhouse. Humidity made it difficult to breathe.

"By the grace of laws of ships and man, this day, the fifteenth of January, nineteen hundred and seventy-nine, aboard the *Penny Dreadful*, pleasure craft, registered the State of Florida, is commenced the trial and court-martial of Philip Williams, accused of mutiny, theft, accessory to the fact of attempted murder, and of Tracey Williams, as she is known, accused of mutiny, theft, and attempted murder."

McCracken paused. His face had a slightly pained expression. His flesh was fully tanned, reddened around the neck, his white hair combed carefully under the cap. Behind him were two flags set in iron deck stands. One featured a blue anchor on a white field. The other was yellow and white with horizontal bars.

"The facts shall be set forth on behalf of the complainant, the owner and maritime authority of said craft, after which defense shall be heard to the satisfaction of the court."

McCracken spoke heavily, as though entrusted with an enormous responsibility, one he had never experienced before. He seemed to have, in his inner eye, an authority of his own, before whom he acted with all the propriety and dignity it was in his power to muster.

Phil watched McCracken as a man might stare into the rifle barrels of his own firing squad. Each second and each word had the delusionary quality of the last seconds of life. McCracken's insanity seemed but a trifle compared with the larger insanity, the arbitrary existence and sudden demise of sentient beings. Phil tried inwardly to call on saints, God, and prophets, but even now they all were fictions to him. In his isolation he called on his family, but they were figures of gray, cardboard beings, lost in the material world. There was nothing to face but the coming pain of annihilation.

He looked at Tracey. She was mumbling words to herself. Perhaps she was fortunate, Phil thought. Her religion would anesthetize her. Her breakdown would help her cross over into the darkness. For Phil it was the worst crucifixion of his mind. He was numb. All things happened dreamlike and slowly with unbearable heat and brightness.

"The *Penny Dreadful*, being outfitted in accordance with the laws of the State of Florida and the regulations of maritime safety, did raise anchor in the lagoon of Coral Gables on the day of January the second, being contracted for a cruise of pleasure."

McCracken seemed to be reading from his sheet of paper. Phil saw notes written in compact script, carefully numbered and outlined. The glare of the paper made McCracken's eyes water.

"Replenishing the stock of foodstuffs, gasoline, and water, and incurring minor repairs, said craft then commenced its voyage east by southeast, as entered in the ship's log. The first two days being passed in merriment and conviviality aboard ship approximately twenty-two miles north of the westernmost shore of the Island of Nassau."

"Cut the bullshit, McCracken!" Phil yelled. "We know your game ends in murder!"

"On the third day of the New Year, brief squalls did force minor breach in seam, aggravated by capped seas and minor gale the following day, measuring a force of forty-four. The craft shipped water, lost its power due to a rupture of the main shaft line."

Phil struggled in his chair, trying to overturn it. It was cast iron, painted white, and securely latched into the deck. McCracken ignored him.

"Generator overdrawn to provide electricity to all decks. Sixth day of January, ship effectively denied any and all power, either mechanical or electrical. Two battery cases damaged, no sabotage indicated."

Sudden cries of island birds restored Phil to his senses.

The jungle was steaming. The glossy leaves glittered in the blue sky. While McCracken droned, the timepiece of his own life was inexorably ticking closer to the end. It was as though he saw a vision, the scene was etched with such a burning clarity. All his fantasies of men's death fell away as thin fictions. The reality of it was extraordinarily brutal.

". . . rationing broken by forced procurement of foodstuffs," McCracken was saying, "necessitating the wearing of ship's armaments. Rowing continued as ordered, with but small assistance from Mr. Williams and none from Mrs. Williams. On the eleventh of January, was approached by freighter bearing the flag of the Union of Soviet Socialist Republic. Mr. Williams attacked the Captain of the *Penny Dreadful*, being subdued only by the quick and forthright action of the first mate. No charges were filed, under consideration of the excitement of the moment and the deprivations of the past week."

"It's good that we die," Tracey said softly. "We leave the world a purer place."

McCracken turned to Penny, rested her more comfortably against the pillows, and gently stoked her face, brushing the hair from her forehead. Penny's eyes stared blankly at Phil. Her nostrils flared slightly and rhythmically, like a soft underwater anemone. They were the only sign that she was alive. McCracken's voice became crisper, lost whatever matter-of-factness it had acquired. Once again, he seemed to be speaking neither to Penny, to Phil, nor even himself, but to some witnesses invisible to all but himself.

"While Mr. Williams remained in violent delusion, no further rowing was possible. Therefore, employing the extreme measure as granted solely by the emergent situation, the Captain did order, and did execute six lashes of the cat-o'-nine, in hopes of reviving Mr. Williams to his senses. Recovery was not successful, as delusions only increased. On the following evening, the twelfth of January, perhaps in consort with Mr. Williams, Mrs. Williams did poison both Captain and first mate with a combination of cognac and an as yet undetermined amount of chemicals from sleeping pills. Theft of essential stores followed, including the ship's dinghy, electronic emergency transmitter, half the remaining water supply, ship's telescope, ship's log, three blankets, two buckets, two life vests, and compass. Captain did emerge from position at foot of stairs, fully recovered, due to excellent moral and physical condition. First mate regained consciousness for two hours, then lapsed into . . ."

McCracken swallowed. He found it impossible to go on. Phil now sensed that behind McCracken's forensic tone was a murderous rage. Why the Captain's need to string out the act of murder? Had he driven every couple to commit crimes against him solely to avenge himself by administering his version of law? What ancient ritual was he reliving to continually justify himself in such a lengthy fashion? This time, at least, Phil observed, one of them was incapacitated, hopefully for good. McCracken might have to play his games alone from now on. Maybe some future guest would complete the job.

"First mate lapsed into coma," McCracken said, his voice cracking to a hoarse whisper, "from which no awakening is likely."

McCracken burst into tears. His shoulders shook. He lowered his face to the table and sobbed. He stood abruptly, tears running in double tracks down his cheek, wiped his eyes with the backs of his hands, and walked away. He stared out at the cove, as though communing with its loneliness.

He walked back and sat down efficiently, with the demeanor of the shell of a man.

"It shall seem strange," McCracken said in a broken voice, no longer reading, "that the hapless victim of the crime be that very person who would have been charged with the defense of the accused. Nevertheless, that is so. Nor would the first mate, I am sure, were she able to communicate with us, deny her best energies, her most eloquent and compassionate mastery of the language, in pleading either for acquittal or for mitigation of sentence. But as circumstances are otherwise—as they are otherwise —the court must, by virtue of fairness and justice, assume this responsibility."

Phil listened carefully. Was there some clue behind McCracken's rambling? Was there a defense? What was it McCracken seemed to want out of this bizarre formality? McCracken stood, paced the floor to the side of the table, extemporizing.

"It is true," McCracken said, his hands extending in debater fashion, "that crimes have been committed. The first mate is living proof. Likewise, the destroyed dinghy, the lost foodstuffs, the ship's log, rescue transmitter, all lost to the bottom of the sea. It would be foolhardy to deny such transgressions."

McCracken paused and licked his lips. His powerful fist slowly came to an outstretched palm, and he was absorbed in his defense.

"But do we confuse two different authorities?" McCracken asked. "There is the authority of the Captain, empowered through centuries by countless governments, who is the sole representative of the State on the seas. In fact, the Captain may be said to be head of a small state in the form of his ship, and his actions, designed to prevent loss of life and property, must and are obeyed as the voice of law. And in this authority, the Captain shall—and indeed must—do whatever his expertise deems necessary, else anarchy and death result.

"Therefore, Captain of the *Penny Dreadful* acted lawfully and courageously in rationing food and water, in ordering the rowing, and in adminstering six therapeutic lashes to Mr. Williams. Similarly, he acted with restraint and forbearance in confining the dangerous Mr. Williams to the hold."

Phil rubbed his wrist against the handcuffs and tried to wriggle his fingers out. The skin of his forearms chafed, bleeding slightly. The veins of his forehead bulged. Mc-Cracken seemed absorbed in his oratory and rarely looked in the direction of Phil or Tracey.

"However," McCracken continued sharply, "does the Captain have the right to punish? Is not this an additional authority? What purpose does it serve to inflict grievous injury or death on a crew member when such injury or death no longer aids in the survival of a ship?"

"Damn right, McCracken," Phil muttered. "If you want us punished, you take us back to Florida!"

"To be sure, captains have flogged their crews, dunked them, keelhauled them, shot them, in emergent situations. But was not this to inspire the force and majesty of the law into the minds of remaining crewmen? And what possible purpose can now be served by the execution of two crew, one of whom is mentally deranged, and the other unable to contribute so much as a hundred yards rowing?"

"You cut off her thumb, you bastard! Who's insane?"

McCracken sat down at the table, facing Phil and Tracey. He spread his hands wide. There was an expression of reasonableness on his face.

"Besides, it is well known that physical privation, thirst, and hunger will derange a man's perception of morality. Acts which once were viewed with justified horror become feasible. Possibly the meaning of death was no longer clear to Mrs. Williams when she attempted the murder of the first mate and the Captain."

Tracey burst into tears.

"Forgive me!" she wept. "Oh, God, forgive me!"

"Let her go, Captain," Phil said, fighting the metal on his wrist. "I can buy you ten yachts. You can set yourself up in Yucatan. Anything you want."

"And there is the argument, which must now be advanced, that Mrs. Williams had incurred what can only be called a diminished capacity to understand what she was doing. Has it been shown that she understood that the combination of cognac and sleeping pill was lethal? Has the court been supplied with an erroneous picture of her true motivations?"

"I didn't mean to do it," Tracey sobbed. "I just wanted everybody to sleep. Just sleep."

"She's lost her reason," Phil said quickly. "How can you punish someone who's lost her reason? Is that the action of a captain?"

McCracken sat back in his chair. His eyes glittered. He made no sign of hearing anyone but himself.

"Fourthly, and in conclusion," McCracken said, almost happily, "is not mercy the queen of virtues? Is not dispensation of her the most human of gifts, next only to that of life itself? Is not the mark of greatness not only expertise, courage, and determination but, aye, that softness of the heart that heals the moral wound? And would it not enhance the majesty of this court to so dispense such balm when it has the jurisdiction and right to impose the ultimate and most final of judgments?"

McCracken's hand slowly floated back to the table. He seemed pleased with himself. Suddenly there was a crash. Penny had fallen against the table and slid to the floor.

"Penny!" McCracken shouted. "Dear God!"

McCracken leaped to the deck. With trembling fingers he lifted the eyelid of his wife. He looked with disbelief. Suddenly, a keening began, a long, low sound that seemed to emanate not from a human being but from the ether, rising higher and higher, a drone of anguish, with neither breath nor tremolo, until it filled the deck and echoed nightmarishly back from the cove.

"Oh God," McCracken wept, bending low to Penny's face. "It was too much this time, my darling! We misjudged. Oh God, we misjudged!"

McCracken was inconsolable.

"My dearest mate," he murmured, insensate. "My dearest . . ."

Tracey shrieked. "She's dead! She's dead!"

Her piercing cry penetrated McCracken. He turned, fixed them both with a black and anguished look.

"Yes," he whispered hoarsely, "While *you* live!"

Phil was taken aback at the murderous rattle in McCracken's voice. McCracken wrapped Penny in the blue blanket. He held her in his arms. He set her in her chair. Phil watched in horror. Penny's face had not changed, except that the eyelids were partially lowered. They seemed to observe slyly the proceedings, waiting for a chance to speak.

"The court shall entertain the arguments as advanced by acting counsel," McCracken said.

McCracken sat in his chair. A quick breeze ruffled the large flags. As it stilled, a murmur of water lapped against the boat. Perspiration darkened McCracken's jacket, beaded his forehead. He was wrapped up in his cause, energetically finding the best words. He seemed moved to perform now for Penny's sake.

"First, as to whether the Captain or designated authority may inflict punishment above and beyond the immediate cause of well-being or survival of the rest of the crew," McCracken said quickly, precisely, looking at the table, seeing nothing. "There is, above and beyond the exigencies of individual trial and suffering, beyond the minute and particular circumstances of any given exertion, the majesty, nay, the divinity of law. The law is the greatest expression of that intelligence which raised the human above the blind struggle for existence. And wherever law exists, human life is glorified."

Phil gazed without comprehension at the figure of McCracken earnestly, deliriously propounding his case. Why did the man feel the need to justify himself before his own conscience? If it had been he, Phil, would *he* have carried out such an elaborate ritual just to prolong the final annihilation? It was a question that Phil, at this moment of his life, could not answer unequivocally.

"Therefore, wherever a representative of the law finds

himself, be he captain, magistrate, or in the employ of the
Congress of Parliament, it behooves him to give a just
account of that law. To sacrifice the law for any individual
crew members, however so much we may find it in our
hearts to bear them love, is a violation of a vastly greater
principle. For no man is above the law, least of all the
Captain."

"You're insane, Captain!"

"And the law in this case cannot be more specific. The
punishment for the enumerated crimes is well known."

"Who appointed you, McCracken! The court sits in
Tallahassee!"

McCracken slammed a hand on the table and glared at
Phil. Surprised that McCracken had listened or reacted,
Phil closed his mouth.

"The Captain aboard a vessel convenes such courts as he
deems fit to administer the law."

Confused, Phil could not find how to argue. Obviously,
McCracken was wrong. But how debate it?

"That's . . . that's old-fashioned," Phil protested weakly.
"Today there's a Coast Guard . . . or a federal court, a
merchant marine . . ."

McCracken slammed his fist on the table. Tracey started.
McCracken leaned forward, veins throbbing in his neck.

"Secondly, no physical trial obviates anyone from moral
responsibility. Why doesn't every coward or no-good murder his captain? Because of the law, Mr. Williams, because
of the law!"

"Not true, Captain! What about drugs, insanity? That's
it, temporary insanity! You know Tracey was not in her
right mind—"

McCracken snorted in disgust. He withdrew, a hand on
Penny's shoulder.

"And lastly," McCracken concluded, "shall we consider
the notion of mercy? Who of us can say whether mercy or
the law is most majestic of man's accomplishments? But is
it not human nature to offer mercy to those in whose

hearts some goodness may yet be seen, in whom the moral degeneration has not taken place to an irreversible degree? How quickly we extend mercy to those truly contrite at heart, and how naturally we withhold it from those who remain hard and obdurate. And from Mr. Williams do I detect no sign whatsoever that he respects the supremacy of divine law. None whatsoever! Mercy is but the acceptance of the right of law. And Mr. Williams has decided, now and forever more, to remain out of its reach!"

"Cut the crap, McCracken!"

"Let the heavens witness! Let the currents of the ocean cleanse his perfidy from these shores!"

McCracken was momentarily overcome. Then he straightened his jacket. He was perspiring freely now. Trickles of sweat rolled down his neck, dampening his collar. Phil felt his tongue swelling between his parched lips. Tracey was slumped as far forward as her handcuffs allowed. She mumbled incoherently, as though pleading. Only Penny's skin was dry and smooth.

"The court will consider the arguments."

"What about us?" Phil demanded. "Don't we get to speak?"

"Are you dissatisfied with counsel?"

"You're a murderer! I read the logbook!"

McCracken paused.

"Then you know with whom you deal."

McCracken went to the stern railing. He knelt on a single knee, his fist resting lightly against his lips. Phil could not see whether he was praying or thinking. McCracken was intensely absorbed in his mental effort. Phil tried to wrench himself off the chair. Violently he tugged at the chain. His cuffs, biting into the metal, banged it against the sharp edge of the chair. McCracken only knelt, looking out from time to time at the dense, glistening foliage that exuded its humidity over the boat.

Showing signs of great stress, McCracken lifted Penny from the chair and carried her into the wheelhouse. Pausing at the door, he seemed demoralized, uncertain what to do next. Going back in, he stood, arms akimbo, looking at Penny. Then he stepped back into the bright sunlight.

McCracken sat at the table, scrawled several words rapidly on the sheet, took the sheet, folded it sharply and placed it in his breast pocket.

"Death by hanging," he said softly.

FIFTEEN

McCracken stood, walked to the stern, and stared out at the cove. He seemed to be looking for a good site, but then he placed his hands against his eyes, as though to blot out the memory of everything that had happened. His back to Phil and Tracey, he held his posture erect, then turned on his heel and went into the wheelhouse. There he lay down on a bench opposite Penny. While Phil struggled and hammered at the chair, his handcuffs, and the short metal chain to the deck, McCracken slept fitfully in the dank heat of the wheelhouse.

Phil could no longer swallow. His tongue was leathery.

Tracey seemed to have dislocated a shoulder, having fallen from her chair, held up awkwardly by the handcuffs. With the cooling of the afternoon came long shadows, sinister as black snakes, writhing up to the chairs. Mosquitoes hovered in dense clouds. McCracken slept in the wheelhouse.

"God," Phil whispered, "help me. Just this once. Just this one time. I'll do anything. I promise."

Tracey observed Phil with pity, and quietly said, "He's coming."

McCracken, a bulky shadow among the shadows, stood over them.

"Though she sees nothing, I shall have the first mate witness one hanging before consigning her to eternity." His

237

voice was thick, suffused with sadness. "It was our greatest round. It was too much for her."

"I have nothing against you, McCracken," Phil pleaded. "Just let us back in the water. We'll swim ashore. We'll live on the island. You'll never hear from us again."

"She was a noble first mate, as noble an officer as served on the sea. And, if I may say so, a fine and beautiful woman."

McCracken turned, evanescent in the twilight as his shadow merged into the darkness at the wheelhouse. Phil cursed and fought furiously at his metal chain. The engines started. With horror, Phil realized McCracken was taking them further up the stream, or lagoon, into the density of the jungle beyond any possibility of help.

They appeared to enter a darkly shrouded small bay. The stars burned coldly. At first, a cold breeze rippled the still water, then it was calm.

McCracken unlatched the handcuffs from the chair. A rough hand seized Phil by the collar and tumbled him across the deck. Three razor-sharp points pushed slowly into Phil's cheek.

"Get down below," McCracken ordered.

Cursing, trying to keep his balance, Phil half fell, half ran down the stairs. He twisted his ankle. The prongs arched into his ruined back. With a cry McCracken raised his foot and pushed Phil into the stateroom, then slammed the door. Moments later, the door was kicked open again and McCracken carried in Tracey, the harpoon pointing at Phil from McCracken's right arm. He laid her on the bed, then retreated to the darkness of the corridor.

"With the dawn," McCracken's voice oozed out of the blackness.

The door slammed. The bolt slid home and locked. Phil leaped at the door and pounded. In the darkness he saw Tracey stir.

"Tracey! This is it! He's really going to kill us!"

Tracey opened her eyes and backed away from Phil on the bed.

"Dear God," Phil begged, "I . . . I don't want to die!"

He fell on Tracey, desperately clinging to her. Her skin was flaccid, clammy. He embraced her and kissed her fervently. She was cool, without muscle tone, only a small shivering. Ashamed, Phil rose.

"God has placed us once again into his hands," Tracey admonished. "This is to punish us, and we do not reject the judgment of God."

"Stop that, damn it! We've only got a few hours! We've got to figure a way—"

"No. I want to die. You must, too."

Phil looked wildly around. He threw a bureau drawer against the wall. He gouged at the wall with the base of a lamp. He tried to squeeze thrugh the porthole. There were only sounds of Tracey's uneven breathing and his own desperate cries. The worn paperback novel by the bed, McCracken's antique instruments on the wall, the maps, the piece of old oil barrel all seemed pathetic reminders of that transient experience of life itself. Phil was headed for a far more permanent blackness.

Phil ran into the bathroom looking for metal tools. All he saw were the tissue holder and the rim of a mirror. He could not dislodge the faucets. The iron edge of the barrel band seemed the only likely tool, and he slammed it into the floor. He reasoned that somewhere below was the shaft, the deck plating, something.

Throughout the night Phil labored with his crude tool. Soon the hardwood floor under the scored carpet was scratched and broken. Below it Phil smelled oily water, a thick, unpleasant odor of stagnation and gasoline. He reached into the darkness, where he felt only another floor. Furiously, he pounded at the lower floor. Soon the iron band had bent. Phil's knuckles bled.

The door opened.

McCracken held the harpoon gun aimed at Phil's knees. There was an amazed twinkle in his eyes.

"You have developed beyond my expectations, Mr. Williams."

Phil threw the iron band at McCracken's head. A flash of light knocked Phil to the floor. His leg spurted blood. McCracken refitted another spear into the breach.

"Bind it!" McCracken said, "or you'll die here in your stateroom."

Feeling faint, Phil tore his shirt and wrapped it around his leg. Tracey sat quietly, blandly observing the two men. Her eyes were vacuous, unseeing. Her mind was off in some spiritual limbo. Phil cinched the cloth tightly around the bleeding wound.

"We got close, didn't we?" he gasped.

"Very close. You were less than five miles from this island. Once on it I might never have found you." McCracken smiled. "No one had ever gotten that close."

"How did you find us?"

"The pulse transmitter, of course. Turning it on was not an act of intelligence."

Phil looked away in disgust. His eyes searched beyond the porthole, smelling the jungle.

"Well, I hope we satisfied you in all other ways."

"Very well."

"What about the next one, McCracken? Mightn't the next one kill you? Somebody just a shade quicker, a shade brighter?"

McCracken laughed softly without humor.

"Then he deserves to win, Mr. Williams."

Even as he spoke, McCracken seemed to be thinking of something else, perhaps his next guests, perhaps Penny.

"A bargain, McCracken," Phil said softly, reasonably. "Free us, and we'll help you. We'll recruit for you."

McCracken's smile broadened. "My guests recruit themselves. As you did."

"We'll help you run the ship. You'll need help now that . . . that . . ."

McCracken's eyes hardened momentarily, then turned softly dolorous. His voice trembled.

"No, Mr. Williams. I shall function perfectly well alone. As I showed you, these boats practically run themselves."

McCracken waited, making no move, seeming to wait for Phil's response. Was it psychological torture the Captain was indulging in? Or was it Phil's turn to dictate the course of the conversation.

Phil finally asked, "Will you tell me one thing?"

"If I can."

"Why do you do this?"

"What an absurd question." McCracken grinned. "But then, you're like a child who simply has to have an explanation for things."

"I mean—these antiques? The prayers? The court-martial? The entire charade?"

McCracken's face tensed. "It's no charade, Mr. Williams. I appreciate ceremony. Most people do."

"But they don't . . ." Phil swallowed the last word.

"Kill? No. Most people remain, like you, on the far side of the chasm. I had almost thought you might have crossed over. When you were rowing, firing the pistol, I thought I detected signs."

McCracken paused. He seemed to be listening, as though for sounds of Penny through the entire length of the boat. Sharply he turned back to Phil, piercing him with his strange blue-gray eyes.

"I could tell you it was because they killed our son. But it wouldn't be true. However, they did, you know. He was crushed loading pipes for an installation in Saigon. We were very bitter about that. We sued, but the military . . . well, it doesn't matter. I could tell you that I see things more precisely than people like you. I can *see* the annihilation that awaits us all. Would that satisfy your curiosity?"

Phil's eyes ferreted about for a likely weapon.

"I could tell you that it has become a drug, Mr. Williams. Or like sex. How can I explain it to you? It's addictive. Life is paltry without risk. Contemptible."

Phil watched McCracken's eyes slowly soften, take him in, focus on his own incredulity.

"In the final analysis, what difference does it make? Let's just say that I enjoy it. I drifted into it, I discovered it over a period of time, and now I do it. Can anyone explain himself more than that? Can you explain why you design leather purses?"

Phil said nothing. McCracken studied him closely.

"I think, in spite of yourself, you do understand. After all, you shot at me."

"In self-defense."

"Come now, be truthful. How did it feel?"

"It felt great, McCracken! I wanted to see your teeth splashed all over the deck!"

McCracken laughed. "Beautiful. You see, Mr. Williams, you can develop. Even you know that."

Phil drew back in his chair, not knowing what to say. Was McCracken trying to convert him? Was it a test? Did it mean that he would not perform the execution?

"So what if you're right?" Phil asked.

"Ah, yes, you've seen the abyss. You felt the bitter wind, didn't you? When you rowed out on the dinghy? Frightening, isn't it? But how did it feel? Weren't you more than a man? Didn't existence itself seem to respond, for once in your life, to your presence?"

"No, it was entirely indifferent to me."

McCracken laughed.

"That's an aspect of it, to be sure," he chuckled. "The great indifference. But it is precisely that which pumps the blood. Have you ever seen such murderous blankness? The ocean, Mr. Williams. We are nothing to it."

Phil waited. McCracken, he thought, would continue to drift into a soliloquy on the sea. Instead, he quietly said, "Come now, be truthful. Can the gentler bonds of life ever again match the thrill of living each second at the edge of existence?"

"I don't know," Phil said cautiously. "You may be right."

"Of course I'm right."

"Okay. What's the next step? What do I do?"

"Do?" McCracken shook his head solemnly. "I'm afraid there are no options left you, Mr. Williams. You've been fairly tried and sentenced—"

"You made a bad mistake this time," Phil said suddenly. "I'm not Charles MacIver, or Henry Ransome, or the . . . the Frenches. People are looking for me."

"Is that so?"

"My name is Sobel. I am the president of a large corporation with connections throughout the northeast and Europe. I assure you, my absence will be noted immediately."

"Nonsense."

"We have outlets in Florida. They'll expect to hear from me shortly."

"You were both very discreet. False names, clandestine correspondence. Nobody knows where you are."

Phil watched McCracken. Perspiration speckled his feverish forehead.

"My staff—"

"Your staff," McCracken said quickly, "functions well without you."

"My wife will—"

"Your wife is well rid of you. Am I right?"

Phil said nothing.

"Yes, to be sure, there will be a search," McCracken continued. "A legal gesture. But what can they find? There is absolutely nothing linking you to me. You will be swallowed up by the outer world. No doubt they will assume you simply absconded. In time they will despise even your memory."

Phil had stopped moving. The remnants of his shirt were

drenched through with sweat. He was afraid a nervous gesture would send the lance into him. But his fingers trembled involuntarily, and his breath came in frightened, uneven gasps.

"Have I cured you of your vanity?" McCracken asked.

Phil licked his lips. He was scarcely conscious of what McCracken said. Ideas did not penetrate his frozen brain. All he saw was the sharp image of the white-jacketed Captain fifteen feet from him.

"I'm a man of means, Captain. I can—"

"You were an inch from becoming a murderer!"

"I can set you up. Anywhere—!"

"—and it thrilled you!"

McCracken turned, looked at Tracey who had awakened. Keepnig the harpoon aimed steadily at Phil, McCracken extended a hand to her.

"Come," he said with inexorable gentleness.

Tracey took his hand appreciatively, rose, and walked docilely ahead of him. Phil screamed and threw himself forward. The door slammed in his face. The bolt snapped shut.

"You can't do this, you bastard!" Phil yelled.

Phil scrambled to the porthole. The waters of the upper cove were rippled in the viscid red of screaming birds that flew out of the thickets. Insects hummed close to the glass. A long black bar lay like a stain on the water. It was the shadow of the *Penny Dreadful.* It undulated very slowly. Through it was visible the shallow water, tiny pebbles and dark sand. It was cold. Phil felt the sting of insects across his forehead and neck.

A faraway voice mumbled words by rote. It was McCracken. A round shadow appeared, moved, stopped, changed shape. McCracken said several more words, reading from a book. Then a second shadow came from the deck. It lay on the water like a fat obelisk. The water suddenly shimmered, disrupting the shadows, slicing into them with dark blue and red shafts of reflections.

"Tracey!" Phil screamed. "Fight! Fight!"

McCracken mumbled several more phrases. In the following silence, Tracey's voice prayed aloud, begged the Virgin Mary for forgiveness, commended her soul unto God. McCracken's shadow placed a rope around her neck. He raised a hand, as though to heaven.

"Tracey! Run!!"

With a violent shove the smooth, shrouded shadow swung forward like a child's swing. It shivered, shook, swung back. Then it swung forward, jerked once, and floated backward, its swings diminishing, until it was a still shadow among the others.

Phil fainted.

When he awoke, the sun poured in through the porthole. Glimmers of light gleamed off the astrolabe, the brass instruments on the bureau, the tiny teeth of the wheels and the incised lines and numbers in black.

Phil sat, drenched in perspiration, on the edge of the bed. He felt as though the blood had been sucked from his veins. He found himself staring out the porthole. It was a bright lagoon, nearly two hundred yards wide, calm and flecked where the breeze crossed the surface. On the far shore was a mass of green vines and grass. Beyond, a brown, bare hill rose in a well-rounded cone.

"It was all a dream," Phil told himself.

He whirled.

"Tracey? Tracey?"

He ruffled his hands through the sheets and blankets. He ran into the bathroom.

"He was playacting," Phil said aloud. "Just another damned charade—to torture me!"

Isolated, Phil stood in the bathroom. The mirror showed a face he did not recognize. It was puffy, red-eyed, and unshaven. It had the desperate look of a madman capable of anything.

Then, like a new system of feeling and thinking, a change rippled through his nerves. To survive, he had to

kill McCracken. There was no more sacrifice, no more
subservience. Like two animals in the pit, the lion and the
panther, if he could be a panther, they would tear each
other to bloody stumps.

Trembling from the self-realization, Phil left the bathroom. He felt stronger. Inhibitions had dropped away. His
blood raced smoothly and rapidly from his heart. Everything looked amazingly clear. The clotted wound in his leg
no longer hurt. He despised everything he had been, everything that he had stood for.

He searched through the room for a weapon.

The instruments had pointed needles, brass rings. He
tore a brass ring from a chronometer and stuck it into his
pocket. A well-aimed blow would draw blood. Suddenly
disfigurement thrilled Phil. He wanted to maim, then kill.
Desperately, he kept Tracey out of his mind. Certainly she
was tied to the salon bench, or in the wheelhouse, while
McCracken carried out one of his long-winded exercises.
Phil picked up what was left of the iron band from the
barrel. It had bent around, and was too soft. He reached
into the floor. Now the light was better. All he saw was a
second floor. He felt along it. His hands came up dirty.
There was no seam, no series of bolts. Perhaps he could
stuff it with newspaper and set it on fire.

There were no matches in the room. Phil pushed the bed
against the door. It was a heavy bed. With him pushing
from behind, McCracken might never be able to open it.
He suddenly realized that by not thinking of this earlier, he
was partially guilty for Tracey's . . . death—? No, not that!
She was alive!—bound and cuffed in the hold. Would Mc-
Cracken torture Tracey to force him to open the door?
Despondent, Phil slumped to the edge of the bed. Mc-
Cracken seemed to have figured it out so well.

Restlessly, Phil paced the floor. Gradually, his blood
warmed again. He was hungry.

Would the porthole glass shatter? Could he fix the
shards onto a makeshift club? Was there a soft spot in the

rear wall? Could he gouge a hole into the far aft of the boat? Could he sink it? Phil remembered that there must be a seam somewhere. After all, it was made of wood. Fatigue clouded his mind. He unhinged the porthole. Perhaps he could use it as a shield for his head.

Phil listened for sounds of Tracey. There was a muffled scrape overhead. Out the porthole he saw nothing. There were no shadows. Straining, he pressed his ear to the outside. The breeze shook the palm fronds on shore.

"It shall be high noon," he heard McCracken say. "Not until then."

Phil was vastly relieved. Who was McCracken talking to, if not Tracey?

McCracken paced the deck. Phil dismantled a chronometer entirely, finding only small springs, an elaborate wheel, and a figure of Neptune on the outer case. A sand glass yielded only small wooden bars, elegantly carved and twirled, that held up the tops. Disgusted, Phil threw the glass at the wall. The glass rolled onto the bed, left the light in a glimmering, yellow curve through the concavity of its shape.

Phil sat on the dressing table and surveyed the silent room. Lack of food had caused a headache that physically pounded through his forehead. Still, he saw things with supernatural clarity. It was as though he and McCracken, by whatever accident of fate or insane destiny, found themselves matched against one another at the edge of the precipice. How trivial his life had been, Phil thought disdainfully. It had been a stunted life, among stunted people. Now, on the edge of his own death, he was not afraid.

He held the hourglass in front of the porthole, hoping to focus the rays onto the sheet and start a fire. It became warm, but no more, and the yellow glimmer of light rolled off the edge of the bed.

"The sun is moving," Phil murmured, his stomach tightening. "It must be close to noon."

Overhead there was a creaking, as though McCracken

had stood up or shifted his position. He was walking across
the deck, after making some kind of preparation at the
davits from where the dinghy had once suspended.

"By the authority of God, His Majesty the King, the
people of the government of these isles," McCracken intoned.

Phil grimaced, trying to hear.

"Though it be not the deep of the sea, the water here is
cool and runs not onto the shore but out into the tide,"
McCracken went on. "Circumstances have forced us to this
last cove, my love. And as my soul is half with thee, and
thine with me, we shall not be parted. But in this foul
barbarity of the world we have done, and conquered, and
no man shall say of us, having known us, having tested
our mettle, that our intelligence was lacking. Or that life
did not run deep and swift through us."

McCracken paused. There was an enormous silence.
Phil thought that the ceremony, whatever it was, had
ended. But McCracken's voice continued, from the same
position not far overhead.

"Therefore, do we commend thy mortal remains, which
did but encapsulate the most noble of souls, to the water
on which thou wast reborn. With neither remorse nor sor-
row, anguish nor dread, do we part. Composite things dis-
integrate, and we are thankful for the life which was
bestowed."

Phil covered his ears. The sound of McCracken's droning voice seemed poison to him, to distill corrosion into his
brain. The jungle birds, raucous in the thick foliage beyond
the boat, screamed for Phil to kill McCracken. Yes. He
would kill McCracken, Phil pledged to himself. Though the
man would beg for mercy, he would destroy him—and
take pleasure in the doing.

Phil ran to the small porthole. He had already removed
the glass, which allowed him a bit of space, enough to
protrude half his face. He saw nothing but the flat, inno-
cent cove, and the inlet leading out to sea.

There was a splash.

Startled, Phil banged his forehead against the iron hinge. He stared. A heavy weight turned over, rolling downward, into the inlet, moving sluggishly toward the open sea.

"Roll on, mighty ocean, roll on. Take this, my own soul, to the farthest deep."

Bubbles circled lazily among the tiny waves. Ripples extended now under Phil's porthole. The glaze of the water hurt his eyes. He pressed forward. Without another word there was a second splash. Phil caught sight of a form wrapped in a blanket, roped around the middle, sliding end over end into the water.

Numbed, he watched it sink, rolling, toward the moving channel and the far width of the bay. Soon the bubbles had trailed down into the bay, moved by strong current, and had fanned out, disintegrated. Phil stared at the motionless, bright horizon.

"It's a trick!" he screamed. "A trick, McCracken!"

His shout echoed across the bay. The hill disdainfully seemed to watch him. McCracken walked over the deck. Phil ducked inside, ran to the bed, and braced himself. There were no footsteps leading down through the salon. McCracken remained on the deck.

Phil picked up the hourglass. Sunlight streamed through the small porthole. Phil broke the frame of the map of the Caribbean and felt the parchment. It was brittle and dry. He tore it into tiny shreds and slivers. He scooped them into a pile, put it on the barrel, and shoved the barrel under the window. He broke the frame into tiny splinters, then listened for McCracken.

The sunlight extended down onto the inner wall, drooping a circle of brightness. Phil poised the hourglass under it, but the crinkle of light fell to the floor in a curved rainbow line.

All his thoughts diminished, focusing onto the object of starting a fire. He had become obsessed. It did not occur to him that he would more likely perish in it than McCracken.

Destruction thrilled him. He moved rapidly, smoothly. His senses were unnaturally sharp. He scraped shavings from the edge of the mahogany bureau, using the brass wheel of the destroyed chronometer. He procured a handful of sawdust and several small slivers of wood. These he piled onto the paper bits on the barrel.

At the far end of the bedroom was an alcohol lamp. He shook the lamp upside down, ripping away the glass and brass base. Only a few drops fell onto the top of the barrel. Phil wiped out the alcohol basin and placed the tissue on the barrel. He tore the paperback novel to shreds of half and full pages and laid them in a loose stack.

The hourglass reflected light in a semicircle past the juncture of floor and wall. Phil put his hand under the light. It was barely warmer than the rest of the room. He tore a light bulb from the bathroom and held it under the light. The light diffused over the barrel, glittering in speckled points.

Phil listened for McCracken.

Inside the chronometer were small pieces of glass tinted navy blue and pink, ornamental figures on their surfaces. Phil held them under the light, but they were flat; only two concentric rings shined onto the pile of paper and shavings. Disgusted, Phil smashed a sextant onto the floor. A silvered mirror flew against the bureau. A small telescope rolled under the bed. Phil dived under the bed. One of the lenses had rolled through the cracked telescope housing. The other he held in his hand.

"Where is it?" he whispered. "Damn—!"

He shook the linen from the bed. He crawled under the bed, pinned below the low mattress, listening for footsteps. In the dusty, humid air his eyes blurred. He felt systematically along the carpet, strands of which he had previously torn from the floor. In the corner he found the glittering quarter-sized glass. He ran to the small porthole.

The light was still a circle but it had angled toward the rear wall. Soon it would rise close to the horizontal, then shift rapidly as the sun rose along the porthole wall and disappear.

Holding a lens in front of the porthole, Phil moved the second lens up and down. A rough circle formed. With his foot he pushed the barrel under his arms. His arms grew tired and trembled. With every movement the circle swung wildly and disappeared. He had to find again the relationship of lens distance. The light constantly changed its angle. Soon it would rise beyond the porthole.

Phil nudged the paper slivers closer. He stared fixedly at the nucleus of light that wrinkled inside a rainbowed hole over the paper. A breeze blew away most of the paper. The slivers contracted and collapsed from their small pile.

"Damn!"

A wisp of air shot upward as the paper curled suddenly. Phil tried to move more paper under the light with his foot but the barrel was too high. He was afraid to move his arms, afraid of losing the heat he had generated from the lenses. The slivers turned away, rolling, browning, leaving a bare surface on the barrel.

Phil suddenly put down the lenses and quickly scraped together all the paper from the novel into a loose clump, adding the small sawdust pile of the bureau. Under the lenses they sat motionlessly in a bright circle for what seemed an eternity. Then, in an agony of heat, a piece of paper twisted and browned. A wavering of light rose over it. Phil's hands began to shake.

One by one the pages made a small sound, flattened, browned, and fell away. A sliver of the map, its flourished inscription still legible, crisped around the edge and blackened. Smoke trailed inches over the paper. Phil blew gently and cinders flew away, leaving unburnt paper. He scraped together the rest of the pages, tearing them into tiny pieces. After a minute he shifted the barrel far against the wall, even put his foot under it to raise the surface to meet the light.

He heard McCracken's footsteps coming down through the salon.

A wisp of bluish smoke rose an inch and abruptly flared outward as a breeze struck it. In the silence Phil heard the paper bend. Dense air seemed to exude from the mass of thick, typed pages crumpled below him. It was a colorless flame. The corners of pages seemed to flow toward the density of air, then more smoke rose. There was a small sound, and below the wavering air was a blade of yellow flame. The acrid smell of the smoke tingled his nostrils. Phil held the lenses with aching arms. His foot was under the barrel, and he dared not breathe. A flame traveled up to the end of a ball of crumpled page, then died out. A small collection of map fragments burst into a short yellow flame.

Phil carefully fed the small flame with pieces of tissue. The tissue held a few soaked drops of alcohol. White smoke twirled up. There was a puff, and the tissue rapidly expired in a wave of flame. He blew gently onto the charred tissue. Embers flared over the pieces of sawdust and burst into flame. Soon several filaments of fire smoothly consumed the paper that he held into the center of the barrel top.

McCracken's footsteps had paused at the rear of the salon, as though he had gone to the galley, but now he was walking through the salon toward the aft stateroom.

Splinters of wood blackened, disgorged minuscule embers, and finally yielded a long, narrow blue flame. More paper accepted the fire. Phil smashed the frame into smaller fragments, driving splinters into his palms. The wood burned in a tiny crossed pile. The air reached to the base cleanly. The fire grew.

There was a knock at the door.

SIXTEEN

Phil fed crumpled pages onto the fire, twisting them into thicker rolls. He found two narrow splinters from the broken floorboards and laid them delicately over the tiny blaze. The barrel's varnished surface was turning black.

The bolt to the stateroom door was snapped back. Phil quietly removed a map of the East Indies from its frame, rolled the entire parchment into a tube, and laid it on the flames.

"Give me a minute, Captain," Phil said to the closed door. "I . . . I need to pray."

"You should have thought of that days ago."

"I need to . . . get right with myself."

"You'll be right enough with yourself soon."

"I beg you, Captain. For your wife's sake. I'm troubled."

Strangely, there was a pause.

"Five minutes, Mr. Williams."

The bolt slammed back into place. The Captain's footsteps retreated. Phil broke the frame into its four parts and laid the pieces in a cross onto the flames. With an iron bar he smashed at the bureau drawer, then used the bar to tear out the molding along the bureau. That, too, he laid over the flames. By now the sun had shifted and the light was high over the barrel on the wall. If the fire went out there was no more light.

The curtains were too thick to burn. The edge of the

sheet browned, but did not flame. The cover of the paperback novel bulged and burst into fire. A lace doily rolled
over, crumbling into black. Wrappers and tissue from the
bathroom burned quickly. The wooden pieces of the hourglass were consumed. Moldings, stripped from the door and
along the floor, bubbled white paint, noninflammable, and
only smoked. Phil ripped a nightgown from the closet. It
was the nightgown he had bought for Tracey at Bonwit's in
New York. As though paralyzed, he stared at it. Some
other arms, it seemed, an animal's, laid it gently onto the
small flame. It curled, then flared into an exquisitely hot
flame. The sheet now turned to fire, and Phil crumpled it
carefully, pushing it toward the center of the barrel. Already the fire was hot enough to keep him at a distance.
The curtains burned. Phil ripped them from the portholes.
Footsteps approached.

McCracken knocked.

"I'm not through, Captain. You don't know what it's
like—"

"I know only too well what it's like, Mr. Williams. I
live with death daily."

"But not me, Captain! Give me two minutes. Just two
minutes!"

"Courage becomes a man, Mr. Williams. Not begging."

Phil threw a cellophane shirt envelope onto the fire. The
barrel top had charred. Smoke rose up to the porthole,
blew in, and stung his eyes. Phil laid a sport hat onto the
flames, and the woven grass tore apart in the heat. He laid
Tracey's blouses, then angled the bureau drawer over the
fire, from the barrel top to the wall.

"You think I'm less courageous than most, Captain?"

"Fair, Mr. Williams."

The bolt slid open.

A crackling sound was audible in the room. The bureau
drawer was charring on the reverse side of the panel. A
pillow case burned. Fingernail polish, dripped over the
wood, glowed with a rush. The bureau drawer developed

blue fingers. Travel folders burned rapidly. Passports, money, travelers' checks, and flight ticket stubs disappeared with astonishing rapidity in the hungry, growing flames.

The door slammed against the bed, refusing to budge.

A second nightgown soared into flame. The contents of Tracey's handbag flew apart in fire. Smoke hovered just below the ceiling, fanning out, slipping through the porthole. Phil coughed, threw the blanket from the bed into the crackling flames. The barrel was spitting puffs of blue smoke along its side. Phil shoved the bureau hard against the barrel, pinning the barrel at an angle between it and the wall. Smoke rolled into his eyes.

"Open the door, Mr. Williams. You must not hold it."

The shower curtain was not flammable but the contents of the small linen closet were. A large plastic bag of tissue rolls erupted in flame and several sheets, loosely unfolded, burned rapidly. Phil laid a second empty drawer onto the fire.

McCracken threw his weight against the door. The bed pushed back a fraction. Phil threw himself against it, slamming it shut.

"I order you to face your fate, Mr. Williams!"

"I'll kill you first, McCracken!"

A violent shove knocked the bed back an inch. Phil pushed it back, then found his feet slipping against McCracken's superior strength. The prongs of the harpoon were visible at an angle through the door opening.

"This is demeaning, Mr. Williams!"

"Am I ruining your ceremony?"

"You are more intelligent than this!"

The barrel split vertically, a burning stave falling to the carpet. The remainder charred rapidly, glowing along the entire side. Phil threw the pillows onto the bureau. One fell into the fire.

"Why will you die without dignity, Mr. Williams? Your wife was a model of decorum!"

Veins bulging, Phil leaned his shoulder into the bed, against the door. The fire burgeoned. He ran, lifted out a drawer and its contents and dumped them into the conflagration. The back of the bureau was black in large, oblong fans of charring wood. The bed violently scraped backward.

"What are you doing, Mr. Williams?"

Phil struggled to push the bed back but his strength was no match for McCracken's. He saw the harpoon pointing toward the small porthole where the lacquer sizzled and bubbled along the edges of the bureau. Paint bubbled, ran down in drops. The sweaters and scarves in the bottom of the bureau disgorged a foul smell, rolling in smoke sucked through the porthole away from McCracken. Phil felt the room grow closer. The heat was now palpable where he stood. When would McCracken sense it?

"What's happening, Mr. Williams? What's that I smell?"

The harpoon was poised. Only McCracken's arm was visible through the opening of the door. Sooner or later, Phil reasoned, McCracken would discharge a spear from the harpoon. In that second, until he could refit another spear, they would be more nearly equal.

Phil reached out and drew to him the brass ring of the ruined sextant. It was sharp but not heavy. A poor weapon. He crouched as far to the right as he could, behind the bed. The fire radiated off his left cheek, singeing his hair. McCracken's harpoon pointed to his left. Phil threw his shoe into the fire. The harpoon jerked but did not fire. Suddenly the glass of the porthole window, lying at the rear wall, cracked with a loud report. Like a nervous reflex, the massive hand jerked. A shaft leaped across the room with a rush. It happened so fast Phil was caught by surprise. The door opened. McCracken turned to the left, a spear already refitted, aimed at the fire. McCracken's mouth dropped as he stared at the flames.

In that moment it struck Phil that, unlike the sea which has no shape, no intelligence, McCracken was a man as he

was. Therefore, McCracken could be defeated. It was not
death itself, but a particularized form of it. Suddenly Phil
understood that the rules had been changed—to his benefit.
It was McCracken's game, but it was Phil's move. With a
shout, hideous to his own ears, Phil hurled himself at the
white blur that was McCracken. He brought down the
brass ring. It felt solid, a sound of hard bone, a surprised
eye. A massive shove threw him into the wall. He ran,
anticipating the triple blade in the small of his back, a blow
that never came.

Panicked, shouting a battle cry, Phil ran through the
salon.

"This is outrage!" McCracken bellowed.

Phil ran into the galley, rifled the shelves for pots, pans,
or knives and found nothing. Hearing McCracken's heavy
tread, he ran toward the master stateroom, past the hold
that had imprisoned him. Turned and trapped, he fled up
the stairs onto the deck.

"Arson!" McCracken shouted.

Phil slammed the hatch door shut. He found no lock. He
pushed a deck chair in the way. McCracken's harpoon
slammed through the wood of the door. Elongated splinters
flew outward. Through the hole Phil saw McCracken appear at the bottom of the stairs. A small appreciative grin
was on his face.

"Well done, Mr. Williams," McCracken allowed.

Phil threw sunglasses and a bottle of suntan lotion
through the hole. They bounced off McCracken's chest as
he refitted a third harpoon spear into the metal band of the
gun. Phil ran to the side railing. Everything happened so
quickly he was surprised by the brightness of the day. A
rope hung in front of him. It ended in a slack noose, a
large, fist-sized knot bulging at the base. It was the noose
intended for his neck.

With a cry of horror Phil ran into the wheelhouse. The
deck chair in front of the hatch door flew across the deck.

Through the streaked glass of the wheelhouse Phil saw

McCracken searching for him, strolling slowly with his harpoon cradled over the crook of his arm. It was a version of eternity. Each second burned with a fullness that suspended time. If darkness was the origin and conclusion of life, then this was its apotheosis. Phil crouched low in the wheelhouse. He drew a screwdriver from the table and clutched it to his chest.

"How does it feel, Mr. Williams?" McCracken's voice called. "Are your juices flowing? And aren't you afraid?"

The wheelhouse heat was insufferable. Sunlight, caught behind the glass of the windows and door, built up in the room. It was hard to believe that they had once shivered in a cold rain and huddled on these very benches. Phil looked for a heavy instrument, but found only the white signal lantern.

"Death, Mr. Williams. Isn't it a fearful thing?"

The signal lantern was not strong enough to blind McCracken when he would burst through the door. Perhaps, Phil hoped, it could surprise him. Was there a shield? Phil tugged at the bench cover, a mat strapped over the supports.

"That this extraordinary experience, this light, should end!" McCracken cried. "Isn't it inconceivable, Mr. Williams?"

Phil tipped the bench mat, support and all, against the long glass of the wheelhouse. He only briefly glimpsed McCracken walking on the white deck, his white jacket soaked through with sweat.

"To look thy last on all things lovely! To disappear without a trace?"

Phil realized that his stateroom was below him. He smelled no smoke, but he prayed the fire had not died.

"Do you sense the injustice—the exquisite injustice— Mr. Williams! Do you feel it in your marrows?"

A harpoon spear shot through the glass, through the supports, through the mat, and embedded itself in the wall above him. Fragments of the window showered over the console. Phil felt a thousand stings over his face. It awoke him from his insensate vision. He crashed through the remainder of the door glass, cutting his arm in several places, and ran desperately out of the wheelhouse.

Phil ran in his stockinged feet, his shoes having been thrown onto the fire. His lungs burning with oxygen short-age, he rounded the cabin wall. McCracken was clearly walking around the wheelhouse, but which way? It was precisely an even chance, to live, to die, to run to the right or to the left. Immobilized, Phil looked for shadows, but the sun was at his back. It was his shadow that stretched out along the deck.

The world was a monstrous arena in which men hunt one another, Phil realized.

Phil leaped from the back of the cabin wall, stumbled, tripped over the deck chair, and catapulted down the hatch stairs. Reeling down the corridor, he found his left knee did not support him.

Gradually an intoxication overtook Phil. It was not only the blood pounding in his temples, the preternatural aura of his vision, but an odor immersed itself into his brain. It was smoke, and with the smoke came the knowledge that the *Penny Dreadful* was probably mortally wounded.

Destruction had become Phil's ally.

He ransacked the cabinets, finding fishing poles, rain gear, hooks. On a lower shelf he found a yellow striped can with a spout. It smelled like kerosene or alcohol. He un-screwed the cap to the spout and threw the entire canister, spurting clear fluid, down the length of the corridor toward his stateroom. It bounced, then rolled into the flaming room.

Phil ran to the stove and turned on all the burners. He turned the oven on. He smashed the alcohol lamps against the sides of the galley. McCracken was lumbering down the stairs. Phil ran into the master stateroom and slammed the door.

"The fire . . . good try!" McCracken panted. "But it won't—"

There was a bang as the metal canister's sides flew against the wall. Phil prayed that McCracken would not notice that the gas jets were on. Perhaps there was no more alcohol in the stove. Phil rolled McCracken's bureau in front of the door, but the bureau was light and would not hold. Where was the hatch to the engine? It was in the corridor. Was there a second entrance? Was there a fuel hold? Spare cans of gasoline? Phil stripped the antique swords from the wall, kept the largest broadsword, its handle carved in the form of an angel, its single sharp side curving upward.

A fire ax smashed through the door. With a cry, Phil brought the broadsword down. McCracken removed his knuckles just in time, leaving blood on the bureau. Silence. Had McCracken left? Phil's heart pounded. He could see through the cracked frame of the door McCracken's retreating form as he hurried to attend to the fire. The fact that McCracken seemed confused burst into Phil's consciousness. There was, he suddenly realized, such a thing as victory. It was possible to triumph in a struggle with a fellow man. Now Phil understood a fragment of what McCracken had obliquely alluded to all those days on the sea.

McCracken pulled a heavy fire extinguisher from a cabinet in the corridor.

Phil threw the heavy ink stand down the corridor. Ink flew out over the floor and the quill floated gently down the wall. McCracken charged into the far stateroom. Then, fighting the flames, he backed away. Phil leaped into the galley. The burners of the stove were alight. He ripped the curtains from the portholes and laid them over the stove, threw paper towels, napkins, a tablecloth, and boxes of spices over the flames. Flared out into a single mass, flames fed by the alcohol seeped up into four wicks. Phil threw dried flowers into the flaming arena, then books from the galley shelf. Then he upended the cognac bottle, still on the counter, over the flames, onto the counter and floor.

In the salon he grabbed bottles of liqueurs and smashed them through the salon door, showering the galley with liquid. Then, Phil saw the white shirt streaked with oily grime and blood, just in time. He threw a bottle at it with all his might and heard the glass shatter against the corridor wall. Particles of nauseating smoke blinded him.

"I'm going to kill you, McCracken!"

Through the galley, a harpoon shaft shot past his neck and exploded a cabinet shelf.

"With my bare hands!" Phil screamed.

Now McCracken hobbled in through the galley side, raised his harpoon, and fired.

Instantaneously, Phil's wrist slammed against his forehead. His wrist, which he had instinctively thrown up against the harpoon, was impaled, if not broken, and it had been snapped back with astonishing force into his face, dazing him. Through a loud ringing in his ears Phil heard separate and distinct ominous sizzlings. They were the wicks of the alcohol-stove, and the fire was consuming the insulation of the wires along the galley roof.

"Cry out, Mr. Williams! Cry out to the heavens! Your last cry—"

"Stalemate," Phil stuttered, seeing that McCracken had fired his last spear.

Bits of his flesh hung from Phil's lower arm, and he could not flex his hand, though the fingers were still loosely intact. "I did well," he gasped hoarsely, stumbling, filling his lungs with the poison of the lead-filled smoke.

"Yes, you did, Mr. Williams," McCracken agreed, pulling a pearl-handled dagger from his belt. "Much too well."

"I gave you everything I had," Phil whispered, not knowing who he was, nor where he was, stumbling backward, his legs no longer part of him. His left arm dangled against his hip. "Everything."

McCracken licked his lip. Absurdly, now that he held

the dagger in his hand, he seemed reluctant to use it, as though there were something distasteful about close combat.

Phil stared at McCracken balefully. His eyes glinted white, sparkling in the thick smoke.

"Admit it, McCracken. There's never been one like me on your boat."

McCracken eyed Phil warily, backing him further and further down the corridor. Phil suddenly bent and threw the used fire extinguisher at McCracken's head. It banged against the wall and rolled clear into the galley.

"Yes, Mr. Williams, we're two of a kind!"

"Not quite. You're a freak! A criminal! Demented!"

Phil threw a pillow from a cabinet the length between them. McCracken deflected it with a quick wrist. Smoke billowed from the stateroom. Phil doubled over in an agony of stomach pains. He breathed hoarsely in a grating, rasping wheeze which roared from his abused lungs.

"And you, Williams?" McCracken shouted. "You're desperate to kill me! Who's the criminal? Fornicator! Adulterer!"

Phil pushed backward into the door. It gave way and he half-fell, half-stepped into the aft stateroom before he realized his mistake. The smoke was pouring in sheets from the wall. The paint ran in rivulets to the floor. The ceiling was flared outward with brown stains.

Coughing, Phil knelt.

"You're a miserable, dishonorable insect if you deny that!" McCracken hissed.

A rushing wind flew into the stateroom. It ignited the walls again. Then there was an enormous sound, a glare of light, and a physical push that threw McCracken off his feet. Phil's ears rang after the explosion. McCracken scrambled to his feet, then knelt. Ears bleeding, eyes dazed, he wildly swung the dagger in front of him.

"Burn! Burn!" Phil exulted. "Look at your boat, McCracken!"

A hideous cracking of buckling timbers rent the growing gloom.

"I made it your coffin!" Phil yelled. "I! Phil Sobel! Not Williams! Sobel! *I* did it!"

"*My ship!*" McCracken gasped.

A second flare of light brightened McCracken's face. Pieces of canister flew into the corridor. A terrible smell of alcohol came at the same instant that a sharp crack reverberated throughout the ship.

Phil crawled into the bathroom, slammed the door shut, and blindly beat at the flames. He turned the shower and basin faucets on and let them overflow. Ducking his face in the water, he gasped for air. He held himself up by his good right arm and sucked in air from the ventilator, from which a gentle waft of clean air issued.

"Williams!" McCracken roared.

"Dear God," Phil prayed, "let the ship go down."

In his hallucination Phil saw a thousand fingers stripping down the door. The varnish was running in strips. Smoke puffed out in gentle patterns from the inside of the door. McCracken had mistaken the closet door for the bathroom and, in his delirium, had slashed the remaining clothes to shreds. Now he righted himself and barged into the bathroom. His white jacket was soiled with black soot, blood, and the smudge of smoke.

Savagely Phil beat him about the neck, hands, and face. The dagger sliced into his ruined left arm. Like a whirlwind Phil flailed relentlessly and unconsciously. He saw only a white uniform gone red, flecks against the wall and the bright squares of the tile. He sensed it was crumpling. Phil dragged himself onto the deck and vomited. His lungs were filled with grit.

Smoke funneled in plumes up from below the deck.

Phil gazed at the smoke, idly comprehending little of what he saw. He felt he had passed through a barrier. He was not the man he had been. He scarcely knew who he was. It seemed natural that he should be looking out on an island that appeared to harbor dense vegetation, snakes, and insects, but no human beings.

McCracken was somewhere below. Dead? Wounded? Smothering in lead-poisoned smoke? Phil did not know. He wandered, strangely relaxed. The sun beat down on the shimmering white decks. Then his heart warmed to the sight of bubbles of paint blistering the stern decking. Black smoke hissed upward through the cracks around the flagpole.

It was like a beautiful dream. The sun heated his skin and invigorated him. His lassitude worked a kind of narcosis on his pain. The blue water of the bay seemed to lap gently at the rich, tangled shores in a steady, rhythmic applause, as though nature approved of everything he had done.

Phil strolled into the wheelhouse through the shattered door. There, he was seized with inexplicable jerks of energy. A memory of McCracken assaulted him and he leaped at the compass, the radio, anything, and destroyed it, smashing it under his heels. Then the feeling left him and he was as before, exhausted, breathing with difficulty, pale, and jumping at every sound.

Dimly, Phil perceived that he was in the grip of something larger than himself. He wondered, as from far away, at the violence in his powerful hands, the calm murder that circulated evenly through his body. He broke all the windows of the wheelhouse and threw everything into the sea. Was there no ax with which to cut through to the floor below to create a draft to help the fire? There was only a short metal pole, an extension to the flagpole. After a few short blows, Phil gave it up. He drifted to the port side. Below him from the small porthole in his stateroom, a foul-smelling column of smoke flowed upward into his face.

Phil crossed the deck. There was no dinghy. He went back to the wheelhouse to get the small pole for a crutch. Could he swim with his injured leg? How deep was the water? Perhaps he could float. Small fish rippled through the shadows, over the sand, creatures with no moral sense, like himself.

Out of the hatchway white smoke flowed like steam.

Phil tossed the deck chairs into the smoke below. Then he lifted the umbrella from its base and rolled that part down the stairs. From the wheelhouse he threw everything that was flammable. He tossed all the pencils, cushions, extra sweaters, even the volleyball net, swim trunks and the gaily colored Hawaiian shirts. Looking into the dense darkness, he could see no flames, but he felt the heat. Suddenly the cushion covers burst into a slow-burning flame. Phil threw down pieces of the door, shattered in the harpoon blast. The spear fell to the deck. He kicked it down the stairs.

Phil walked over the deck.

Smoke poured from the roof of the burning hatch. Flames licked at its base. Phil kicked the rest of the deck chairs around the hatch door. The smoke roared out through the door like a low whistle. Phil looked for other things to burn—a rolled piece of canvas used to shield the wheelhouse door from rain, the drawer from the wheelhouse desk. He tried to drag out the desk, but the legs were stuck in the door.

Phil broke the desk apart with the pole. He littered it with towels, sandals, and the legs of a miniature telescope. He went to the hatch. Flames ran in smooth sheets up the tunnel of the hatch. The heat billowed across the deck like an invisible curtain and drove him away.

The *Penny Dreadful* shifted, bumped forward.

Phil watched calmly. Smoke surged through the deck flooring. It was invisible directly over the varnish, but it coalesced several inches higher and flowed smoothly into the air. The deck chairs burned. Everything was satisfactory.

The *Penny Dreadful* jerked like a dreaming dog.

Falling dishes and glasses clattered from below. Phil ambled to the flagpole and took in the flags. He threw one on the wheelhouse pile of debris, the other into the scorched hatch. The breeze turned against him, and the fire exhaled a stinking, vacant breath in his direction. Amused, he watched as he retreated from the heat.

Flames rolled down the deck, sending off flares that disengaged, distended against the blue sky. Black smoke puffed irregularly at the forward end. The *Penny Dreadful* seemed to be moving. It jerked from side to side. There was a violent hiss. White steam added a humid smoke to the fire. Phil found that by leaning against the rungs of the accommodation ladder he could hold himself by his right arm, lower his right leg, thus maneuvering his way down. Unwilling to let go, he hung at the bottom rung. He could see now that it was far deeper than he had thought. A trick of the light showed the sandy bottom. Through the unnaturally transparent water Phil saw the stones and sand clearly. The shadow of the *Penny Dreadful* gave off a kind of flare in an evanescent shadow of smoke and steam.

It was difficult for Phil to breathe. The fire sucked up the oxygen. The hull of the ship beaded, its paint resisting the flames. It became hot.

Phil weakened. His consciousness segmented. All he saw was the dark pebbles in the water, the shadow of the boat and, above him, the roaring, sucking sound of the fire. The universe had retreated to a space no more than ten feet in radius, and it was filled with pain and—something akin to satisfaction. His trembling arms were giving way. His numb hands were cut in a dozen places, polluted with oil and smoke. A glittering path of reflected sun hit his eyes. He felt he was slipping into something warm, soft, and infinite. But it was not the future. His future was of no interest to him now. That could only be a pitiful, miserable abstraction. Instead, a great shouting seemed to invade his ears.

"I won!" he said aloud.

Distantly, he felt his fingers relax from the rungs. He sensed a push against his face and body. It must have been a wave. Floating, he saw sky, smoke, flame, fish, jungle, and his bleeding arm. At the same time, he thought he heard his name called. The clear water enveloped him. He turned deliriously. The *Penny Dreadful* had lost its anchor. Cable lay on the deck. The boat was sliding, listing heavily, into the main body of water. Black smoke billowed out at Phil. Its heat stuck to the water in the form of an oily scum of black particles.

"Mr. Williams—!" echoed a gritty, animal voice.

At the stern of the listing boat a bulky mockery of a man's form crawled slowly. Its huge, shapeless flesh was blackened with smoke and burned cloth and the hair matted in spiky clumps over a blood-speckled forehead. A white space—an open mouth—worked convulsively.

"Mr. Williams—!" cried the shape, struggling to upright itself.

Phil's hands paddled dreamlike. Neither went forward nor backward. His broken leg moved like seaweed with the gentle currents of the water.

With a small burst of the floorboards, the shape fell. A captain's cap rolled into the water. The *Penny Dreadful* was now twenty yards away and drifting faster toward the wide mouth of the bay. Through the smoke was a movement of the heavy form, a glimmer of still-white shirt, and the blistered outcroppings of McCracken's square face.

From afar, came McCracken's hoarse shouts, dying slowly over the water.

"Congratulations, Mr. Williams! You're a . . . ten! An *absolute . . . ten—*!"

The blaze of the explosion illuminating the *Penny Dreadful* seared Phil's eyes. His face blistered as, triumphant, he was propelled backward with a rush. McCracken's words echoed, tingling, snakelike, at the roots of his brain.

He blacked out.

SEVENTEEN

BOAT SINKS, THREE LOST

MIAMI, Fla. (UPI)—Bahamian authorities announced today the release of the single survivor of a fire which apparently claimed the lives of three at sea. Philip Sobel, 38, chairman of Sobel Industries, a well-known fashion center in New York City, was treated for first-degree burns, arm and leg injuries, exhaustion and smoke inhalation. Mr. Sobel was found in poor condition on the beach of an uninhabited islet about ten miles east of Nassau. A passing private plane notified authorities of the burning vessel, the 78-foot pleasure craft *Penny Dreadful*, and investigating officials followed the oil slick up to the bay of the islet where Mr. Sobel was found. The three victims of the disaster have been described by Mr. Sobel to be Mrs. Tracey Hansen of Manhattan, and John and Penny McCracken of Coral Gables, Florida.

According to Mr. Sobel's initial account, the *Penny Dreadful* shipped water and was disabled at sea shortly after reaching international waters. He told authorities of rowing toward the islet where the vessel was eventually moored. Mr. Sobel appeared distraught and confused and refused to speak further until granted immunity. He was questioned for three hours by Bahamian authorities and then released to U.S. authorities.

Upon investigation it was ascertained that there is no registration of a craft named the *Penny Dreadful* in Coral Gables, and John and Penny McCracken are presumed to be aliases.

After six hours of questioning by the Federal Bureau of Investigation, Mr. Sobel will be released in Miami, pending further medical observation.

IN MEMORIAM

MORRISTOWN, N. J.— Memorial services were held yesterday at the Holy Cross Catholic Church for Tracey Elizabeth Hansen, 28. Mrs. Hansen was among those lost at sea during a fire several miles east of Nassau two weeks ago. Mrs. Hansen was a graduate of Bryn Mawr and taught English for two semesters at Hunter College in 1974. In addition to being a devoted horsewoman, she was a former member of the Morristown Chamber Ensemble where she played the flute. She married Lawrence Foster Hansen, then a graduate student of electronic engineering at M.I.T., in 1975. Mr. Hansen is currently an analyst for the Defense Department. The Hansens made their home in Manhattan. They had no children.

In attendance were Mr. Hansen; Mrs. Daniel Farrier, mother of the deceased; Isabel Harding Cutler, a sister; Janet Farrier, a sister; Ralph Hansen, brother to Lawrence, and Philip Sobel.

DEATH BOAT SURVIVOR DIVORCED

NEW YORK, N.Y. (UPI) —Philip Sobel, 38, sole survivor of the burning pleasure craft *Penny Dreadful* off the coast of the Bahamas last January, was formally divorced from his wife of ten years, Barbara Ann Stroud Sobel on the grounds of adultery. Mr. Sobel surrendered custody of his two sons, Mark, 4, and Philip, Jr., 7, as well as any share in the Sobel Design Center which remains in the control of his wife.

Sobel was found four months ago, bleeding and incoherent, on the beach of a small island in the area east of the Bahamas. No bodies from that wreck were ever found. It was revealed that Sobel's companion was Mrs. Lawrence Hansen, 28, of Manhattan. In addition, authorities speculated on the possibilities of violence or arson, though no charges were formally filed. Sobel's testimony has been contradictory and confused and it was never made clear as to what the *Penny Dreadful* was doing in such an isolated cove. Charred remnants of flesh were found on floating segments of wood several miles from the island.

Mysteriously, an ancient chronometer, developed by the Royal Navy in 1737, was found inside a floating cabinet. This kind of chronometer has not been in use for 200 years. Sobel left many questions unanswered regarding the disaster but no further investigation was conducted.

The divorce settlement was reputed to entail an undisclosed sum paid to Sobel in lieu of alimony, while the entire holdings of the Sobel Design Center and its subsidary enterprises, as well as all of its foreign stock was retained by Barbara Sobel.

At the divorce trial yesterday, Sobel appeared for only ten minutes, at which time the settlement agreed upon was filed with the court. His present whereabouts is unknown.

Barbara Sobel will revert to her maiden name, Stroud, and has moved to Manhattan where she will preside over Sobel Industries, now renamed Hudson Valley Design.

Sarasota Yacht Sales
Licensed and Bonded Ship Brokerage

State Reg. No. 30655

INVOICE
63064

21212 Sunrise Beach Road
Sarasota, Florida

September 7, 1980

Name of Yacht: <u>ABSOLUTE TEN</u>

Construction
   Builder: American Boat Works
   Length: 59'
   Beam: 17' 6"
   Draft: 6'

Double-planked mahogany decks
Bronze fastenings
Oak frames
Fire retardant resin

Engines
   GM 8V-71 twin diesel 300 HP
   Cruise: 15 knots 1900 RPM 20 GPH
   Maximum: 18 knots 2300 RPM

Electrical
   12/32/110 — (6) MD batteries
   Auxiliary: Kohler 10 KW
   Inverter: 12V to 110V

Apelco MS 252 fathometer
Apelco radio
Datamarine digital depth sounder
Apelco ADF
Apelco radar mod. ADR7 12-mile
VHF 12-channel
Autopilot (Bendix)
Hartman hailer

Equipment and accommodation
   Fiberglass unsinkable dinghy (minus outboard at request of purchaser)
   Automatic CO_2 fire extinguisher system
   Triple tanks: fuel 250 gallons
                water 100 gallons

   Sleeps four, master stateroom forward, double bedroom aft. Two-burner
electric stove. Salon amidships with built-in barstools. Stereo. Large
hanging closets, tiled heads in each stateroom. Enclosed helm. Extensive
cabinets, stainless steel double sink in galley. Harriman fishing seat
with safety belt and mounted harpoon gun. Nonflammable paneling.

   Total price: $234,000

   Purchaser: Mr. Philip Williams
               Casa Grande Hotel
               Sarasota, Florida

Other Arrow Books of interest:

VISIONS OF TERROR
William Katz

'Mummy, Mummy . . . I saw Daddy.'

It isn't a dream – it's a picture. A picture that only Annie can see, and that only her mother believes. For when Annie sees her Daddy she sees him lying down, his head injured. When Annie sees the picture of her Daddy he is dead. Annie can see the past, the present and the future. And what she sees are visions of terror.

Since her husband's disappearance, Vera has tried to keep life normal for her daughter and herself. Vera has always believed that Harry would return – and that life would be what it once had been. But then everything begins to change . . . as an undreamt of evil transfers a pleasant community into a dungeon of horror.

And caught at the very centre of the terror stands one tiny child.

£1.25

THE EIGHTH SQUARE

Herbert Lieberman

From the bestselling author of CITY OF THE DEAD

How could a peaceful walking holiday so easily become a
nightmare of fear and claustrophobic terror? It began so
innocently, and now they were lost – totally and horrifyingly
isolated in a maze of uncharted paths. And without a guide.

They had been lifelong friends, until one appoints himself
leader – driven by a sinister and ungovernable desire. As hours
stretch into days, old hostilities become hatred, and fear
escalates into paranoia.

The climactic step into the eighth square is one of paralysing
and remorseless horror . . .

£1·30

CITY OF THE DEAD
Herbert Lieberman

Once again his gaze drifts past the Chief to the reconstructed corpses, the gobbets of flesh and bones still in trays all about him. . . . 'Why the hell do you do it?'

He does it because it's his job. Paul Konig is Chief Medical Examiner, New York City. Each day's grisly workload of strangled whores, battered babies and dismembered corpses is just routine to him. Contemptuous of the police, the public and his fellow doctors, he presides over the morgue like a monarch. But things can go wrong, even for Konig . . .

Suddenly, a piercing, wrenching scream, followed by a lewd giggle in the background. 'Dr Konig . . . that was your daughter.' Another loud, wrenching scream. Then the phone is slammed down.

Not only has Konig's daughter been kidnapped, but he's up against a dead-end in the most gruesome multiple murder case of his career.

'The toughest, most harrowing, most gruesome novel in a long, long time' *Publisher's Weekly*

'The shocker of the summer' *Time*

£1.60

FALLING ANGEL

William Hjortsberg

It begins with a missing crooner.

But what starts as a routine investigation leads to a nightmare of murder, mutilation and satanic evil, culminating in a breathtaking climax of sheer terror.

Falling Angel is one of the most haunting and original novels of the occult ever witten.

' . . . A spellbinding adventure in suspense that rollercoasters the reader toward an ending that is the equivalent of hitting a brick wall at 90 m.p.h. . . . This is a book that you don't walk away from' *Richard Brautigan*

95p

BESTSELLERS FROM ARROW

All these books are available from your bookshop or news-
agent or you can order them direct. Just tick the titles you
want and complete the form below.

☐	BRUACH BLEND	Lillian Beckwith	95p
☐	THE HISTORY MAN	Ma colm Bradbury	£1·25
☐	ENTERTAINING	Robert Carrier	£4·95
☐	A LITTLE ZIT ON THE SIDE	Jasper Carrott	90p
☐	AUCTION	Richard Cox	£1·25
☐	FALLING ANGEL	William Hjortsberg	95p
☐	AT ONE WITH THE SEA	Naomi James	£1·25
☐	IN GALLANT COMPANY	Alexander Kent	85p
☐	METROPOLITAN LIFE	Fran Lebowitz	95p
☐	AFTER THE WIND	Eileen Lottman	£1·95
☐	THE BETTER ANGELS	Charles McCarry	£1·50
☐	SPORTING FEVER	Michael Parkinson	£1·25
☐	THE MASQUERS	Natasha Peters	£1·95
☐	STRUMPET CITY	James Plunkett	£1·95
☐	A SHIP MUST DIE	Douglas Reeman	£1·10
☐	A JUDGEMENT IN STONE	Ruth Rendell	95p
☐	TO THE MANOR BORN (Book 2)	Peter Spence	£1·00
☐	THE FOURTH MAN	Douglas Sutherland	£1·25
☐	THE YEAR OF THE QUIET SUN	Wilson Tucker	80p

Postage

_____

Total

_____

ARROW BOOKS, BOOKSERVICE BY POST, PO BOX 29,
DOUGLAS, ISLE OF MAN, BRITISH ISLES
Please enclose a cheque or postal order made out to Arrow
Books Limited for the amount due including 35p per book
for postage and packing for orders within the UK and 45p for
overseas orders.
Please print clearly
NAME ....
ADDRESS ....
....
Whilst every effort is made to keep prices down and to keep
popular books in print, Arrow Books cannot guarantee that
prices will be the same as those advertised here or that the
books will be available.

261 - 3653